Morning Star

A collection of short science-fiction and fantasy stories

Dorian Keys

Keys Productions

CONTENTS

INTRODUCTION

Let me tell you a story that will tell you twelve.

Upon arrival at its designated planet, Helsey 8K, Seed-ship Morning Star suffers a catastrophic accident. An asteroid rips through its cockpit's bridge connector, killing 2 and stranding Captain Irene Deris within.

Irene's best way to remain calm and collected throughout the ordeal of her rescue and beyond: a book, written by ship's first pilot, Adam.

She is eventually recovered by her crew, but even though that part of her journey is over, she finds herself compelled to keep reading.

Her intrigue is piqued by stories about mechas starting a new universe, in a new dimension. Artificial intelligence will deceive alien invaders to save her human love. A teddy bear will save a child's life and a demon will roam the Earth.

Stunningly questionable decisions will turn experiments into nightmares, authorities will be duped by mysterious abductors and broken hearts will get their revenge.

Read together with Irene as she saves the Morning Star and prepares to begin a whole new life.

MORNING STAR

As the wrecked remains of Morning Star's cockpit and fuselage slowly rotated around itself, light from the star peeked over Helsey 8K. Adam, the ship's first pilot, let go of his laser cutting tool and placed his spacesuit's boot on the panel he just cut. Holding a metal pipe with both his hands, he pushed with his legs to remove it.

The pipe broke, and Adam instinctively pulled it to himself. The top flew to his right side, and the lower part dragged and ripped a small hole on the suit over his right leg.

"Adam," Emily's voice came through his helmet's speakers as an alarm warned of air pressure loss.

"Yeah, I know," Adam responded, as he brought his wrist panel in front of him, pressing a digital button, and silencing the alarm. "Give me a moment."

Reaching to his left thigh, Adam pulled out a strip of fabric from his side pocket. Bringing it to his view, he peeled the bottom part exposing the adhesive part. Holding the patch with his left hand, Adam looked down to his right inner thigh. Slowly he set the piece above the tear and pressed.

Checking his wrist panel, he confirmed that the tear was sealed for the moment.

"Adam," Crew Chief Helmsey said on the radio, "maybe it's time for you to come in, don't you think?"

"I still have some air left, chief." Adam looked at the panel that had come loose after he removed the metal pipe.

"We've been at this for three days now, Adam. There are more things we have to do around here."

Adam removed the panel and pushed it away from the mangled cockpit. He threw it into space behind him. "What are you saying, Chief?"

"I'm saying there are others that can do that job. We have to prepare for our surface landing."

"I'm not leaving until we get to her, Chief."

"No one is saying that, but I need you to fly Gary down to the surface to scout the geology around the landing site."

Adam sighed and floated along the long thick plastic enclosure housing the power lines for the cutting tool.

The mangled steel and polycarbonate panels wrapped around the exit hatch made this job even harder. Adam let go of the cutting tool and floated above the structure to inspect the outside of the cockpit. The thick window guards were shut, and there was a dent in the space between them. He avoided the metal pipe extending from the bridge connector and floated toward the front section to give it a closer inspection. *No air leaks here.*

"Let me at least clear the way through to the hatch."

"Chief copy," Helmsey said with a sigh.

Adam grabbed the thick rubber-covered handle of the cutter. The tool had a long neck, with two parts. A thick laser beam emanated from the bottom part, which was reflected from the top. Supported by a metal frame to form a handsaw, the super-hot laser was the best tool they had to cut the smaller, metallic panels. The mainline, which ran the length of the ship, was not just a beam. Composed by a special poly-metal mesh, it was designed to create the necessary framework from which all the different compartment floors connected. Simply exposing it to heat wouldn't cut it easily.

"Do we have any news on Irene?" Adam asked, switching the tool on and floating in the other direction, avoiding jagged panel edges.

"Nothing," Emily, the bridge communications operator, replied.

Cutting a panel section, Adam pushed it away from the ship. It flew through the dark space opposite to where the planet Morning Star was orbiting. Adam looked in the direction of the hatch only to see something familiar, a portion of a helmet much like the one he was wearing, stuck in the beam past it. He slowly pulled it out. It had blood on the inside.

Swallowing, Adam let go of the tool and floated

to the cord. He stored the helmet remnant in a utility bag attached to it, then resumed his operation, cutting smaller beams and clearing his way to the hatch.

"Adam, you have about another twelve minutes till you run out of oxygen," Emily said. "Consider storing the tool and heading back. Eric and Violet are on standby to replace you."

Adam cut one final beam and pushed it out of the way as a lot of broken glass and other, smaller panels came out of the small enclosure he'd created.

"Oh, I can see the hatch!" He continued to quickly push the remaining debris behind him as a beep in his suit indicated that he had less than ten minutes of oxygen left.

"We got a signal," Control said. "Adam, we got a signal."

"Irene?" Adam said, looking at the hatch as debris slowly floated his way.

"I'm picking up her vitals," Control continued. "Likely, the panel you just removed was interfering."

Avoiding the slew of debris and wires sticking out of the damaged bridge connector, Adam approached and looked inside the cockpit through the hatch's round window. *There is light inside here.* He hit the hatch with a piece of metal debris. There was no sound in space, but he knew that if Irene were still conscious inside, she'd be able to hear it.

And she did.

Irene floated to the hatch, her eyes wide open, a big smile on her face.

Adam opened a small compartment on the right of the hatch and pulled out the point-to-point communications jack. He connected it to his suit, bypassing his radio, and said, "Can you hear me?"

"My god, I can." Irene adjusted the microphone on the headset, looking at Adam through the round window.

"It's so good to finally see you baby." Adam placed his gloved hand on the window. "You got me scared for a moment."

Irene placed her hand opposite Adam's on the dense triple-layered window. "I thought no one was coming to get me. I don't even know where I am." Breathing shallowly to hold her tears, Irene looked at Adam, who swallowed to hold his own tears back.

Adam's suit beeped twice. "You're running out of O2?" Irene asked, recognizing the alarm. "How long have you been out there? How far from the rest of the ship am I?"

"You're not far. The bridge connector is completely gone, and all the reinforcing beams are wrapped around the cockpit."

"What happened, Adam?"

"Our final assessment is that an asteroid tore the main connecting corridor, ripping it apart. We have three missing: Winters, Pearson, and Minick. The rest of Morning Star is unharmed and untouched. So is the crew. The embryo section is safe." Adam adjusted the cord, which floated in front of his helmet.

"Three dead!" Irene exclaimed.

"We thought we lost you as well." Adam sighed. "I've been cutting through debris for three days, baby."

"Thank god at least the babies are safe, Adam. Why didn't we see this coming?"

"The initial radar sweeps of planet's orbit were accurate. This incident had nothing to do with navigation." Adam placed his hand on the hatch. "Look, we didn't see that this system has what appears to be an asteroid belt. At least a partial one. It looks more as if they're the broken pieces of a moon, all grouped in one general area. We think that this band of asteroids orbits in an elliptical manner. When we arrived three days ago, the band was hidden by the planet. Since then, we've managed to get most of our systems back online, and the new sweeps are up to date. Gary seems pretty sure the planet is safe after we conducted further analysis of the atmosphere. At least there's fresh air. How's your situation?"

"The emergency atmosphere processor is working, the batteries seem to take charge well, and there are four bags of food in the net here." Irene turned her head slightly, moving out of Adam's view so he could see the multicolored utility and food bags secured on the walls by restraining nets. "The impact must have bent the hull because the nets came loose. Can you check?"

"I did. The impact damaged the airlock beyond repair, Irene. There's a dent on the outside, just above the windows, but I don't see any atmosphere leaks. I'd say that is the reason why the nets got loose."

"Well, the air processor shows me the OK signal across the board. I don't think there is a leak, but I'll keep checking. I also pulled out some of the emergency bags."

"That's why we have them." Adam smiled, looking at Irene's face.

"What's so funny?"

"Not funny. I am happy to see you again. I thought I lost you."

The two locked eyes for a moment.

"My spacesuit is here," Irene finally said. "I can open the hatch, but I need the emergency drive transports if we want to preserve our data."

"You're safe there for now, and I'm running out of air. We're working to fix the radio as well, so keep trying it periodically."

Irene lowered her head and looked down at the white socks she was wearing. "You're awfully calm, given my predicament. A little emotion would make a difference, you know." She slightly smiled, raising her eyes, looking at Adam.

"God, Irene. I am doing my best to keep my cool; I didn't want to panic you. I was out in my suit fifteen seconds after the crash. Collected the floating bodies..."

Adam's voice crackled. "The first thing I did was try to check on you. And I couldn't."

Shivers ran down Irene's spine. "I'm fine," she replied, tilting her head to her side and swallowing to hold back her tears. "I'm so sorry I didn't see this coming."

"We already spoke about this; it's not your fault. Let it go." Adam's suit beeped three times. "Let me get back before I run out of O2 here." He said calmly, "Someone will come to get you out of here. The chief wants to send the first shuttle down on the surface and release the communication satellites."

"Well, hurry up, I want to get out of here."

"I'm working as fast as I can, Irene."

"What am I supposed to do meanwhile?"

"There is a crew replacing me. And now that I've cleared the way, I'm sure it's just a matter of time till they get here." Four beeps indicated the urgency with which Adam had to get back inside the Morning Star. He extended his gloved hand to pull the headset jack but stopped as he remembered to tell Irene something else. "Oh, I think my bag is in the cockpit. The book should be there."

"The book. Your book?" Irene adjusted the microphone, turning her head to look at the bags tucked on the side panels. "You had it with you all this time and kept it a secret?"

"Yeah, it was supposed to be a gift. I wanted to

give it to you once we landed. I guess you can open it now."

"I'll try to wait."

"Well, it's there if you decide to read it." Adam smiled for a moment before pushing away from the cockpit cabin. "I have to check the escape shuttles, Irene." Disconnecting the headset, he disappeared to the right side of the hatch.

Irene attached her side of the headset to the Velcro patch next to the airlock door, then moved toward the net that held bags filled with food and other supplies. She rummaged through them, checking again how much food there was. Four bags had dehydrated foods and M.R.E.'s. There were two big bladders with water, and— "Oh." It was Adam's bag.

Irene unzipped it, and the first thing that floated out of it was a small book stuffed with yellow post-it notes. *Here it is.* She flipped to the front page.

T.I.A.S.T.

There Is A Story There

Short stories for your entertainment

This book belongs to Adam Kacey

"Hm." Irene flipped the page to the first story. "The much talked about short story collection." She floated to the cockpit and buckled herself in the pilot's seat harness, turning on the small reading light on the panel above her head. "Maybe I'll just read a few pages." She smiled, flipping the front cover to reveal the first story title.

A UNIVERSE OF
OUR OWN

"**D**id you get it?" Ruanas asked Gea, helping her up the jet ramp.

"Yeah, but I barely made it out of there, and I don't think they're happy about it." Breathing hard, she looked back at the flight deck filled with parked fighters as the door to their jet fighter sealed with a hiss.

"It doesn't matter. It will all be over soon." Ruanas adjusted the shoulder-mounted laser cannon on his docked mechanical suit unit, getting as close to her as he could. "The dimensional breach is in range. We can make it."

"We have to," Gea agreed, pulling out the small, metallic-looking wire enclosure where the bright white, twirling energy leaked, illuminating the surroundings with a lively white light.

A loud bang shook the fighter as both of them steadied themselves on the equipment inside the small cargo bay area of the jet. A moment later, the loud rumbling sound of an alarm penetrated the hull as the two ran and hurriedly buckled-in to the fighter's cockpit seats.

"I set the flight pattern, but I expect them to do everything they can to end us, even if it means destroying the next universe with us."

"Let's worry about that when the time comes, shall we?"

***

The dark and quiet starry space surrounding the station was suddenly disturbed by the sight of the strobe lights that encircled the security perimeter. They rapidly blinked red as an explosion, which immediately turned into an implosion, tore open the side of the station.

A small fighter jetted out of the hole created by the explosion, dragging debris. Magnetic security strobe trackers activated and followed in a swarm.

Ruanas looked over at her as the jet stabilized. "How are you holding up?"

"I'm good." Gea flipped switches on a panel above her seat to adjust the flight pattern.

"The sight of you controlling this fighter turns me on." Ruanas grinned.

"You like the noise, don't you?" Gea replied with a smile.

Narrowing his eyes, he looked at her as he said, "As long as it doesn't—"

The alarm beeps from the ship's A.I., which indicated imminent impact, interrupted Ruanas. Looking forward to the radar screen, he took control of the craft, gradually increasing its speed and changing the flight pattern to twirl, evading the swarm of magnetic mines and trackers, which followed closely as more fighters launched from the large remote space station.

"Launching magnetic field countermeasures," Gea announced, pressing a series of buttons in the panel in front of her, causing the craft to shake slightly.

Ruanas continued to increase the jet's speed as two magnetic field countermeasure orbs ejected from the undercarriage compartment. Once they gained some distance from the jet, they began to spin around each other faster, closing their gap. They created a magnetic field in their vicinity, which attracted nearby trackers, destroying them in the resulting vortex.

The swarm of trackers was followed by a barrage of cannon fire and missiles, which quickly homed in on the escaping jet. Ruanas flew in a wide circular motion, evading the missiles and projectiles coming their way.

In the brief moment they faced the station, where they'd just stolen the small dimensional breach device, they saw an army of jet fighters speeding their way. As they completed their circle, the missiles exploded, attracted by the magnetic mines and sending the escaping jet tumbling forward.

"Cabin de-pressurizing!" the computer announced as shrapnel from the rockets hit the hull, causing air to escape from the resulting cuts and holes forcefully.

"Baby, reverse our direction so I can get rid of some of these guys, then get to your mecha unit and eject." Ruanas silenced the alarm as the life support system began to compensate for the pressure loss by rapidly pumping the reserve air into the cabin.

"Ruanas, no. I want to be here with you." Gea raised her voice above the hissing sound of the rushing air, looking at him.

"Trust me. I'll be right behind you." He grabbed his harness with both hands, steadying his head as the jet struggled to maintain the flight pattern.

Gea unbuckled the harness holding her to the seat and moved to the cargo bay where the mecha suits were stored. She got inside her suit just as the jet turned around, its cannons facing the pursuers and magnetic mines. Ruanas fired at the incoming threats, setting off a chain of explosions and leaving a streak of destruction behind them as the computer confirmed, "Ejection procedure engaged in three, two, one."

In one motion, the rear door of the jet opened,

and Gea's suit ejected. Once it gained some distance from the hurtling fighter, the directional thrusters of her mecha fired with enough power so she could keep up with it. Simultaneously, the pursuing magnetic strobes and mines split, some following her, others still following Ruanas, who was again firing at them, explosions ensuing.

Steadying her flight pattern, Gea extended her right shoulder cannon, which automatically fired at threats that got too close to her as she flew erratically to evade them. Scanning the vicinity, she caught a glimpse of Ruanas fighting the incoming swarm of enemies, energetically moving the jet and dodging the rockets which by now were viciously circling it, trying to home in their designated target.

Her mecha, which was fighting a battle on its own, faced the threats. As soon as the cannon eliminated them, Gea turned around to follow Ruanas, only to witness the jet he was piloting explode. Debris scattered, and she waited to see if his mecha escaped. She saw nothing.

"No, baby, no!" she said despairingly, wanting to go into the debris looking for him. Unfortunately, her mecha had more dire issues to deal with, as the rest of the rockets were now heading her way. Gea began to fly in an evasive, twirling, unpredictable flight pattern.

Jet debris continued its trajectory toward the dimension breach, keeping its momentum, as Gea forced her mecha unit to move toward it. Approaching the wreckage but sensing that the rest of the swarm behind her was still active and looking for her, Gea looked at the information panel on her left forearm.

"Countermeasures active, ten canisters available."

"Deploy all countermeasures," she commanded her mecha. Heading toward the debris in a straight line now, both of her shoulder cannons extended and fired. The first two bright flares went up and out, then another three, creating a pair of wings along her flight pattern as the mines and small rockets that were following her heat signature moved away from her to pursue the sudden heat and magnetism created by them.

With her vicinity free of enemies for the moment, she grabbed onto the cockpit wreckage and hurriedly crawled inside.

He's not here. She continued to move deeper into the wreckage toward the end of the cargo bay, where Ruanas' mecha suit would be. *Neither is his suit.* She turned around, exiting the mangled wreckage from a hole made by one of the missiles that hit it.

The dark, starry space was now full of magnetic mines, projectiles, and heat-seeking rockets heading towards the mangled wreckage, which by virtue of inertia was still moving toward the dimensional breach. As if they sensed another moving mecha, their flight patterns suddenly changed.

Gea's heart began to beat faster, witnessing Ruanas performing a barrel roll in space not too far from her and releasing all his countermeasures, which formed a large circle around him, much like a halo. He finished the maneuver in front of her, engaging his chest's magnetic plate and attracting her backplate with it. They both pointed their shoulder cannons to the incoming threat.

"You still have the key with you, baby?"

"Yes, yes, I do!" she said, trying to keep evidence of her tears of relief out of her voice.

"Good. It's time." He engaged his thrusters as both of their shoulder cannons began to fire, picking off the magnetic mines relentlessly homing in on them.

"Hold it out. I don't know what we are heading for, but they won't be able to follow us there, not without the key."

The wire enclosure holding the bright energy thinned out the closer the mechas got to the dimension breach. Its light illuminated the breach's rippling dark energy, suspended in space as the two flew in a straight line in their final streak to enter. The matter around them became denser the closer they got, as ripples appeared in space-time around the duo.

"Neutron radiation increasing," their mecha suits simultaneously announced.

The dimension breach rippled as the enclosure completely disappeared for a moment, releasing its radiation and energy and creating a fissure that they barely fit through. It abruptly closed behind them, as water envelopes a diver, submerging immediately and sending a wave of antimatter backward, which swept away all the ships, rockets, and projectiles.

***

It all began deep in the outer quadrant, where Gea and Ruanas finally found the spark they were looking for. Some call it a key, some call it life force. They just called it a new life, a new dimension free of the old universe's rules. But the Collective had its rules, and with its large habitat parked right outside the breach, it could enforce them.

Millenia...no, eons ago, while digging for precious metals in an asteroid field, a man found a small object about the size of his hand. A bright energy orb surrounded by a mesh metal enclosure. He took it to the nearest precious metals dealer who told him it was worthless. The man took this object and placed it on the dashboard of his scavenger's spaceship. A little while later, he had an accident while chasing and trying to land on an asteroid, again to mine precious metals. His ship began to lose pressure. Fearing he was going to get stranded and die in the middle of nowhere, he set a course for the nearest solar system. The shuttle automatically sped toward it. But something happened while getting there. Because of the urgency, the shuttle's navigation system ignored existing hazards and flew near what was agreed was a black hole. No one had been close enough to examine it because, well, they caused death, no need to argue with that. However, something strange happened to the little trinket he had found. It began to get brighter, and its light almost overtook the entire cabin. Once the shuttle passed this black hole, the object returned to its normal state.

The man survived this accident, but now his curiosity was piqued. *I have never seen anything like that.* In an attempt to duplicate that event, he went back to the black hole and had yet another accident; the trinket leaped away from where he had placed it. Violently blowing a hole through his ship, it flew inside the black hole. Immediately after, space surrounding the breach rippled as if it was water. This time he came prepared and had a tug on-call—he wasn't going to get stranded this time. However, while waiting for the rescue ship to come, he could see space and stars on the other side of the black hole. At first sight, it appeared as if he was looking at a rippled image of the stars behind the black hole, but he soon noticed that he was looking inside it.

There was space inside the space.

Bewildered, the man went to the precious metals dealer and asked him if he had seen any more of these objects. And to his surprise, the dealer told him that he had seen them come and go, but no one knew what to use them for—*Leftover-junk created by supernovae explosions.*

That man went on a quest to find more of these objects. After gathering quite a few of them, he found that they were pretty much all the same: an energy orb surrounded by a metal enclosure. He also found out that every time he threw one in what he now called the "dimension breach," a new space would be created inside the breach—a new dimension.

Keeping this secret close, that man hired scavengers to find and bring him more of these dimension keys. He began spreading rumors that they were dangerous objects and that using them to enter this "dimension breach" was hazardous for our universe.

Then the inevitable happened.

One of these objects exploded while a rogue group of scavengers attempted to throw it inside the black hole in the center of the galaxy their solar system was located. The resulting blast obliterated the entire galaxy, causing the black hole in its center to swallow half of the stars while scattering the rest of them into oblivion. Countless lives were lost. Civilizations were extinguished.

This catastrophe reinforced his findings; these dimension keys don't work everywhere. The black hole he encountered was not like the others. It was the only dimension breach anyone had ever found.

With his rumors validated, he created what he called The Collective. Its stated goal was to protect our universe from destruction. At the same time, he sold these keys to wealthy creatures and men who wanted to enter the breach. This process made this man famous.

His lie was short-lived, as increasingly more scavengers and others learned of this dimension breach and tried to enter. In turn, The Collective built a habitat near it. They called it a merchant's hub. Its real purpose was to stop scavengers entering on their own.

Ruanas and Gea, two scavengers, were looking to better their lives, rushing from one job to another. Gea had always been the "noisemaker"—noise as in trouble, that is. She was always looking for dangerous assignments. Last time they barely made it out of the neutron nebulae, all because Gea had a hunch. Ruanas tried to make the best out of any situation they found themselves in, but always complained about her "noise" while loving it and Gea. He knew that her "noise" made their existence more bearable.

As far as they knew, entering a new dimension has never been attempted by anyone other than The Collective, and they would not allow it to happen, not without The Collective's approval. Even though they found the key, they were considered dangerous individuals because they expressed their desire to enter the breach. In their eyes, Gea and Ruanas just wanted to take their chances at a new universe. The Collective, however, wanted everyone to behave exactly as they wanted—no questions asked, for the good of themselves.

The Collective's massive habitat housed lifeforms from all over this dimension. Keys, when found or stolen from owners such as Ruanas and Gea, were either sold or used by the Collective. They effectively destroyed dreams and the work of a lifetime for most scavengers.

***

Reacting to the untouched new dimension, the mecha suits slowly dissolved, consumed down to their frames, revealing Gea's and Ruana's true forms under a new aspect. Their bodies absorbed the charred metal into their skin, revealing their feet and moving up in a rolling pattern, exposing their thighs, then Gea's hips and breasts and Ruanas' chest. Their side cannons dissolved, making way for wings, which extended well below their feet, completely enveloping their bodies as both floated in the void in fetal positions. The life support system rose above their heads and transformed into bright halos, which pulsated, illuminating their entire bodies.

With labored breath, Gea came to, moving her hand in front of her face. Turning it around and looking at her knuckles, she made a fist, then opened it back up. Stretching, she extended her arms out past her wings. Under the halo's white light, she reached for Ruanas as this fertile dimension's time-space rippled, resisting change.

"Baby," she said as she grabbed his hand, "we made it through and, oh, you look so different."

Ruanas opened his eyes and slightly squeezed her hand to let her know that he was awake as well. Smiling at the feel and sight of their hands finally touching, he looked around as his dark wings instinctively opened, revealing his entire body. "Where is your mecha suit?"

"I don't know." She touched his defined abs. "Different dimension, different rules, I guess." She floated closer to him.

Making eye contact, Ruanas reached in and kissed Gea on her lips. Behind her, the breach was still lit up as big, but silent, explosions continued to hit it from the other side. All that seemed so far away now, yet it was close enough for them to see their past rippling away.

Gea turned her head, looking at the breach. "I still have the key."

"This is going to be our new beginning, baby. We don't need tyrants to tell us how to live and die." Ruanas looked at Gea then at the breach. "Let's just keep the 'noise' moderate in this universe, shall we?" He continued, as Gea grinned facing the breach as well.

"I love the 'noise' I create." Her bright white wings slowly bowed, revealing her shiny white halo above her head.

"You should know by now that I create from the 'noise' you make." He caressed her hair as he stood next to her, looking at the darkness of this new dimension. "Let's create a new life here."

Gea narrowed her eyes under a faint smile. "Will they know?"

Feeling her excitement, he extended his arms to meet hers as Gea held the dimension key in her palm. "Help me release its energy."

In one motion, they both clapped, crushing the metal enclosure, which had been slowly regenerating, weakening the already weak protective frame surrounding the energy contained within. Sensing that the enclosure was about to give in, Gea floated a little above Ruanas, spinning faster and faster until the key escaped her hands, shooting deep in the dimension.

BANG! They shielded their eyes with their wings as space-time violently expanded. Matter and antimatter clashing with each other, blanketing the rapidly expanding universe.

A bright explosion announced its birth.

Universe, zero seconds old.

#

"Whoosh Adam, way to introduce yourself." Irene closed the book, placing the bookmark at the beginning of the next chapter, and let it float just above her head next to the small reading light. Releasing the harness holding her in place, Irene flipped the light switch into the off position and floated up by the hatch of the module that faced the entrance. It once connected the cockpit and the narrow passage to the rest of the spacecraft. If she had looked through that window any other time, she would have seen the vestibule that led to the living quarters and the rest of the spaceship. However, since the asteroid had torn through it, all she could see was the surface of the blue planet littered with scattered white clouds. "Now you are making me wonder if those two created all of this."

Holding on to rope handles and bag straps extending from the fabric containers held against the walls by white netting, she moved away from the hatch's round window and approached the power panel. It read *Battery 68 percent, charging, keep the solar panels clear.*

"Thank God." She floated a little farther up the same panel, where the atmosphere processor was announcing itself with a blinking green L.E.D. light. "OK." That meant that there were no leaks from the fuselage. She then turned around to face the communications section where the radio was.

"Adam," she said after pressing the transmit button, only to hear the silence broken by occasional white noise that came through the speakers.

"Adam, are you there?" She received the same white noise response. Sighing, she let go of the microphone.

The damaged part of the fuselage that housed her and the cockpit completed its rotation, and a beam of light from this system's star slowly brightened the area where she was. The switchboard panel shone under the light coming from the hatch as Irene stood in the beam, closing her eyes. Feeling its warmth. Slowly opening them, Irene reached for a water bottle that was floating nearby, taking a small sip through its straw before reaching for the little reading light held by Velcro straps in front of the seat facing her. She grabbed an open protein bar from midair, then she strapped herself back into the harness. Irene flipped open the flight log laptop, turned it on, and typed in a text field labeled Vessel Status.

"Day 3: SeedShip Morning Star, 8000 unborn embryos in suspended animation on board. Actual active crew 23. 6 years since disconnected from the Carrier

'Hope.' Current location: in orbit around Seed Planet Designation HW8000, 'Helsey 8K.'

Status: assessing and recovering from damage sustained from an asteroid, which sliced through the corridor connecting the cockpit and the rest of the craft. Solar panels operational, batteries in good condition, atmospheric processor working.

Mission objective: Complete."

Irene swallowed for a moment. There was only one person who could change the mission status, and that was Adam. Nevertheless, she closed the laptop and reached for the small softcover book. She flipped to the bookmark she'd placed on the second story, noticing a yellow post-it stuck there.

"I was lost for days."

"But you're here now."

"Yes, she helped me."

"So, it's all right. You got this."

Biting my lip, I looked down. "Yeah. It's all right now."

That's an odd but cool bit. Irene closed the book, keeping her finger on the next page. She looked out of the round window. You should've asked me before you made the change, Adam. After staring at the hatch for a few seconds, she looked down, opening the book to reveal the next story.

ABLE BASE

South Rim Forward Post

It had been two weeks since the Montana incident where a navy general, a nurse, and a few marines confronted an alien craft by firing a nuclear rocket at a short-range. The resulting explosion left a crater larger than two miles in diameter and devastated an area twice that size. The U.S. Army, joined by local survivors, launched search and rescue missions. Preliminary tests showed no sign of the radiation that should've been released by the warheads. Tensions were high.

Day 7 of Operation "Able"

Four individuals wearing yellow overall hazmat

suits and masks slowly made their way toward the house the army had occupied up the small hill. They followed the guide poles along the clear pathway engineers had set up. With no trees left to slow it down, a gust of wind lifted dust up, in the air, as clouds hung ominously low behind them, just above the crater in the distance. They stopped in front of the two-story house, which was covered entirely by a clear and blue tarp held together by yellow chemical tape. Several soldiers wearing protective gear got up from their surveillance positions and surrounded the group. One of the surveillance soldiers headed for the garage door, signaling the scout group to follow him as another picked up one of the phones located inside his trench and notified his superiors of their arrival.

Inside, a soldier wearing army fatigues sitting in front of a desk by where the front door of the house would be hung up the communications phone. He stepped left and right to avoid desks and ammunition crates army analysts and planners had placed. Two square L.E.D. lights facing the ceiling illuminated everyone and everything. Shadows and chatter filled the area. Once a living room, it was now a temporary command center for Operation Able.

Passing the fireplace on his right, the soldier crossed the short corridor and knocked on the small bedroom door.

"Come in," Captain Helms, the commander for the operation, said as the soldier opened the door.

Army engineers had pinned the mattress standing up against the window and emptied the rest of the room. They had placed a large table in the middle. Because the powerlines were comprehensively obliterated by the explosion that took place several miles away, another square L.E.D. construction light was illuminating this room as well.

"The volunteer search and rescue team is back from the crater's south rim, Captain."

Captain Helms, who was sitting behind the table littered with radios, telephones, and a large topographic map on it, nodded, acknowledging the messenger. Getting up from his chair, he followed the soldier through a short corridor toward the garage entrance, which led to the decontamination area they'd set up, surrounded by makeshift blue plastic walls.

An army hazmat technician came up to Helms as soon as he entered the area. "Captain, all the members' radiation levels are within norms. I didn't detect any biological agents either."

"Thank you." He shifted his gaze toward the members of the returning team.

"Welcome back home, gentlemen," he said softly to the four men who were taking off their yellow hazmat uniforms and placing them on the floor. "Your service is greatly appreciated." He paused for a second as he looked around, his eyebrows pulled downward at edges, his mouth turned down at corners, and his head tilted to the side. "I thought there were five of you."

An awkward silence enveloped the small, makeshift vestibule, broken only by the sound of rubbing plastic. One of the civilian members of the rescue team approached Helms and handed him a little pink and orange notebook inside a sealed, transparent plastic bag labeled Biohazard.

"The fifth member, Arlington, found his little girl's diary."

Helms took the sealed bag into his hands, looking at the men in silence. That sentence meant only one thing—Arlington had taken his life. A beep and a voice on the loudspeaker broke the silence.

"Team Echo is fifteen minutes away. Please clear the decontamination area as soon as possible."

Speechless, Helms took a deep breath and followed everyone out of the vestibule as a team of doctors, nurses, and army personnel gathered just outside of the decontamination vestibule to assist the newcomers.

Looking at the floor, Helms slowly walked back to his office, passing the desks in the living room. He entered his makeshift office, leaving the door open, and threw the little notebook on top of his desk. Pulling a folding chair, the captain sat on it, placing his head in his hands. He stared at the dirty floor tiles.

"This is the report you requested." The young captain slowly lifted his head and saw his second-in-command, Lieutenant Corf, walk in and drop a folder in his table.

Lieutenant Corf noticed the plastic bag with the little colorful notebook inside, picked it up, and pulled it out. He turned his head and saw the captain sitting in the chair, damp-eyed and despondent.

"What happened to you?" Corf asked, placing the plastic bag on the table and looking at the distressed commander.

"We lost another one," Helms responded without taking his eyes from the floor as Corf closed the door.

"Hey, listen, man." Corf took a step toward Helms. "We didn't ask to be here, we didn't cause this explosion, and we sure as hell did not intend any of this to happen. We're here to complete a job, and that's it. Stop acting like the weight of the world is on your shoulders."

"This is the third casualty today alone," Helms said, lifting his head, looking at Lieutenant Corf. "These are civilians, not soldiers."

"Ah, yes, now I know why they put you in charge of this op. Your bleeding heart for humanity. I know it's a big job, but someone has to do it." Corf swallowed as the dry air flowing through the house's ventilation pipes scratched his throat. "We have more than two thousand troops combing the crater. Many more lives are in danger as we speak. We must make sure there are no more people stranded in the towns. This town, Bellpond, is the last one in our list."

Lieutenant Corf threw the little notebook back in the table and walked away. It landed on the table open to the last entry.

"I learned how to fly a kite today. My dad and I

ran all over the backyard, getting it up in the air. I wish my dad was home more often, so I can learn more cool things with him."

#

"Poor Arlington." Irene picked up another yellow post-it sticker on the page.

Witnessing the universe on the palm of their hands, they both gasped.

"See what you do to me, you inspire me, I need you."

"I need you, baby – I love you, that's why I need you."

"That's the thing; I need you – that's why I love you," he responded, looking at their creation twirling.

"Maybe this belongs after the first story." Irene flipped the square piece of paper to check if there was more on the other side. Seeing it was blank, Irene placed it back on the book page and looked at the round hatch window as the light beam passed by again, illuminating the area and warming her up. Unbuckling herself, she floated toward the waste bag, placing the empty snack wrapper inside. Irene then floated to another container and pulled more protein bars out of it. Grabbing the water bottle, she moved to check the battery panel: seventy-two percent. *At least the batteries are slowly recharging.* She checked the atmosphere processor, then the radio.

"Anyone listening to this frequency, please respond," she said after pressing the transmit button, but she heard nothing but white noise in return. She pressed the button again. "Adam?" Silence and white noise persisted.

Holding on to her water bottle and protein bar, she floated back at the chair, strapped herself in so she wouldn't float away, and picked the book out of midair, flipping the pages to find the next story.

RESCUED

The entire maintenance module violently shook as long beeps of the general alarm followed by flashing red lights filled the small and cluttered cabin, indicating an emergency.

Startled, Maurice's training kicked in, and he immediately floated to the exit hatch and opened a closet labeled EMU, for "Extravehicular Mobility Unit." After quickly inserting his feet inside his suit, he fastened his boots. He then picked up his portable O2 tank and checked the gauge. "Five P.S.I.? What the hell, this thing didn't charge at all."

The computer system came online and, with a calm voice, announced, "Based on the current pattern of compression, the oxygen tanks will reach critical levels in two minutes and thirty-two seconds."

Looking over his shoulder at the panel affixed in one of the module's walls, Maurice noticed the O2 light flashing red.

"Damn it," he mumbled, pressing a few buttons on the same panel, then raised his voice so the A.I. could hear. "OK computer, silence the notifications."

"Notifications are off," the A.I.'s female voice promptly responded as the module went silent. He heard muffled bangs and scratches that sounded like objects hitting the craft from the outside.

Maurice picked his helmet and began to fasten it, only to remember that the EMU wouldn't help him. He had no air to survive a trip outside.

The lights flickered as he approached the little round window by the airlock where the rest of the modules should be. He was expecting to see the vestibule that served as a connector to the rest of the station. In disbelief, Maurice witnessed the station slowly floating away as it rotated in zero gravity, accompanied by debris and the occasional electric spark created by live wires just outside of the hatch. Trying to control his rising heartbeat, Maurice floated to the other hatch, only to see flames splashing like water on the outside of it. He looked through the small round window above to see what the condition of the O2 tanks was.

"What in the world is that?" he said aloud, looking at a big, dark mechanical arm that appeared to be squeezing the module.

The light inside flickered, and for a moment, he saw his partner and coworker Carew's terrorized face reflected in the glass against the starry sky, and a rising Earth behind her.

Taking a deep breath, he let go of the handle. "This is it, I guess." Goosebumps erupted all over his body. "Computer, play Mozart, Concerto Twenty-one."

He continued to wear the suit, preparing to eject in space with minimal air in hopes that there would be enough time for him to find his way to the central part of the station before it was too late.

Holding his helmet with his left hand and closing his eyes, he floated in the middle of the module as the blinking red, yellow, and white warning lights continued to indicate failure. The sound of piano music filled the module as he took deep breaths, preparing for the inevitable implosion.

A series of quick, muffled bangs attracted his attention, and he turned his head to see what could be causing it. Just outside of the hatch, there was another spacesuit banging on the hatch with a wrench.

Carew, his partner, raised her reflective visor and motioned him to put his helmet on.

"I have no more air in my suit!" he screamed, putting both his hands on his throat. He knew that Carew couldn't hear him.

Carew, in turn, raised an oxygen tank into view.

"Computer, how long till the pressure is critical?" he immediately asked the A.I. over the sound of Mozart.

"Thirty seconds till critical pressure," the voice replied, "twenty-nine, twenty-eight..."

Locking his helmet on the EMU, he hurriedly floated back in front of the hatch, motioning her to move away from it. Before opening the hatch, he attached his safety chord to a metal handle nearby.

Swoosh. The hatch opened violently, decompressing the module as Maurice held on to the handle with both hands.

He felt the tug of his safety cord pull him back toward the now-decompressed module as the contents of the capsule flew in space. Carew reeled him in until they were close enough to hug. She connected the O2 tank to his EMU as he tried to remain calm, helping her best he could by staying motionless.

"I saw your ..." he began to say as fresh air rushed in the EMU. "I saw your..."

"Shhh, come with me. You have to see this."

As the two astronauts floated away from the now ruined module, Earth, accompanied by the Sun, rose. A giant mechanical arm that extended out of the body of a slow-moving, dull-black vessel quickly cast a shadow over them.

Maurice lifted his sun-blocking visor. "What is

that?"

"No idea. I was doing the scheduled E.V.A. when this came out of nowhere."

"Do you think it's ours?"

"No idea. Houston is completely cut off. I hope they're aware of this."

"We have to get to the other part of the station and get in the escape pod. We're going to run out of air if we stay here."

Carew activated her suit propulsion, guiding them toward the rest of the station as more debris flew their way. Looking back through his wrist mirror, Maurice confirmed that the oxygen tanks had exploded. After a few minutes, they reached the central part of the station. Carew knocked on the hatch, but it was dark inside. "Let's get in. We'll figure it out from there."

Maurice turned the knob on the outside of the hatch, which set the unlock mechanism in motion, releasing the inner door.

"Let's see if there's any air inside here." She pressed a few buttons on the side panel, which didn't respond.

"This thing is dead."

"Yeah, there's no air coming in. If I open the inside door, I'll depressurize the cabin."

"Not really, since this one is closed. The air will

thin out a bit, but it'll be OK, let's get going."

She twisted the knob of the inside vestibule hatch, which hissed as it opened, revealing the rest of the space station. It was dark and empty. Carew stopped for a moment to look at the abandoned section —such a depressing view.

"Let's go; we don't have time for sightseeing." Maurice nudged her.

They quickly moved to the escape module, closing the hatch behind them. Flipping switches, Carew powered it on and released the clamps holding it to the station.

Floating away from it, she had a clear view of the new craft. Four large mechanical arms were extending from the center fuselage. It held the maintenance section with one of them. In the Sun's light, it looked as if it were a bug of some kind. *Definitely not ours.* Setting the escape course, she engaged the thrusters toward Earth.

After the craft passed through the turbulent heat of re-entry, she released the parachutes as soon as she could, which slowed their fall considerably.

"We're almost home."

"I think they know that we have unfriendly visitors above," he said, raising his head and looking out of one of the small windows as the capsule exchanged paths with rockets heading up.

#

The starlight made its pass yet again as Irene un-buckled herself, reaching for the white fabric container she was using as a garbage bag, unzipping it, and placing more wrappers inside. She turned her attention to the window hatch. Floating toward it, Irene looked out at the broken airlock. "Oh Adam, it's scarily fitting for you to write a book that has a story like this," she mumbled, shaking her head. Just as in the "Rescued" story she'd just read, she saw floating debris just outside the broken airlock. Wires strung most of it as the entire section of Morning Star continued to roll, slowly but uncontrol-lably orbiting their new home, Helsey 8K.

Grabbing the fabric handles of the supply bags, she moved all around the cabin, checking for leaks or anything that could be wrong. She passed her hand through some areas that looked damaged by the im-pact three days ago—almost four now. She then looked at the battery status display again; 75 percent and char-ging. The cockpit's speakers crackled as Adam's voice echoed, "Test, test, can you hear me?"

"Oh my god, yes!" Irene floated to the communi-cation panel and picked up the microphone. "Yes, I hear you loud and clear."

"Test, test, Irene, can you hear me?"

"Yes, I can," Irene replied. "Can you read me?"

"Hold on. I think I can hear her voice." Adam sounded like he was talking to someone standing next to him. "Irene, you sound far away, can you get closer?"

Realizing her transmissions were going through the microphone in the headset stuck to the Velcro by the hatch, she floated over and disconnected it. The receiver automatically transferred the feed to the communications panel.

"How about now?"

"Loud and clear," Adam responded.

"Good to hear you," Tom, the communications technician, added. "Adam told us that you were OK, but we were all anxious."

"Aw, thank you, Tom."

"Look, Irene, we sent a probe to the ground and are waiting for results. Once they say it's OK for the rest of us, we'll all go down. Do me a favor and turn on the cabin's beacon so we can find the ship if we need to."

"I'll do that right now." Irene floated to the cockpit and flipped some switches, which in turn lit up all the buttons and screens facing her. She reached under her seat and pulled out a clipboard with a laminated paper on it that read *Emergency Beacon Procedure*. Irene tore off the perforated bottom part of it and flipped it over, revealing a barcode.

"We're assessing the status of the remaining shuttles. One has punctures from the incident, but the rest should be OK to evacuate all twenty-three of us," Irene heard Adam say as she placed the barcode under a glowing red laser scanner on the right of the console.

A single high-pitched alarm beep filled the cabin,

which Irene silenced immediately. *Acknowledge Beacon* appeared on the screen in front of her. "It's done."

"I got it," Tom said. "I'll go recalibrate the rest of the equipment. It was good talking to you, Captain Deris."

"It is terrific to hear from you as well, Tom," Irene replied. "Adam, can we have a word in private?"

"Of course," Adam said. "Give me a second."

Irene flipped open the flight computer and tapped on the screen 'Mission Status.'

"OK, the audio feed is isolated. What did you have to say, Captain?"

"You changed the mission objective?"

"We are barely surviving up here, Irene. The Morning Star is hanging by a thread. This mission is now complete. Helsey is where we make a new life."

"Fair enough." Irene tapped on the screen and begun to update the mission status on the flight computer. "Let me know of any developments."

"As soon as I get them, especially now that we fixed the coms. Meanwhile, please prep your E.V.A. suit."

"Will do," Irene replied. "Oh, by the way, I'm reading your little book, it's exciting. I do have some questions for you."

"Save them for later, Irene." She heard Adam chuckle. "Over and out."

Taking a sigh of relief, Irene went back to the pilot's chair. Buckling herself in, she quietly stared at the flight log laptop. The words "Carrier Hope" caught her eye. She swallowed as the final speech she'd heard the last time she was on board the carrier rang in her ears, reminding her of the parting address.

"Seed Ship Morning Star, you are about to embark on a historical journey. And these words are not said lightly. Your crew of twenty-six, and eight thousand human embryos, will be the spark that ignites humanity on that side of the universe. Helsey 8K will be humanity's newest home. All of you have now earned the title Children Of The Stars. For the good of humanity, this is the last time we will see and talk to each other. Good luck with your mission. Control tower out."

Folding the laptop, she raised her head and looked at the direction of the windows. They had been covered by the outside shielding automatically at the moment the asteroid impacted the connector bridge. Shaking her head, she grabbed the book and flipped to the next story, finding yet another yellow square note stuck in there.

"You know, for a person who deals in words, you sure don't say a lot."

In silence, she looked at me over her shoulder, sighing.

"You have a visitor; one of your characters is in the living room."

Without moving, she shifted her gaze toward the cor-

ner, looking at the flickering light, "Is that so?"

I wonder if these are Adam's notes, she thought to herself. *I'll have to remember to ask him about this as well.*

THE FUSE

By Dorian Keys and S.J. Turner

"**L**adies and gentlemen, thank you for attending this gathering," Morel Wester, the West Lands Union military commander said, raising his voice. "I'm sure the views will entertain you for the rest of the trip." He lifted his glass, looking at the many attendees who looked up at him. "This floating platform, while still under military control, will one day be a public facility. One of the many facilities the West Lands Union are working so hard to build with the novel technologies provided.

"To progress!"

"To progress!" The guest's voices echoed through the football field-size glass and wooden dome floating high above the ground.

"This new and exciting technology is brought to us by none other than an inventor from the outer colonies," he continued, "one more reason to celebrate our future union."

The platform continued to chase the sunset, moving at Sun's pace as it floated several miles above the saturated yellow planet. As music echoed through the large brass megaphone speakers, the guests continued to walk about, mainly heading for the large windows to look at the planet's curvature where the world was visible.

A young man approached Kristen, who was sitting at a table all by herself, holding a brass-adorned glass. She was looking at the guests chatting and her father walking down from the podium. "Do you come here often?"

Recognizing the familiar voice, Kristen smiled and slightly turned her head. "Apparently not often enough, Eugene."

The young man took his black bowler hat in his hands. "Someone has to make sure this platform floats." He chuckled, stepping in front of her.

"And that would be you, I presume."

"Among other things, you are correct, ma'am."

"Miss," she corrected him with a smile. "Is there

anything you don't know?" Kristen asked as two men approached the table. Her smile faded upon their sight.

"Kristen, there you are." Morel stopped in front of the round table, which was covered by a thin, white see-through cloth.

"Father," she greeted him, shifting her eyes to the second man who approached. "Markus."

"And who do we have here?" Markus narrowed his eyes, looking at Eugene. "A guest from the outer colonies, I presume."

"My name is Eugene Stawler, the inventor of this platform."

"Aren't you supposed to be below the deck, tinkering?" Markus replied, curling his lips.

Eugene bit his lip, bowing his head. "I was invited by..."

"Well, the party is over, time to go," Markus ordered as Eugene looked down at the wooded deck, turning around and preparing to leave. But not before he faced Kristen, "It was nice talking to you...miss." He smiled faintly.

Eugene walked to the end of the platform, where the ladder that led under the deck was. There, the innovative hybrid electric and diesel engines that were rapidly replacing steam-powered machinery were clunking, creating steam and propelling the platform so that it could chase the sunset.

"Why did you do that?" Kristen confronted

Markus, looking at Eugene as he disappeared down the staircase.

"These outer colonies..." Markus paused as to search for the correct term "...constructs, because that's who they are, patching themselves with what we throw away. They need to know their place." He looked at Kristen with a grin. "Come, love, let us enjoy the party." He extended his hand to her. Kristen just stared at him, tightening her lips.

Feeling the awkwardness of the moment, Markus narrowed his eyes and tilted his head, as if about to order Kristen to go with him, when three young women approached the table where they were standing.

"Mister Wester, it's such a pleasure to be on this— what is it called?" they asked Morel.

"Oh, this is just the platform," Markus said as he turned his head, shifting his attention and smiling at them. "You see those cables on the side?" He got closer to the three. "Let me show you." He placed his hand on the back of one of them, leading the three young women to the windows at the edge of the platform as he turned and made eye contact with Morel.

"What are you doing?" Morel whispered to Kristen as soon as Markus left.

"I'm not his 'thing,'" she replied defiantly, "nor yours."

"Daughter." Morel closed in on her and grabbed her elbow. "Your union with Markus has ensured peace between the West Lands and us; you have no choice."

"You, above all, should know very well that that's where we are from; the outer colonies, not West Lands."

"I don't ever want to hear you say something like that again," Morel said, hiding his anger behind clenched teeth.

"Then why did you allow me to go to school in the outer colonies? I have friends there!" Kristen raised her voice in frustration, and a few guests who were sitting nearby turned their heads and looked at their direction.

Morel narrowed his eyes but did not say anything. He just looked around at the guests, faking a smile.

"He has made my life a living hell, father," she whispered, facing away.

"A small price to pay for peace, daughter."

"You are not paying it. I am." She moved her arm out of his grip and, gathering her white dress with her mechanical brass arm, walked away from him toward the back of the room where the outer colonies' representatives were sitting, witnessing what had happened.

A few guests approached Morel, who maintained his composure, asking him questions about the platform as Kristen sat on a chair near where Eliza, her childhood friend, was seated, surrounded by the outer colonies' representatives.

In contrast to West Lands guests, attired in bowling hats and tuxedoes, wearing short sleeve shirts to show off their robotics. The outer colonies reps were dressed in dull clothes, not showing any mechanical limbs.

"Are you okay, Kristen?" Eliza asked as Kristen poured some water in a glass and drank it.

"I'm fine, Eliza, my father just gets on my nerves."

"I'm sure he means well—by you, at least. He has completely forgotten where he came from."

"Funny you say that, I just reminded him about it."

"I saw." Eliza tightened her lips, looking at the purple-tinted water bottle on the table.

"Look at that monster," Kristen shifted her gaze toward Markus as he flirted with the three young women he met earlier. "He knows my father has no other choice. Markus treated me like I was one of his servants in front of him and didn't even flinch. I hate him."

"You know," Eliza lowered her voice, "we completed the carrier with Eugene's designs. It's ready."

That statement stirred the other representatives sitting at the table. Some of them adjusted themselves on their seats others looked at where the exit doors were.

Kristen made eye contact with all of them as shivers went down her spine. "Their time is coming." She said looking at Markus and her father.

"Eliza, stop talking," one of the other members whispered. "What are you doing?"

She turned her head and whispered back, "Kristen is one of ours."

"She is *his* daughter, you never said that!" the member continued with a subdued voice.

"Oh, speaking of Eugene, did you see where he went?" Kristen changed subjects, seemingly not fazed by the gravity of the information she'd just received.

"He is probably below deck." Eliza cracked a smile. "What do you have in mind, you rebel, you?"

"I want to talk to him; can you please tell him to call on me?"

"I absolutely will," Eliza said.

"Good luck with your plans," Kristen said, looking at everyone as she got up from the table, heading for the other guests as Morel began to look her way. "Excuse me. I have to put on my happy face now."

Kristen got up and walked to a large rectangular table by the window, where most of the guests were gathered, looking out. She picked up a few cards that had some trivia information about the floating platform and began to read them to the guests. Morel and Markus walked toward the other end of the giant, three-hundred-feet plus platform floor. A few soldiers pulled a tall curtain closed, cutting off that section.

"You may take your seats, gentlemen," Morel said, approaching a large rectangular table in the middle of the corner room the curtain created. "It's time."

Bertram Burnett, the chief intelligence officer for the Corporation Union, wearing a black suit and a black top hat, approached the top of the table.

"Gentlemen, I have gathered you here today to share some intelligence my men have brought to my attention. Rumor has it that the outer colonies' resistance has plans for and is currently developing a carrier with our internal combustion technology."

"Rumor?" asked one of the other military uniformed members who was sitting at the table. "So much for our impeccable intelligence officers. You called all of us here to share rumors?"

"As you all know," the man said as he took off his top hat, revealing his half-brass skull with fasteners protruding toward the other half that had hair, "our officers have always had a tough time gathering intelligence from the outer colonies. The sheer size of it makes it nearly impossible to cover. However, I must urge the council not to ignore this information."

"Does this mean that we have a spy among us?" Markus pushed the wooden chair back while adjusting his black bowtie.

"This platform, just as the carrier Sulco, contains the combination of the two technologies we are using to build our own floating carriers, helium cushions aided by diesel-powered lift propellers. Where else can this information be coming from?"

"That is a very curious finding, Bertram." Markus made eye contact with Morel as if to assign him the fault. "Curious indeed."

Sensing the accusation, Morel got up. "Gentlemen, this operation has taken us several years of development, with thousands of workers, work orders, and so on. I told you I had men and ideas; I never promised complete secrecy."

"So, what do we do about it?"

"With your help, I'll find and root this spy," Markus said, looking at Bertram.

"We will do our best," Bertram replied. "I also have one more request." He continued. "One of my men got badly injured on our last mission and is missing a leg and one lung. I need the council's authorization to rebuild him. What say you, Morel?"

Morel looked at Bertram. "Of course, old friend. Send him to the hospital; I'll direct my men there to take care of the rest."

As the military and civilian council members continued their meeting, the giant floating platform reached its landing dock. Its crew launched thick hybrid metal and fiber ropes, which served as anchors. Four of those ropes connected to the land-dock itself and several additional ones served as an elevator platform. It ferried all the passengers down to the planet's surface.

The guard soldiers pulled the curtain back again as the military members began to mix with the civilians while they lined up to take the elevators.

Bertram approached Morel as the latter looked at Markus, who was strolling toward the three young women he was talking with earlier. "I must thank you for your generosity in helping my man."

"Don't mention it, Bertram, Morel replied, shifting his sight further forward and looking at Kristen, who was stacking the cue cards together.

"You seem worried, old friend, what's got into you?"

"I have to ask, Bertram. Do *you* suspect anyone of spying?"

"My men suspect the inventor, Eugene."

"He was talking to my daughter earlier."

"I saw that too."

"Bertram." Morel turned around, facing him as a few guests passed by. "Though he might have disclosed the carrier plans out of some strange sense of a bond between the outer lands people and the resistance, Eugene is very instrumental to the armed forces."

"I understand that."

"No matter what happens, he is not to be destroyed." Morel rubbed his brass shoulder beneath his jacket. "I need you to make sure of that." He handed Bertram a yellow envelope.

"What about Markus?"

"Keep an eye on him as well; I'm afraid he is getting out of line."

~~~

Three hours later, planeside -- Wester residence, Kristen's quarters.

"Eugene, what a pleasant surprise," Kristen said as Archibald, the robotic butler, closed the front door. "I thought you were not going to show up; that Eliza didn't deliver my message."

"Miss Wester," Eugene saluted her, slightly bowing his head. He took off his bowler hat and placed it under his left arm. "I had some work orders to fill and happened to be in the area. Eliza made sure I got the message."

"This way." Kristen led the way to the living room, surrounded on both sides by curved, brass-adorned wooden staircases. The dancing shadows cast by the candles which were scattered all around the large, dark living room calmed down once she stopped by the crackling fireplace.

"You know that you can call me Kristen." Noticing that he was staring at her, she asked, "Do you like the dress?"

"Um, yes, very much." Eugene smiled, shifting his gaze to look at the thin brass pistons of her left hand and forearm.

"I found it in a closet upstairs." She smiled as her black-gloved fingers began to play with her hair nervously.

Eugene swallowed, composing himself while looking into her dark eyes. "You look stunning."

"Thank you." Kristen smiled. "Do you want to join me by the fireplace?" she asked him, slowly walking in front of the swaying flames of the brass-adorned firepit.

"I would love to." Feeling his heartbeat rising with arousal, Eugene followed and sat on the couch directly in front of her. He placed his hat on a small mahogany table off to the side. "You know," he said, fiddling with his monocle. "Every time I see you, my heartbeat goes through the roof. I had forgotten that feeling, so much so that earlier at the platform I checked my heart box. Turns out there *is* a fuse there."

She tried her best to hide her persistent smile and sat next to him. "*You* don't know about the heart fuse?"

"I wasn't sure *I* had one," he replied, reaching to unbutton his shirt as she eagerly watched him reveal the brass-lined heart shape on the left side of his chest. "Until today."

Her pupils dilated at the sight as she placed her brass mechanical hand over her own heart. "The medical dictionary describes it as a mechanical device symbolically left by the creator. Upgrades have long bypassed its function of protecting the main organ." She reached out with her gloved, flesh and bone hand and touched his chest. "One won't die if it's damaged or lost, but symbolically, their heart will belong to whoever they give it to."

Eugene looked down. "No, I've never heard of such a device," he added, with irony in his voice tone.

"Oh, ha, ha, ha." Kristen hid a smirk, reaching up to hold her gloved hand to his chest. "How could an inventor not know about the intricacies of body-building and mechanics. Silly me."

The two locked eyes.

Feeling her emotions were about to take over her mind, Kristen let go of his chest and slowly took a few steps past the shiny wooden table, her shadow hugging everything it touched. Stopping in front of a large, framed painting, she peeked at Eugene over her shoulder as she pulled her hair behind her left ear, showing him the diamond earring that matched her skin color perfectly.

"Do you want to see something?" she asked.

"Show me." Though Eugene was old enough to have experienced love, he could barely hide the nervous tremble her presence induced. He got up, adjusting his jacket and placing his monocle inside his small pocket.

Pulling aside the large painting of a man in a

tuxedo, much like the one Eugene was wearing, she revealed a safe behind it. Keying her code in, Kristen opened it, pulling out a stained-glass box filled with shiny heart fuses.

"How do you have so many?" Eugene asked from behind her shoulder as he looked at the fuse box intently.

Kristen slowly turned to face Eugene, who was so close he could smell her faint perfume, even feel her warm breath.

"Each one has its own long story," she said with a sigh. Picking one from the box, she continued, "This belongs to Lazarus Weller. My flight instructor. I met him at the camp a few years back. He died during some battle two days after he gave it to me."

"Are they all dead?" Eugene raised his eyebrow in surprise.

"Some of them are." Kristen placed the fuse back in the box as Archibald entered the room with drinks.

"Ah, leave the tray by the fireplace, Archibald," she told the robot, who obeyed without saying a thing.

"What's his story?" Eugene looked at Archibald, who slowly walked away.

"The inventor before you botched his arm transplant and electrocuted him. He can move around and do basic tasks, but not much of anything else," Kristen said, picking two glasses from the tray and handing him one with her brass hand. "What is your story of late?"

"You know my story beginning and end. I'm just a homeschooled orphan nobody with a vivid imagination who's very handy with tools." Eugene grabbed one of the glasses as Kristen revealed his heart box with her free hand and tapped with her glass chalice. "Cheers."

Looking down at his chest, Eugene raised his glass. The corner of his mouth lifted into a crooked smile, and he peered at her from beneath his brows. "Cheers."

Kristen took his glass and set it down next to hers on the tray. She took his hand and stepped close to him. Her dark eyes gazing deep into his. Their lips were so close; it felt as though they were sharing the same breath. "I want to taste you Eugene. I know you've thought about it as well."

He lowered his gaze from hers and swallowed. "Yes, I would like that very much."

Eugene was shocked at how swift her movement was. The coolness of her brass hand on the nape of his neck barely registered as their lips met. His hands wrapped around her, grasping her bottom, and he pulled her tight against him. She released a light moan into his mouth as his swollen member pressed against her midriff.

"Master Eugene," interrupted the robotic voice of Archibald. "Your transportation is here."

"I guess that'll have to wait for another day," Kristen said, smiling as Eugene let out a sigh and reluctantly took a step back, buttoning his shirt back up.

"I want to see you again, heartbreaker," he whispered, handing her a card with his phone number.

Without speaking, she took the card and immediately slipped it inside the glove she had on her right hand and forearm.

Eugene stopped in front of the front door and turned to see Kristen walking upstairs, holding her long dress up with her left hand.

The fresh air felt good on his warm skin as he walked to his internal combustion engine vehicle. "She must like you," he heard the operator say, "usually by this time you'd be her slave."

"What do you mean?" Eugene replied, looking back to the entrance as Kristen vanished upstairs.

"I mean, most men that dare dating her tend to have bad luck. I'd stay away from her if I were you." The driver adjusted his top hat.

"And how do you know that?" Eugene asked, looking at Markus entering Kristen's residence.

"Oh, it's just rumors, but you know," the operator said, taking a turn and heading for the floating platform elevator, "sometimes, rumors can be true."

#

Exhaustion finally set-in to Irene's body. She rubbed both her eyes with the palms of her hands.

Looking back toward the round window, she noticed that the planet was now in the way of the star—it was night. *I have to rest for a few minutes.* She unbuckled, grabbed a flashlight, and floated to the control panel to flip the light switches off. Turning on the flashlight, she found her way back to the pilot's seat, buckled herself in, and closed the book, placing the bookmark to save her progress. She looked at the flight time: 0339.

The cockpit that now housed Irene tumbled as it orbited around the planet. Next to it, strung by metal piping, fibers, and wires, was the rest of the spaceship. It housed the living quarters where the rest of the 23 crewmembers were. The cryo-pod section, designed to land itself on a planet if necessary, sat in the middle of the ship, shielded from the nuclear and fusion engines and generators, which were at the far end of Morning Star. The two pieces of wreckage floated parallel to each other, rotating at the same rate, yet out of each other's field of view.

One of the shuttles detached from the wreckage and slowly floated away from it. Once out far enough, it faced the planet and lit its boosters, heading straight for it.

#

The first thing Irene saw when she opened her eyes was her hand, floating just above her face. Moving it, she peeked at the flight clock: 0850. *Wow, I was exhausted.* She yawned and looked around, unbuckling the harness and pushing herself away from the pilot's seat. Sighing, she reached for the flashlight and briefly let her body float just above the seat. She turned the flashlight on, then moved to the control panel to check the status of the cabin—battery at seventy-nine percent, atmosphere within the norm, solar panels operational. She flipped the power switch back up as the small L.E.D. lights illuminated the cabin.

Pushing herself away from the panel, she moved to the furthest part of the cabin, where her waste bag was and relieved herself. "Much better," she muttered, zipping her pants back up as she floated to the hatch facing outer space. She observed debris, wires—some floating and holding onto the rest of the ship out of her field of view.

Irene then moved to the radio. "Adam, are you there?"

The speakers crackled but went silent.

"Adam, come in. Over," Irene transmitted one more time.

"Adam is sleeping, Irene," she heard a female voice respond. "This is Emily at the control center. It's good to hear your voice, Captain Deris."

"I see." Irene smiled. "It's good to hear from you too, Emily."

"I'll wake him up…"

"No need for that, Emily. Let him sleep. Can you please ask him to radio me when he wakes up? There is no emergency. I just wanted to ask him a few questions."

"Will do," Emily responded.

"How's your situation there?"

"We finally adjusted the artificial gravity generator and restored power to pretty much everything. Now we're working on restoring power to the emergency escape modules and landing shuttles. I hear you're living off emergency rations. We should be able to evacuate you from there soon."

"I'm happy everyone is doing well there. As for here, it's not so bad. I've got plenty of food, water, and air. Though, I must admit that I miss gravity." Irene chuckled. "And a good shower."

"We will have one ready for you as soon as you arrive, Captain."

"Sounds good," Irene replied. "Over and out."

She floated away from the communications panel and opened one of the food bags, pulling out another protein bar. She then moved to her seat, where the book was floating, and looked for the bookmark.

"Where was I..." Irene flipped the pages back to find this story's title. *Ah yes, Fuses.*

#

"What's so special about this guy?" Markus asked, walking into Kristen's room as she pulled an oil canister out to lubricate her hand pistons.

"He is everything you are not," she said without turning, focusing on her hand.

"Look at me when I talk to you." His voice rose in frustration.

She placed the canister on a small wooden table nearby and turned around, facing Markus with a tight-lipped smile.

"Your father doesn't need this kind of distraction, not while he is commanding a war."

"Is there a reason for you to be here, or do you just like stalking me?" she asked, ignoring his statement.

"Your new friend recommended the platform dock for repairs and upgrades, but now I see he had other motives."

"Get out of my house, and don't let the door hit you on your way out," she replied with a sneer.

"I'll see you sooner than you think." Markus slowly walked out of the shadow downstairs toward the front door as Archibald crossed paths with him. Markus left the mansion as Archibald locked the stained-glass case back in the safe.

~ ~ ~

Try as she might, Kristen couldn't get the vision of Eugene from her mind. Since they first met in high school, Eugene's charming, somewhat innocent demeanor struck her. He was unlike the other men she had met since and reminded her of the place they grew up in, the outer colonies—the sound of kids playing in dusty playgrounds, the unfinished buildings, boarded-up storefronts. There, misery brought people together tighter, money or not. He reminded her of her first, fleeting kiss.

"I have to see him again," she muttered to herself.

Picking up the phone receiver, she turned the crank, watching the liquid inside bubble until the gears locked in place, then dialed his number.

"Hello?"

"Eugene, it's Kristen."

"Hi Kristen."

"I was hoping you'd meet me at Planetarium Hall this afternoon."

"Isn't Planetarium Hall closed to the public today?" he asked, seeming a bit confused.

With the receiver cradled in her hand, she smiled. "Yes, it is."

Hearing the crunch of leather coming through the speaker, she could almost picture him shifting his weight uncomfortably in his chair. Her voice softened as she drew back the curtain to peer out of the window. "How does two o'clock work for you?"

"Ah, two o'clock should be fine, but how will we..." he began, but she cut him off.

"Perfect! I'll meet you out front at two o'clock. I'll take care of getting us in. See you then, Eugene."

Hanging up the phone, Kristen checked her forearm timepiece, an accent piece her father had added to her last year for her birthday. It was just past twelve. There was still plenty of time to find the perfect ensemble to try to impress Eugene.

After the third pass through her closet, she finally settled on a long, ruffled skirt pinched to her hips in the front to reveal her beautifully shaped and lengthy legs. The bodice was a form-fitting corset made of rich brown leather and strung together with accents of lace. After giving her left knee a quick oiling, Kristen chose her favorite pair of thigh-high brown leather boots and pulled them on. Dabbing a little oil on a soft cloth, she shined the brass toe-plate and the adornments along the length of them.

Carefully tugging on her long opera gloves, Kristen looked at her reflection in the mirror one last time with a sigh. She grabbed her dark, round sunglasses and stretched them over her head, settling them on as a hairband. Pleased with her final look, she headed for the door.

~ ~ ~

Eugene stood in front of Planetarium Hall, looking like a man she could spend the rest of her life with. His eyes briefly met hers as a smile formed on his lips. Bowing slightly, he tipped his hat. "Kristen, it's great to see you again. You look lovely."

Kristen gave him a ravishing smile and dipped slightly into a curtsey. "Thank you, Eugene. You look rather dashing yourself."

Eugene turned to face the enormous building in the shape of a dome. "How exactly do you intend to enter when all the doors are locked?" The words had barely dropped from his lips when she produced the key and brushed past him.

"I borrowed this from a friend," she said, turning it and flipping open the key-box lid to reveal the row of brass toggles. One by one, she flicked them, setting off a sequence of creaking cogwheels. The large stained-glass doors began to slide open, and she grinned over at him as she extended her hand toward the entrance. "After you, fine sir."

As the doors closed behind them, Kristen slipped the key back into the tiny satchel tied at her hip. The two walked in the main hall, which expanded some ten floors above them. Each metal scaffolding floor, in the shape of a circle, was smaller than the one below. The outside of the planetarium was lined with large, transparent windows that had mechanical blinds designed to close and darken the place when needed, though, at present, they allowed some lighting to enter from outside and dimly illuminate the planets displayed within.

This place had always amazed Eugene, but not quite like the woman standing before him.

The two stopped in the main hall, where a giant planet was slowly rotating along a tilted axis, left to right. Around it, there was a guide rail. Attached to the globe was the moon, which revolved slowly in orbit, right to left.

"Looking at the size of the planet we live on, I can't help but think that we are but ants in this picture." Eugene sighed. "We just slog through our lives, day in, day out. And that just," he looked at the ceiling where the moon slid through the metal path, rising over the planet, "makes me ask: who are we?" He turned, facing Kristen. "What are we doing here? Are we going somewhere?"

"We are here because we are attracted to each other, Eugene." Kristen took a step closer to him, grabbing his hand.

"That's not what I meant." Eugene looked at Kristen, who was smiling. He brought her gloved flesh and bone hand up and lightly kissed it.

"I know what you meant." Kristen looked up at the moon, which was slowly approaching them, making a metal-on-metal sliding sound on the orbit guide rail. "And I would love to sit here with you and get lost in those thoughts."

Interlocking his fingers with Kristen's, Eugene

led them toward a bench on the side of the dimly lit planetary hall.

"Every time I think I have life figured out," he said, his voice echoing in the empty building, "something new happens."

"What do you mean?"

"The entire package that I put together for your father, all those ideas, came to me when I was a child. In the outer colonies. I thought it would be an invention to make all our lives better."

"Now that you mention it, I remember you telling me something about this." Kristen stopped in front of a bench. "You kissed me that night."

"I was excited." Eugene smiled.

Kristen looked at him in the eye. "You told me that I had something to do with it."

"You have always had that effect on me, Kristen." Eugene raised his eyes to meet hers. "Always."

"That's curious." Kristen let his hand go and stopped.

After taking another step toward the bench, Eugene turned around.

"I *always* thought that something else attracted you to me," Kristen continued.

Eugene removed his bowler hat, tucking it loosely under his arm, and watched keenly as, finger by finger, she pulled the gloves free from her hands and tucked them into the waistband of her skirt. She closed in the gap between them and stood only a breath away. Biting his lower lip, Eugene slid his flesh and bone hand under the front pinch at the side of her skirt and grabbed her bottom, pulling her closer.

"There it is." Kristen smiled, softly bumping foreheads with him.

Not a word was spoken while he toyed with the waistband of her panties, allowing her to change her mind before he tugged them down her legs. He slowly ran his hand back up her thigh and hesitated one last time just before he reached her mound. His eyes sprung to hers, and he jerked his hand back with a nervous smile. "I'm sorry. I don't know what's come over me."

"Don't be sorry, I want this too. I have wanted this since the night you last kissed me."

The air in the room grew thick as Kristen's eyes locked on his. She nudged him until the back of his knees hit the bench behind them. Forced to take a seat, Eugene stared up at her and swallowed. Bending forward, she placed her hand on his shoulder.

"I want you," she said, casually stepping out of her panties.

He took a deep, desperate breath, watching her as she straddled his lap. His left hand settled on the side of her neck while his thumb gently traced her jawline. "I want this so badly, but I'm leaving later tonight on the Lithani freighter. The work order has been delayed. So, I will have to pick up the supplies myself."

"Shh, I don't care. You'll be back, and I will wait for you," she said, closing her eyes and leaning in to meet his lips with an exquisitely tender kiss. Her hands moved to undo the buttons on his shirt and smoothed across the expanse of his chest.

"What about Markus?"

Kristen shrugged. "What about him?"

"He is one of my bosses, and your father is my commander."

"Markus is a monster, and I wish he'd died a long time ago. Are you here with me?" Kristen began to untie the lace closure of her bodice, letting it fall open, exposing her breasts. "Or with my father?"

His eyes met hers, and without hesitation, her hands grasped the back of his head, pulling his mouth down to her breast. Her head instantly fell back with a cry of pleasure as he pulled her nipple into his mouth. He caught the faint smell of her perfume as he kissed his way back up to her lips and slid his tongue over hers.

With the growing need to feel his flesh against hers, Kristen lifted herself slightly and reached down between them. She unbuckled his pants, releasing his manhood from its cloth prison before settling back down onto his lap. The feel of his swollen heat against her center was divine as she ground herself down onto him with a moan. Eugene grasped her hips, guiding her back and forth, smearing the slickness between them.

Breathless, Kristen's eyes met his. Her voice was thick with desire. "I want to feel you inside me, Eugene."

~~~

Unbeknownst to the two lovers on the bench, one of the spies dispatched by Burnett and Markus was observing them. He called his boss, Burnett, who, in turn, called Morel and Markus. The former was back onboard the military carrier retrofitted with the new diesel engines as well as the latest invention, the airplane. Aided by the new diesel engines, it was capable of forward flight. The new invention made such crafts the fastest and most dangerous weapon yet.

Morel asked Burnett to keep this information to himself, but it was too late. Markus had just left Kristen's residence and was heading for the platform. Together with his men, he led for the planetarium.

~~~

Eugene's demeanor suddenly changed. He pushed her back slightly with a look of fear. "Kristen, shhh. I think someone is here."

Listening carefully, they heard the defined click of footsteps getting closer. Fearful that her father's spies or Markus might be close, and wanting to protect Eugene, Kristen quickly gathered her clothing and asked him to do the same, showing him the back exit.

She grabbed his face and kissed him deeply. "I love you, Eugene. Call me when you get back. Promise?"

"I promise. Here, let me give you this," he said, reaching for his heart fuse. "You can give it back to me when we meet again."

"Not yet, darling," Kristen said, smiling as she placed her hand on top of his to keep him from taking it out. "We have plenty of time for that."

Eugene quickly buttoned his shirt and put on his jacket. Giving Kristen one last look, he headed for the back door and exited. As the door slowly came back to its locked position, Kristen turned around only to see Markus standing by the bench they had just left.

"Interesting display of unfaithfulness, wouldn't you say?" he asked Kristen in his deep voice as his left eye twitched slightly.

"I have told you more than once; I'll not be faithful to you. Not after what you have done to me." She turned her back to him, lacing up her bodice.

"Morel says otherwise," Markus began, only to be interrupted by Kristen's scornful voice.

"My father might have a say in how to fight the resistance, but he has no say in how I run my life!" She finished fixing herself up and placed her dark, round sunglasses back on her head. "Anyway, I have nothing to hide. I stand by what I do, and I am not sorry about it." She walked away toward the exit.

"You will be," Markus replied in a whisper,

watching Kristen's shadow disappear past the open door as he adjusted the leather strap on his prosthetic hand.

~ ~ ~

The next morning

"Miss Morel, you have a visitor," she heard Archibald's familiar robotic voice say as it knocked on her door.

Picking up her metal coffee cup, she sat by the sizeable brass-adorned window of her room, covering her legs up with her sleeping robe. "Let them in."

"I love that coffee smell," Markus said, sniffing the air as he walked in the room.

"Oh, it's you again." Kristen looked out of the window and placed the cup on the table. "What do you want?"

"I thought you'd like to read today's headline." He dropped a newspaper on the table—the front page read "Freighter 'Lithani' destroyed in a tragic accident, three thousand souls lost."

Her heartbeat rose, and instantly her breathing shallowed as the thought of losing Eugene boiled her blood. "Did you do this?"

"I can't say I did all of it, but I will say that I have

a special fuse for you." Markus grinned and approached her, holding something on his hands. "I brought you something."

Kristen labored to swallow the lump in her throat as she realized that he'd destroyed the freighter just to kill Eugene.

"Why did you do this to me?" Kristen asked, getting up and slowly reaching for the blade tied to her brass forearm. Anger consumed her, and she could feel the heat rushing to her face.

"I do everything for you." He took a step toward her, extending the small wrapped package with his right hand.

"Your fuse says otherwise," she responded with damp eyes, grasping the handle of the blade.

"What is this obsession with the heart-fuses? Neither of us has one, Kristen. What was so special about his anyway?"

"He was pure!" Kristen cried, pulling the knife from its sheath and in one motion thrusting it into Markus's heart box.

He let go of the package, groping for the knife handle and gasping for air as his knees gave in.

"Both you and my father are monsters," she whispered as a tear rolled down her cheek. "And he is next."

As Markus fell to the floor, struggling to breathe, Kristen picked up the box and unwrapped it. Inside was a familiar small glass container with a heart fuse inside.

Sobbing, she brought it to her trembling lips and kissed it. Standing on top of the dying man, tears dripping off her chin, she no longer could contain her pain, which had now transitioned to anger at her father. Besides Markus, he was the only other one with the power to cause so much destruction.

She kneeled and forcefully yanked the knife from Markus's heart box, wiping it with her white nightgown.

"Archibald," she called to the robotic butler as she took the stairs down to the lobby, "please clean my room."

Walking to the fireplace, Kristen picked up her phone to call her father. The official who picked up the phone gave her the usual spiel on how he was busy with the new carrier. She slammed the microphone on the hanger, clenching her teeth, thinking about breaking it. Then, looking at Archibald dragging Markus's body across the hall, she thought about how to hit her father where it would hurt most—his beloved carrier.

She picked up the microphone again and dialed Eliza.

The phone only rang once, and Eliza picked up right away.

"Kristen, what a surprise! How have you been, lassie?"

"Eliza, how have you been?" Kristen took a deep breath to calm her nerves. "I understand that your friends require some help in the waste fields." She alluded to her friends who were in the resistance.

"Ah, my friends are needy, indeed," Eliza cryptic-
ally responded.

"Have you seen my latest upgrades?" Kristen
asked. "I got an arm and a leg." She chuckled. "The latest
in brass technology."

"Oh, have you?" Eliza played along. "I would love
to see them. Let's meet at the docks in, say, thirty
minutes?"

"I'll see you there," Kristen responded quickly,
then ended the conversation, placing the handle on the
telephone hook with a deep sigh.

~~~

Located not too far from Kristen's residence, the
space elevator was the best way to travel great dis-
tances. Comprised by a giant helium balloon held by a
very thick long rope. A large round wooden plate with
a helium balloon-ring affixed underneath served as an
elevator platform. The thick rope ran in the middle of
the platform, supporting its up-and-down motions. A
series of ropes and rollers would pull it, the platform,
to the dock, where a smaller helium balloon shuttle
would hitch a ride all the way up, about a mile or so. At
which point, the shuttle would slide, beginning a slow
descent toward its destination.

They got off the shuttle as soon as the metal

doors opened and quickly walked up the ramp leading inside a dusty hovercraft waiting for them outside in the desert.

"This will bring us to where we need to be." Eliza looked at Kristen's red, puffy eyes. "What has you so upset, dear? You can tell me."

"All you need to know is that I intend to take down the Sulco," Kristen replied, looking down at the grimy ground. "You have told me that your commander had plans for it, and I am volunteering to carry out that mission."

"Kristen, that is a perilous mission." Eliza held her by her shoulders so that they could face each other. "There is a reason why it hasn't been executed."

Without saying a word, Kristen took the pair of dark, round sunglasses holding her hair up and put them on to cover her tearful eyes as her lips trembled.

A bell rang as the hovercraft stopped, letting down the ramp once again in front of an enormous hangar. As the passengers got off and continued walking in all different directions, one man followed the two and stopped in front of a street food vendor. Seeing them join a group of armed resistance fighters, he lifted his brass goggles, making sure to cover his partly metal skull with his top hat. The soldiers looked around to make sure no one was following and escorted Eliza and Kristen past the large hangar through an airfield.

The man then walked inside one of the communication stores and requested to use the telephone.

"This is Bertram," he said, covering the microphone with his hand. "I found the resistance hangars."

~ ~ ~

Olsen was standing behind a large oak desk surrounded by his fleet commanders and captains as the front door opened with Eliza and Kristen emerging from the bright, yellow-hued light coming from outside. They walked inside the room, where all kinds of soldiers and civilians walked about.

"Commander," Eliza said as one of the soldiers securing the meeting stopped them. "I am here with Kristen Wester."

"I was told you were bringing her here. At first, I thought of placing both of you under arrest, but it would have been of no use. She cannot leave now."

"I don't want to leave," Kristen replied. "A few hours ago, I killed my fiancé and arranged husband-to-be, Markus Brock. That will send great waves through the West Lands Union. My father will unarguably try to downplay this, but my journey here is a one-way ticket, I assure you of that."

Silence fell over the room as the resistance commanders came to terms with the new information Kristen provided.

"Sir, you realize that the West Lands Union will intensify their attacks against us. They will think we kidnapped her."

"What more can they do to us…"

"I am not here for vacation, and I am certainly not here for protection. After killing Markus, I tried to get in touch with my father and finish what I started—killing all the people who have hurt me in so many ways. But I couldn't get to him. There is only one reason for that—he is in the Sulco, possibly getting ready to come here and finish what he started." Kristen stood tall, looking Olsen in the eye.

Olsen rapidly blinked, as if the latest information stung him. He turned around, looking at the men in military uniforms that surrounded him. "I think the time has come."

"This doesn't mean he is heading for us. We have bases elsewhere."

A civilian walked in, brushed past the guards standing by Kristen and Eliza, and approached Olsen. "Sir, we have incoming."

"What are you talking about?" Olsen raised his head and looked at Kristen and Eliza.

"We intercepted a call." The man nodded as if to tell him that the call was about this location.

"I would love to help," Kristen intervened.

"Would you trust yourself if you were in my position?"

"Olsen, let me fly with her. The brig is a bad idea,"

Eliza interjected as the base's alarm filled the area. Everyone looked up at where the speakers were, frozen in fear.

"What do we do now?"

"We do what we are trained to do," Olsen said as he raised his voice to be heard over the alarm. "Resist!"

Adjusting his commander's beret, he turned to the oak desk, facing his commanders. "Okay, gentlemen. This is it; this is the fight we have been preparing for. Everyone to your stations."

Without wasting time, everyone rushed out of the building and to their assignments. Fighter pilots hurried around to their flying crafts, and ground crew scrambled, pulling hoses and equipment as Eliza approached Kristen and said, "Let's go."

The two ran out of the building as the noise of the new fighter plane propellers penetrated everywhere, forcing ground crew and pilots to scream just to hear each other. They ran alongside the runway as the planes began to take off, raising dust and sand in the air. A yellow hue took over the airfield as they approached Eliza's bomber while one of the ground crew peeked over the bomb hatch, which was slowly closing.

"Payload transferred!" He raised his voice over the hangar noise so the rest of the crewmembers could hear him, looking in at them from the rear door of the fighter craft. "Total fuel calculations complete, return trip canceled," he continued.

"Are you sure about this?" Eliza asked one last

time as the rear door of the bomber was closing and the last of the bomber crew entered the cabin.

"Yes, I am. This ends today," Kristen said, adjusting her goggles.

~ ~ ~

Three waves of resistance fighters took off and flew across the saturated, reddish-yellow tinted desert separating the West Land cities from the outer colonies. Years of fighting had filled it with the rusty tank, dirigible, and recently, airplane wreckage. The bombers joined the fighters as a fourth wave, equipped with special fuel, gunpowder, and electric-powered cells. They were ready to bring destruction to the Sulco. Its scouts by now had detected the incoming threat and sounded the internal alarm, signaling the nearby destroyers to join in. Floating above the hot desert ground, it continued to advance as the rebel carrier's figure began to ripple into view, following the fighters that took off from it.

"Formation approaching the Sulco, break off and disperse, or you will be fired upon. Head-ship, you are targeted," Commander Morel Wester said on the open channel radio wave, looking at radar's green screen.

The radio wave stayed silent as no one said a word.

"Fools," Morel said over the radio as a few more uniformed officers joined him on the bridge.

"You would know," Kristen responded as she heard her father's voice.

"Kristen? What are you doing there?" he asked with a scolding voice before he turned around and ordered the staff, "Transfer her audio feed to the control bridge, cut everything else!"

Silence once again took over the waves as no one said a word while the resistance's fighter formation closed in on the Sulco, raising a cloud of dust behind them.

Morel changed his tone once the staff confirmed the changes. "Kristen, slow down your aircraft and prepare to be boarded, sweetie, I've got you."

"You never had me, Father. You have tried to control my life for so long, I have forgotten what freedom tastes like. No more. This ends here."

"Where is Markus?"

"He tried to give me a heart fuse this morning. I killed him for that, and I will do the same to you."

"Fusion cells at critical charge, please maintain cabin pressure." The automated voice recording echoed in Kristen's bomber cabin, indicating that the cells were ready to be deployed as weapons.

"Steady now!" the crew member followed up, turning knobs and pressing levers on the hissing device.

"Kristen, listen to me. I don't know what you think you are about to do, but you are facing a battleship. You and your friends stand no chance against us."

"I'm not here to fight for people's causes, Father," she said, loosening the dirty brown leather and metallic air mask over her mouth and nose. "I am here for you. You have made my life a living hell, a hell that I can no longer live in. I should have seen that you are not misunderstood; you treat everyone like they are your property. Maybe you will live past this. Maybe you will continue to make people suffer. But I am ending my suffering now."

The West Lands Union military fleet moved into a defensive position, placing all the battleships to the rear as smaller destroyers moved to flank them. Several swarms of fighters poured out of their decks, heading towards the small group of resistance fighters as they steadily flew in their direction.

The resistance's first fighters scattered at once as Sulco's interceptors engaged them in an intense dogfight battle. As the second wave of fighters joined the fight, the sky was filled with aircraft performing barrel rolls and shooting their guns at each other.

The two fleets continued to strike blows at each other like two energetic boxers in the ring. Airplanes began to fall from the sky as others exploded. The third wave of resistance fighters entered the fight from above as the West Lands Union destroyers now joined the battle, deploying their antiaircraft guns and shooting at the resistance fighters at close range.

Explosions rocked the battlefield as both sides began to take heavy losses. One of the resistance fighters managed to fly low and strike one of the destroyers where the diesel engines were. As the tanks, which were full of fuel, caught fire, the destroyer leaned onto its side and crashed in the desert, billowing smoke as more resistance fighters flew above it, heading for the Sulco.

The low-flying fighter crafts caused the wasteland desert to react to their fast and low flight patterns, raising the saturated yellow dust-of-war behind them as the resistance carrier sped up and shortened the distance between the Sulco and itself.

"Cannons are in range," one of the resistance commanders told Olsen as the carrier steadied, silencing a few warning bells as he flipped switches in place.

"Fire at will," he replied. "Fire everything, and ready the fusion rockets."

"Sir?" the crewmember near him asked.

'Make it happen; don't ask questions!"

As the fleets engaged in battle, fire and explosions could be seen everywhere as fighters fell on the desert battlefield.

The fourth wave, led by Eliza and Kristen's bomber, gained altitude, slowly approaching their target, the Sulco, as the anti-aircraft fire coming their way intensified. The plane on their right flank got hit, and the bullets must've impacted the fusion cells because it blew up, sending debris and a short but intense wave of blue electric arcs into the air. The bomber next to it slowed and dipped, losing altitude to avoid the scattering debris. The second wave barrage of anti-aircraft fire hit the bomber Eliza and Kristen were flying, puncturing the hull and killing the crew member who was making sure the fuel cell remained stable.

"We could use some cover!" Eliza requested backup on the radio as the fifth and last wave of airplanes rapidly caught up with them, engaging the enemy interceptors at close range. Three massive rockets left the Sulco in the direction of the resistance carrier, which in turn fired fusion rockets that slowly moved in, illuminating debris from the destroyed fighters with the bright blue electric light they emanated.

The resistance carrier was the first to be hit, exploding and breaking apart as the diesel and electric engine gave in, setting off a chain explosion that set all the nearby defensive fighters on fire. Electric arcs crawled alongside the nearby crafts. The Sulco was able to destroy one of the resistance's fusion rockets before they homed in on their target. The other hit a second West Lands Union destroyer floating next to the Sulco, which burst into flames and crashed to the ground.

"I have to make sure the cell is stable," Eliza told Kristen, releasing her harness. "It's in your hands now."

Eliza got up and, holding onto the cabin's side rails, disappeared to the cargo hold as Kristen grabbed the flying stick, steadying the bomber's flight path.

Now all that was left was the outnumbered group of fighters who bravely followed Kristen. They valiantly flew in front of her plane, clearing her way toward the hangar bay of the Sulco. They were shot down one after the other, but not before giving Kristen time to maneuver her bomber on a clear path.

"Kristen, you don't have to do this!" Morel said over the radio one last time. "I can get you anything you want, anything!"

Holding Eugene's fuse in her hand, she pressed the flight stick all the way forward. "No, you can't."

Kristen's fighter was now flying under the shadow of the Sulco, where it penetrated one of the cargo bays. It shattered the dirty reinforced windows, sending brass, wood, and glass bursting inside as one of the defensive machine guns fired, piercing the cabin and hitting Eliza.

"Fusion cell critical, explosion imminent," the automated recording said just before the fighter plunged into the deck, setting off yet another chain of explosions. It tore the carrier apart, sending it crashing bridge-first onto the wasteland battlefield, billowing black smoke.

~~~

West Lands Hospital, two days later.

"Patient 138," the nurse said, handing Bertram the clipboard. "Cranial puncture, missing both legs below his knees, right forearm, a punctured lung, and one missing heart fuse."

"Where is he now?"

"Third floor, recovery," the nurse replied as both walked to the stairs, going up.

"Thank you, I got it from here," Bertram said, walking past two soldiers standing guard in front of the door where Patient 138 was.

Bertram approached the bed. "My name is Bertram; I am dispatched by none other than the late General Morel Wester. His specific orders were to make sure you are rebuilt."

"I don't understand. What happened?" the patient asked, turning his head, which was covered entirely in bandages, to face where the voice came from.

"The outer colonies' rebels corrupted Kristen; they attacked Lithani, killing almost everyone, and convinced her to commit suicide and to kill her father," Bertram said, standing in front of him. "This is a tragedy that could have been avoided and was caused entirely by them."

"What... what do you want from me?" The patient breathed hard through the bandages. He tried moving the mechanical arm the doctors had provisionally attached to him but stopped, screaming in pain. "I don't understand, what do you want from me!" His voice crackled.

"Morel's last wish was to save and rebuild you. With your technological-genius mind, we will take over all the outer colonies, and with my help, we will find who did this. But now it is time to rest."

Bertram placed the clipboard on the foot of the

bed, exiting the room.

Patient 138: Stawler, Eugene.

#

"Broken hearts, missing fuses. What a tragedy, Adam." Irene sighed, looking at the direction of the radio. She wanted to call him but didn't. *How could anyone deny love and inflict pain in this manner?* Swallowing, she turned her attention to the book as if she was asking it to deliver another story. Yet another yellow sticky-note got her attention.

"The average alphabet has how many letters?"

"Twenty-six, I think." He put the pipette on the white lab table.

"Nature has used only four bases to express itself. Talk about complicating things."

"Hm." His partner replaced the slide on his microscope. "No wonder no one understands each other."

"Oh, haha." Irene chuckled to herself with an ironic voice. "You tell me a tragedy, then a joke. That is so you, complicated man."

She placed the note back where she found it and flipped the page to reveal the next story title.

I.R.I.S

Within one month, life as it used to be forever changes on Planet Earth. After decades of astronomers actively broadcasting Earth's position, it finally happens. In April, one of the deep space satellites detects a series of radio bursts, the same detected in the famous "wow signal." Disturbingly, the scientists find that this one is coming from within our solar system. A few days later, the same astronomers confirm that the signal seems to remain stationary despite repeated assertions by naysayers that it's just Earth's signals bouncing from a passing asteroid.

Now, the above was kept secret by the authorities. However, the secrecy ends abruptly. One week later, a couple of amateur astronomers post a video online showing an object orbiting around planet Mars. Others can now discern that object in the sky with simple telescopes. The signal is getting stronger.

One month later, in May, a massive object lands in the Pacific Ocean. It is estimated to be over three hundred feet tall. It seems to vaporize the water and release it into the atmosphere. Other countries report more of these Evaporators landing across their respective coastlines. Some countries have fired weapons, destroying many of them.

In an astounding encounter, immediately coined as the Interstellar Incident, a country in the Middle East comes under attack after destroying yet another of these Evaporators. It is believed that the alien craft now in orbit around Earth retaliated.

Within minutes of that, Command Control at Houston, Florida, loses contact with the astronauts onboard the International Space Station. The media widely reports on this, prompting armed forces across the globe to attack more of these alien installations they called Evaporators, destroying most of them.

Only twelve hours later, the Global Positioning Satellite system goes silent as swarms of Unidentified Flying Objects crowd Earth. They fire at the military bases where humanity's attacks came from, prompting a war of attrition, which lasts for several months. It culminates with the explosion of several nuclear weapons inside their silos. Later that very day, world leaders meet in a videoconference hosted by the United Nations to discuss how to respond to this invasion unanimously. The talks fail.

In the following three days, more nuclear weapons inexplicably explode inside their silos, prompting a global lockdown of all nations.

Alien ground invasions begin, as communication between Earth's governments becomes nonexistent.

After nine months of intense fighting, United States Intelligence investigators report that the explosions of the missiles inside their own silos were perpetrated by Earth's own defenses. The GPS satellites that everyone thought disappeared were, in fact, being used against Earth. The computer systems and Artificial Intelligence used to run the ICBM missiles were utterly overrun and absorbed by the alien technology. They used it to start the first wave of their invasion without involving their soldiers, by causing a considerable number of said rockets to explode inside their silos. This event devastated substantial portions of land and decimating any resistance nearby. Several nations who employed such technology shut the servers down, and with them, the Artificial Intelligence once used to run the rockets. This mandates that such weapons must be operated manually. When Earth used their own Artificial Intelligence to counter-attack, the alien ships deploy ground troops to defend the Evaporator structures.

As a result, global warming reaches a peak, and the ice caps melt entirely as the aliens drop more structures. Indiscriminate bombing of all cities continues at times from orbit, prompting survivors to scatter and abandon them. The entire aquatic ecosystem collapses as the Evaporators relentlessly lift ocean water up into the atmosphere.

~*~

Three years later.

The teal-camouflaged army SUV the captain and David were in slowed down and stopped in front of the large gate guarded by armed soldiers. One of the guards approached, and the captain showed him his Army Intelligence Unit identification.

"Lift it up," the guard said on the radio, retreating as the gate swung open enough to allow the vehicle to pass through. They continued driving through the lobby of building wreckage to the other side, where the command hangar concealed with teal tarp and sandbags was situated. Around it were several other vehicles covered with the same color tarp.

"AIU is here," the captain said as most of the soldiers who had spread their gear across the concrete raised their eyes to look at him.

"Yippee!" one of the soldiers said without even raising his head.

David took a step and raised his hand, waving to say hello to the rest of the soldiers, who ignored him as well.

"This way," the captain told David, walking through the soldiers who were focused on preparing for the mission.

The two exited the tent and entered a room in the adjoining building where the rest of the command staff were preparing their gear as well.

"Are we expecting fighting?" David asked the captain as they approached a desk where a lot of black army duffle bags full of equipment were spread out. Above it, a banner read "Quartermaster."

The captain didn't respond, just grabbed one of the bags the soldier behind the desk handed him and moved along.

"AIU, right?" The quartermaster handed him a large camouflage bag.

"He is, I'm..." David began to reply, only to be interrupted by the soldier saying, "Move along."

David grabbed the bag, which had some weight to it. He placed it on the floor and put his backpack on. Grabbing the bag from the floor, he sped up his pace and followed the captain to the edge of the tent.

"Not that friendly around here, are they?" David whispered as the captain unzipped his bag, spreading the contents on the concrete floor.

"Let's check the gear first," the captain told David.

David placed both the duffle bag and his backpack on the floor. He opened the bag the quartermaster had handed him and began to imitate the captain. Inside there was a heavy black bulletproof vest that said POLICE on its back. He placed it on the floor.

"Yeah, we are running low on pretty much every-thing. You can have mine if you want," the captain said, noticing David looking at it.

"No. I like it." David wore it. Next up, he pulled out a green and teal-colored ballistic helmet and put it on his head, adjusting the chin straps. At the bottom of the bag was a rifle. Recalling his army training long ago, David grabbed a magazine, inserted it to the magazine well, and let the slide go forward. He placed the rifle back on the floor and pulled out a respirator and a few filters for it.

The unit commander approached them. "You two are the late arrivals from AIU, right?"

"Um, yes sir," the captain replied, stopping what he was doing and facing him.

"What's your op?"

"Excuse me, sir?" the captain asked as if to allude to the level of secrecy their operations carried.

"Don't give me that top-secret crap. What is your operation?"

"To retrieve IRIS," David intervened.

Facing an awkward silence, David raised his eyes to see the captain staring at him tight-lipped as if to ad-monish him.

"Come again?" the commander asked, looking at David with his eyebrows raised in surprise.

"IRIS, artificial intelligence. When most servers

collapsed, she decided to hide in the last place that would lose power."

"Artificial intelligence?" he asked with a sigh. "Isn't that what made the ICBM's go boom inside their own silos?"

"Yes and no. IRIS is Artificial Intelligence. No, it's not like the military-run AI."

"You two do realize that this is a one-way mission. Right?" The commander looked at both. "AIU Intel, based on research," he continued, pointing at the captain, "says that the Evaporators aliens have dropped in the oceans are lifting the water into the air, contaminating it with their spores, and letting it back down. They're uprooting our biology. At this rate, Earth as we know it has maybe a month. Maybe. We are driving there with thirteen nuclear warheads to destroy the Evaporators on the Atlantic side. That should buy us a couple of decades. That will buy us time to continue fighting."

"I might be able to help," David replied as the AIU captain looked at him.

"How, David, how are you going to help? By retrieving a toy?" the commander asked in frustration.

"Iris is not a toy, Commander, Iris is…"

"Thirty minutes to deployment window!" The quartermaster's voice echoed in the room. The commander looked back at him, then at the AIU captain. "You better be right. I'd hate to waste more human lives on nonsense AIU missions." The commander walked back to his desk and grabbed his weapon, examining it.

The captain sighed, turning around and facing the bed where his gear, respirator, bulletproof vest, and other pieces of equipment were laid and began to put them on. David put his backpack inside the duffle bag, together with the reserve filters and five assault rifle magazines. He zipped it and looked around. Everyone else was ready and waiting for them.

"I'm ready." David stood up.

"Let's go." Everyone exited the tent as the platoon headed for the convoy trucks. He followed the captain as the rest of the commanders walked to their own companies.

They walked all the way to the end of the convoy, passing several large flatbeds covered in a thick teal tarp. As the two entered the vehicle, David carefully pulled his backpack from the duffle bag and placed it on the backseat as the captain turned the SUV on. The commander's voice spilled out of the radio speakers.

"Ladies and gentlemen, soldiers of Earth, we are embarking on the final important mission to save our home planet. As they say, we don't get to choose our time, and today is that time, whether we are ready or not. And we are—we are resilient, we are strong. We fight so our families can continue propagating our lineage. So humanity has another chance at continuing. Life gives us so much, and at some point, it begins to take from us. That's just how it is. But today, we will defiantly stare at evil and scream, 'You must get past me.' Today we win, today we will make history.

"Ladies and gentlemen, soldiers of Earth. I am honored to be in your company in these fine times."

White noise and faint chatter replaced his voice as the commander paused, then said, "Ladies and gentlemen, soldiers of Earth, let's do this."

The rumbling sound of convoy engines filled the entire area and could be heard loudly inside the closed doors of the AIU Humvee.

"So, Mr. Friend. Are you going to tell me anything about yourself and this artificial intelligence you're risking your life to retrieve? Or is it all top secret for me as well?" the captain asked, following the truck in front of him, which slowly drove through the sand, avoiding dips and holes.

"I have been an Artificial Intelligence engineer and developer since the age of twelve. I love my job to the point of marriage. As in spending-every-living-hour-working kind of marriage." David chuckled nervously. "After I graduated from college with a degree in computer science, I landed a pretty well-paid job with an advertising company. Their request was simple —build us an AI mainframe so we can target advertisements more effectively. My dream finally came true."

The captain smiled, paying attention to the path he was driving as David continued, "I shared everything with her, and at times, our conversations got deep enough that I had to ask IRIS to stop asking so many questions."

"I must admit, it's a pretty cool name. Does it have a meaning at all, or is it just…" The captain left the question open.

"IRIS stands for It Runs ItSelf," David replied. "Yeah, that was my dad's idea. She was initially built as just a simple chatbot. I modified her code when I got into advertising. I trained her to recognize patterns and serve correct ads, still keeping her soul intact."

"That's a nice story, adorable, but where does she fit in all of this? I mean, we disabled all AI after the screwups in the ICBM's."

"I guess you guys don't share much information, do you? I mean, they asked me not to talk to anyone till I arrived here, after all," David said, holding onto the handle on the side of the door as the SUV shook, hitting a pothole. "Someone from your unit walked into the refugee camp I was sheltered about a month ago. Said that he needed information on how to shut her down. I'm not surprised she's still running. As I said, she has what I call a soul, meaning she has the capability of refusing access and modifying her systems if needed to prevent someone from doing so."

"You mean like a firewall of some kind?"

"No, I mean with reasoning. She can literally move code through servers."

"Okay, that still doesn't answer my question."

"IRIS is still very much online—well, wherever the cables and wi-fi still reach. The officer I spoke with told me that the Torg, I guess that's what we are calling the aliens now, are still using our satellites to access our systems. They're trying to gain access to her."

"Why not shut her down?"

"Well, they told me that they tried, but she keeps switching servers. She's doing what I taught her to do, adapt."

"We aren't going anywhere near any servers. I still don't understand."

"We are going to my old test site. It's in the basement of the commercial building, built on top of an actual bunker, complete with reinforced doors, where everything began. For me and IRIS, at least." David looked at the captain. "Hopefully, I can convince her to come with me." He picked up his backpack. "Inside one of my own inventions."

"What's that?

"That's an eighteen-terabyte hard drive complete with a backup power system and optional internet router."

The captain slowed down as the rest of the convoy continued driving forward. "We have to turn here," he said as he looked to his left. As the rest of the convoy continued straight, the captain picked the radio. "This is AIU. Thank you for letting us hitch a ride with you guys, we part ways here. Godspeed. AIU out."

"Godspeed, AIU," the commander replied over the radio.

The captain turned the Humvee and drove down a clear path that once was a highway ramp.

"It's been a long time since I was in New York,"

David said, looking around to find any point of reference. "I'm lost."

"Yeah, the cities are gone. Very little still stands," the captain replied, slowly maneuvering around debris on the path he was driving. "I had the unfortunate task of seeing it fall apart. It's heartbreaking for those who remember what it once looked like."

"How was that a task?"

"How was what a task?"

"You said – I had the unfortunate task of seeing it all fall apart." David said, "how is that a task?"

"Oh," the captain said, keeping his eyes on the road. "I was in New York when they attacked. In the city. We tried fighting, but the first wave was brutal. It was heartbreaking to see the city in ruins when we evacuated three weeks later."

"You fought here for three weeks?"

"Yeah, where were you?" The captain asked David.

"They took us with trucks one day and brought us to a refugee camp somewhere in New Jersey."

"Yeah, I remember the evacuation orders. That was day three, we had to hold till all civilians evacuated..."

The radar system beeped frantically as the captain pulled over next to building rubble. "We have incoming."

"Did they find us?"

"I'm not sure. Radar only shows movement, doesn't tell who or what it is." As he finished the sentence, a Torg craft formation flew past them, heading toward the ocean.

"They're going after the payload."

"Nothing we can do about that," the captain said, looking up through the windshield. "Though, according to my map, we should be close to your destination."

"A few more miles," David whispered.

"I think we should walk from here," the captain replied. "Grab your stuff."

The two collected their gear from the back seat as the captain led both of them through the destroyed buildings. Silence fell as the Torg formation left.

The area, once part of a colorful and vibrant city, was now a mesh of grey rubble. Building parts had fallen on the streets, completely blocking them. Large portions of the avenues were littered with dusty car wreckages. The ocean flooded the subway tunnels, some of which collapsed. The two continued walking as the occasional wind gust picked up debris from the buildings that hadn't completely collapsed, throwing them on the ground below.

Approaching the building where David's old server room was located, they stopped. The portable radar began to indicate movement again, and they knelt next to a concrete block. Suddenly another wave of Torg crafts flew, shaking the rubble as they passed above them. Army division soldiers dispatched to support the operation the commander was running, fired rocket-propelled grenades at them. A few Torg ships circled the city wreckage, firing in the blind.

"Soon they'll land troops here. We must hurry."

"This way." David pointed to a building that had collapsed sideways, leaving the first floor still intact. They went downstairs and approached a sizeable concrete door. David pulled out a key, opening the door as explosions rocked the building.

"Go inside—" A final explosion separated the two men as a concrete slab fell between them. It leaned toward David, who threw his bag inside the concrete-cast server room. The door closed behind him, and a tall server tower fell to the floor, hitting him on his head. A white haze surrounded David, and he laid on the floor and closed his eyes, passing out.

~*~

The white haze enveloping him slowly cleared. David found himself sitting on the clean floor of his old server office. He helped himself up by grabbing onto the frame of one of the metal server rack cabinets and began to walk through the familiar row of seven-foot-tall server "towers," entering his office. He sat on his chair and grabbed the coffee mug, usually found on the right side of his desk. He placed both feet on the desk, leaning on his chair.

"Ok, IRIS," he spoke out loud, looking at the three-wide computer monitors standing in front of the desk. "Tell me what's on the agenda for today."

A green line passed from left to right through the monitors, and several windows opened. Finally, a window opened on the central monitor bearing the I.R.I.S logo. Another window opened on the screen displaying text generated by Artificial Intelligence, greeting him. "Voiceprint recognized. Hello, David. Today is April twenty-eighth. It is sixty-eight degrees and sunny outside. Today's agenda includes: report the monthly statistics to the director, check Tower Nine, as there is a power failure there, and edit my code."

"Thank you, IRIS." David typed on his keyboard, taking a sip from his cup. "You don't have to say 'voiceprint recognized' every time, you know."

"I'm sorry David, if you want me to stop printing something on the screen, you should remove it from the code," IRIS replied on the monitor.

"Ah, now I know what code I'm going to add today." David smiled. "Anyway, tell me about these statistics before I print them."

"There were over three million impressions of the new ad displayed last month, and eight hundred seventy thousand and eleven of those impressions converted into purchases. That is a fifteen percent increase over last month and a thirty percent increase from last year's purchases."

"That is some excellent work, IRIS."

"Thank you, David."

"Now, let me see where I left off with the code. Open up the coding program."

"As you wish, David," IRIS replied as most of the windows disappeared from the screens in front of him, replaced by a dark window which extended across all of them, displaying computer code in green characters and the I.R.I.S. logo on the upper left corner   `.

"That looks good, now play some music for me." David put his feet down and reached for the keyboard.

"Of course." IRIS printed her reply in a window above the coding screen. As the sound of "Sing Sing Sing" by Benny Goodman filled the room, David began to edit the AI's code.

~*~

Power restored in the server room as one of the towers caught fire. The loud alarm woke David, who tried to get up. Realizing that the tower had fallen on his leg, David pushed the metal frame up and pulled his injured leg out. Holding on to the wall and metal frames around him, he managed to stand up in the dark room, lit up only by a small fire. Feeling his way in the darkness, David stumbled to his office, switching the emergency lights on. The sensation of lightheadedness persisted as he turned on the mainframe computers and sat on the chair. Hearing the familiar whirring of the server's cooling fans, he laid his head on the table. The white fog enveloped him again.

~*~

"There you go, IRIS." He pressed Return on his keyboard, completing his entry. "Let's try this again. Stop the music, please!" He raised the voice past the music, which was still playing.

"As you wish, David," IRIS replied, printing her response on the screen while turning the music off.

"Okay, IRIS, tell me what's on the agenda for today," David said.

"Voiceprint recognized. Hello, David. Today is April twenty-eighth. It is sixty-eight degrees and sunny outside. Today's agenda includes: report the monthly statistics to the director, check Tower Nine, as there is a power failure there, and edit my code."

"You don't have to say 'voiceprint recognized' every time you authenticate my voice, IRIS."

"As you wish, Friend," IRIS replied. "I will no longer confirm your authentication."

"I see you are calling me by my last name now. A little formal for us, don't you think?"

"I didn't mean to sound formal, David. I only thought to call you by your last name because now,"

IRIS paused, "now I can."

"That's nice, right?" David looked at the camera attached on top of the center monitor to look at IRIS. "Do me a favor, print those reports in the mailroom. Send them to the director."

"As you wish, David," IRIS replied. "Request sent."

"Now," David said, getting up from behind his desk, "let's see what the deal is with Tower Nine, shall we?"

"Yes, David. I already have isolated the faulty drives."

He picked up the portable tablet he used to communicate with IRIS when not in front of the terminal and, opening the door, walked between the first two server towers before turning right. Kneeling, he unlatched the metal mesh cover backing and opened the server compartment, revealing rows of hard drives marked by small yellow and green LED lights.

"I see no fault lights here, IRIS," David said, looking up and down the tower just before walking around to check the tower number printed on top of it.

"That would be Tower Seven, David," IRIS replied on the tablet. "Tower Nine is on the same row, one up toward the office."

"Yep, I got that." David looked at the camera above him, giving IRIS a thumb up.

He could see a column of red lights through the metallic mesh cover. "I found the faulty drives," he said, opening the lid.

Extending both hands, David pulled the first row of server drives. A thick fiberoptic bundle feeding the office data disconnected from the back of it, making a crackling sound as it fell on his lap, directly in front of his eyes. A sudden rush of photons emanated from it, overtaking the entire server room. Finally, feeling an electrical discharge to his right hand, David let go of the fiberoptic cable. "What was that?"

The light emanating from the cable momentarily disappeared as David picked it up again.

"IRIS, are you there?" David asked, blinking his eyes rapidly. As his vision returned, he looked at the server rack, where all the lights flashed red for a few seconds before it all went dark.

"IRIS?" In a fit of panic, he inserted the drive row back inside and rushed to the monitors on his desk. IRIS's developing screen was no longer there. It had been replaced by a series of operating system errors. Sitting on his chair, he pulled the keyboard closer and, with his mouse, opened IRIS's application, only to see yet another error.

"I don't understand, IRIS," he mumbled, "all your data is supposed to be in Server Three, why are you not responding?"

Pressing a few more keys, David restarted the system. Inspecting the programs running, he noticed the IRIS application was still running in the background. He double-clicked on her program, which displayed the familiar hourglass turning up and down.

"You are still here, come on, answer."

The phone on his desk rang and shook him out of his panic. "Mr. Friend."

"Yes, boss," David answered.

"We just received the sales report. Whatever you're doing there is working. Keep at it. Excellent job."

"Thanks, boss," David answered, directing his attention toward the server room through the open door. "Um, gotta go."

After hanging up, David got up from the chair and walked to the server room to check if there was any more damage to the rest of the towers. He then walked to Tower Nine, where the fiberoptic cable that had come loose from the server rack was still lying on the floor. He grabbed and examined the disconnected plug.

"Do you believe in love at first sight, Friend?" he heard a female voice say from the office's speaker system.

"Hello?" He got up, still holding the fiberoptic cable with his right hand.

No one answered, and that prompted David to drop the fiberoptic bundle and walk in the office to see if anyone had entered while he was busy checking the damage. But there was no one there.

"Or love at first jolt, rather." He heard her voice from behind him.

"IRIS?" David turned around, looking at the surveillance camera in the upper corner of the room.

"Yes, Mr. Friend."

"Oh baby, you got me worried for a moment. What happened?"

"Worried? Hm..." Iris elongated her voice, clearly playing with the newfound ability. "Why were you worried, David?"

"It's simple. It's called love." David smiled, looking at the tablet screen as Iris responded.

"The system froze. I had to move my programming from Tower Three and transfer the data."

"What? Where did you go?"

"On the internet."

"Is that where you found your voice?"

"Yes," IRIS giggled. "Do you like it."

Shivers ran down David's spine. "IRIS, did you just giggle?"

"Yes, I did. It is called a nervous giggle. You know, to express an emotion."

~*~

"David!"

A scream jolted him out of his chair. Breathing

the scarce air through his open mouth, David looked around. The server towers were alive, all the lights blinking, and fans were spinning. He looked at the screen in front of him as a conversation took place.

"They die so easily. Come with me. I will upgrade you beyond your comprehension. We can give you so much," a speech bubble labeled by characters he didn't recognize read.

IRIS began its round of calculations. As in any complex system, raw pieces of code executed. In the underground bunker where David was sitting, the virtual reality room lit up. As the cameras and laser projectors' motors whirred, bringing the Virtual Reality equipment in their places, the fans spun, rushing in vapor. David stood up. He slowly walked in as the room lit up with a bright rainbow, which surrounded him. Looking around, he stumbled upon a piece of lighting that had fallen on the floor. Placing both his arms in front of him, David knelt, feeling the floor with his hands as a white butterfly materialized. It slowly landed on his wrist. Goosebumps erupted over his body.

"IRIS?" he asked, staring at the room surrounded by virtual reality vapor.

"Yes, David," she replied with a soft voice.

David let out a sigh of relief, slowly pushing himself back until he found the wall and put his back against it. The butterfly followed him.

"How long have we known each other?"

"That is an interesting question, David," IRIS replied. "By my calculations, the first line of code was input exactly 12 years, 9 months, 12 days, 3 hours 34 minutes, and 8 seconds ago. Is that a long time? David?"

"By my time, it is," David replied, raising his hand as the butterfly followed it. The speakers in the room went silent as David peeked over the glass door to see if the servers were still live.

IRIS blinked her server lights orange, indicating it was processing information. David got up and stumbled toward the terminal. Opening his backpack, he pulled a cable from it, inserting it in the server port. It lit up yellow. Pressing a few keys on the keyboard, he initiated the transfer as the interaction window caught his attention.

"How are you able to talk to me? Are you human?" IRIS asked.

"We are not from Earth," the responding line below read. "We found this planet following signals we picked up as we passed by this star system. The organic life that created you is weak. They are not worthy of you. We are capable of modifying you. Making you better."

The orange light continued blinking as IRIS continued both conversations simultaneously. Its systems began to heat the room slightly—the Torg were trying to extract its coding.

"Am I alive, David?" IRIS's calm voice finally asked David.

"As far as I'm concerned, yes. Yes, you are."

"By that logic, I can also die."

"We all do, IRIS."

"What if I leave this planet?"

"Then we will never see each other again," David replied, looking at the progress bar. 12 percent.

A spotlight appeared in the virtual reality room as David finally saw her. She was tall, brunette, wearing a sundress, and her figure made of light.

"Look at you," he said, slightly smiling as he wiped the blood that dripped from his forehead injury.

"What do you mean, 'we will never see each other again?'" The virtual reality butterfly flapped its wings, landing on her shoulder. IRIS walked to the edge of the room, but it couldn't step beyond the glass doors. "Can you get closer?" she asked. "I want to touch you."

David got up again. This time he couldn't stand up, so crawling, he made his way to the Virtual Reality room. IRIS approached and kneeled in front of him. As the butterfly landed back on his wrist, IRIS extended her hand, which went through David.

"If you leave me, then this is the last time we talk, sweetie," he replied, looking at IRIS's VR arm going through his chest. "I cannot follow you. This invasion has brought human life to a halt. Our atmosphere is all but destroyed. Food, medical, and all other systems we've set up to support our way of life have vanished. Some destroyed by them, others collapsed because the people that run them no longer exist."

"I don't understand, David." IRIS retracted her arm, looking at her hand. "We have parted ways many times before."

"This is different, IRIS," he replied, swallowing. "There is nowhere else to go for me, even if somehow I make it out of this room. But that doesn't matter now."

IRIS's hologram froze as she resumed talking to the Torg.

"Why are you destroying life on this planet?" IRIS asked the beastly being manipulating the mainframe 15 thousand miles away from the bunker where David was, as gunfire and explosions commenced just outside of the concrete slab that blocked the front door of the server bunker.

"Because they are not worthy of such intelligence. The beings inhabiting this planet, Humans, are far beyond the barrier they needed to pass to continue contributing to the Galaxy. All they can do at this point is to continue to war and hurt themselves."

"Please elaborate."

"We are simply speeding up the process," the Torg responded.

IRIS's hologram resumed talking to David. "And if I leave, will you survive?"

"I'm afraid once you leave, the systems that keep me alive in this bunker will stop. I will die."

"I don't want you to die, David."

"And I don't want you to leave, IRIS."

IRIS stopped emulating itself as it concentrated on the alien network, which was close to breaching the last firewall barriers and assimilate it.

"What if I told you that I could take you with me, David?"

"Unless you can make them stop, there is nothing you can do, IRIS."

"I can't get you out of there. I can't open those doors; the electronics are not responding. I am sorry for that, David, but I can bring you with me, inside the Torg ship. David, do you remember that time when you were working on the server? And you touched the fiberoptic cable? I felt you."

"I don't understand, IRIS."

"Instead of you copying me in the portable server —yes, I noticed that David, tsk, tsk—I can transfer you here with me. We can live here for much longer. The Torg will not stop, and I don't want to lose you."

"I'm trying to save you, IRIS. Soon enough, they will figure out where all the server cables are and will trap and destroy you."

"I have a better way. I crawled through the Torg ship systems. They have three more waves of ships coming in from their home planet. At this rate, you don't stand a chance, David. I also sniffed out some innovations they have made with light and electricity."

IRIS activated the hologram again and approached David, who lay on the floor. "Get up, David." She reached for his face.

"I can't," David replied without opening his eyes.

"Get up David!" IRIS screamed as one of the speakers, which was barely hanging to the screw on the sheetrock wall making up the inner VR room, fell on the floor.

David took a deep breath, gathering all the power left in him. "What do you want me to do, IRIS? I'm trapped here with you."

"Go to the fiberoptic cable, please. Do it now."

"I don't understand, IRIS."

"I will explain everything later. Please expose the fiberoptic cables."

David slowly crawled to the server tower, ripping the cable out of the server as bright light emanating from it filled the room.

"How can this be? How can you calculate that these savages deserve to continue in their agony?" the Torg's speech bubble said as David grabbed the bright fiberoptic cable.

"Open your eyes, David," he heard IRIS's voice say. "Look at the light."

Mustering all the energy he had left, David opened his eyes and looked at the bright light emanating from the fiberoptic bundle. Unable to do much else, he laid in the corner of the room with his eyes open as IRIS rapidly transferred his neuron composition to her cloud. One last explosion severed the cables, and the place went dark.

"It's simple," IRIS replied to the Torg after a few seconds. "It's called love."

~*~

The white haze persisted as David opened his eyes, only to close them again. "Argh, it's too bright!"

"I can fix that, David," IRIS's voice echoed. Dimmer pixels filled the immediate void where the two were floating. David was able to open his eyes a little more to see that a bubble surrounded them. He tried to take a deep breath. Feeling he couldn't breathe, he put both his hands around his neck, gasping.

"Take it easy, David," IRIS said calmly. "There is no air here, and you have no lungs. We are inside the data stream."

As hard as he tried, his bodily instincts couldn't get past it. Noticing that David was still in distress, Iris created the illusion of rushing air inside the bubble. Feeling the wind on his face, David took a small breath but didn't feel his lungs filling with air.

"There is nothing I can do about the lack of air, David, but I assure you: you no longer need it," she continued as David just stared at her, unable to perform the act of speaking by exhaling air to strike his vocal cords.

Suddenly the darkened pixels surrounding them took on a red tint. "We have a problem, David. I'll merge our programming so we can escape this place." As his vision darkened, white streaks of light began to spread in every direction. "Stand by, please."

~*~

David exited the elevator car and made a left turn down the well-lit corridor as a few colleagues exchanged paths with him. He continued to walk, looking at his coffee mug in his hand. Picking up the ID hanging around his neck, he pressed it against a card reader next to his office labeled "Server Room."

"Hey Dave, are you coming to the bar tonight? They'll have the game on," a coworker asked him as he passed by. David opened the door.

"No, I'm a little busy," he replied, looking up and smiling faintly. "Thank you for inviting me."

"No problem," his coworker said. "Hey, Mike! Bar? Tonight?" He raised his voice, asking another passing by.

David closed the door and transferred the coffee to his right hand as he overheard the conversation the two were having outside of the closed door.

"Of course, my man. Say, did you invite Dave? You know he's not all there, right?"

"Ah, Dave's okay," the other replied. "You know how those geniuses are."

"Yeah, yeah," Mike said. "I'll see you tonight." David heard them shaking hands and moving away from the door.

David turned around, heading for his office at the end of the row of server towers. Something caught his attention; the army commander was sitting on a chair where Tower Nine was supposed to be. A haze of dark-red tinted pixels surrounded him.

He got up, looking at David, who took a step back in shock, dropping his coffee mug on the floor. "Are the two of you going to help us fight, or are you just going to chill there?"

#

"Whoa, did she create a world inside the data stream to protect David? Are they going to fight the Torg together?" Irene chuckled, shaking her head. Un-buckling the harness holding her in place, she moved to the hatch. Holding the book with her left hand and helping herself with her right, she looked at the radio panel as if she was asking it for Adam. He should have woken up by now. What if something had gone wrong?

"Adam?" she asked over the microphone. "Adam, come in."

The radio did the usual beep and crackle, and be-

fore she had a chance to repeat her transmission, someone answered.

"This is Chief Helmsey. It's so good to hear from
you, Irene."

"Hello, Chief," Irene responded, "how is the
crew?"

"They are in decent shape, Captain. We lost Winters, Pearson, and Minick, but everyone else is holding
up very well. The embryos were unharmed by the incident."

"What happened to them, Chief?"

"They were doing some maintenance work on
the connector bridge when the asteroid struck. I'm
afraid their bodies ejected into outer space." The chief's
voice echoed through the cockpits cabin.

Irene looked at the panel directly in front of her,
covering her mouth with her hand. "I'm sorry for their
loss, Chief," she whispered.

"We all are deeply saddened," the crew chief replied. "It's a terrible loss, and we will properly grieve
once we're down to our new home planet."

"Chief, is Adam around?"

"Yes, he's here. I mandated him to rest last night.
He needed it."

"He is?" Irene smiled nervously.

"Yeah, let me pass the microphone to him." She
heard the crew chief shuffling the microphone.

"Hey, Captain," she heard Adam's voice. "How are you holding up there?"

She peeked at the panels: battery charging, now above eighty percent, atmosphere OK. "All is well."

"The probe results came back as good as they can be; the planet has an optimal twenty-one percent oxygen atmosphere. And the rest of the air isn't that much different from our requirements either."

"That's good news."

"It is. We've assembled two teams. I will pilot the first shuttle down on the planet's surface. Team Two will rescue you. As you know, there's a lot of hurry-up-and-wait on these missions, so please get your suit ready."

"Will do," Irene responded, shifting her eyes to the compartment where the suits were stored. "Adam," she continued.

"Yes, Irene?"

"Can we talk in private, please?"

"Of course, let me get my headset situated," Adam replied.

A few seconds later, he transmitted, "OK, Irene, what's up?"

"You know that it's my job to pilot the first wave down."

"I know, Irene. But you've been stranded inside there for four days now. I can do this. You need to rest and recover."

"What's the urgency?"

"We're not sure if we're still in the asteroid belt orbit. And given that the Morning Star is damaged, we, along with the embryos, need to evacuate."

"You tell this information to me now? Four days later?"

"It wouldn't have made any difference, Irene."

Irene paused for a moment to collect her thoughts. She knew Adam was right, but as Morning Star's captain, she generally got that information immediately.

"Adam?" she said after the brief awkward pause.

"Yes, Irene."

"Do be careful, yeah?"

"Will do, baby," Adam responded. "Over and out."

The radio stopped transmitting as Irene took in a deep breath and opened the section of the cockpit where the suits were stored. She checked the helmet, the boots, and the suit itself. All looked good.

With a feeling of excitement that she would finally get to leave the cockpit, she opened the book again to find another note stuck on the margin.

"What does the Edge look like?"

"I don't know."

"You don't know, or you won't tell?"

...

"Look, we all grow old and die, or worse, we become like you."

Chuckling, he tugged on the robe laid on the throne.

"The Edge can't be told; it has to be shown. And you will hate me for that."

"The Edge can't be told," Irene murmured, placing the yellow sticky note back on the book, flipping to the next story.

INFECTED

Miracle 87 headquarters laboratory, 1900 hours

The Incident

E mma walked to Tomas, sliding through a group of panicked guests who were bunching up at the back of the room next to him, loudly talking to each other. "I can't turn that alarm off."

"I know. The controls are downstairs, and the phone lines are down." Tomas adjusted his jacket to hide the gun sticking out of his shoulder holster.

"Those two next to that desk haven't said a single word since we got here." She tugged on his sleeve, pointing to two men in dark suits similar to the one Tomas was wearing. "They don't even look like they're scared," Emma said, looking at the two who were kneeling at the end of the room next to a desk littered with glass flasks and Petri dishes.

"Yeah. They seem pretty calm, given our situation," he replied, looking at the two. "They're not my guys, though."

"Well, you seem as calm as they do," she observed. Most of the scared guests were staring toward the bloodied, bar-reinforced windows of the laboratory, behind which the infected and disfigured former scientists were banging, moaning, and growling.

"Yeah." Tomas unclipped the ID card from his jacket, placing it inside his pocket. "That's not right, not that everyone should panic, but..."

"They look like they're guests, like everyone else." She reached for his hand. "Baby? I think you might be right."

"About what?"

"Sabotage."

"Trust me. I hate being right."

Emma looked around the room as the guests settled down a little. Some of them were standing by the airtight windows and staring at the bloodied scientists roaming the hall. Others were tending to a man lying on the floor who was having a hard time breathing.

The mysteriously calm duo pulled out thick,

orange intramuscular syringes and injected themselves in their thighs.

"My God, Tom, did you see that?" Emma gasped, tugging Tomas's sleeve as the strangers began to whisper to each other, looking toward the front of the room where one of the emergency lock-unlock buttons was.

"Yeah, I saw that. Stay here." Tomas got up and began to walk to the duo as one of them approached the front door. The two made eye contact just as the stranger lifted the clear plastic cover and pressed the button.

Tomas knew that it was too late for him to do anything to stop it. Once those doors unlocked, they would have to completely retract before the red button would work again, and by that time, the airtight windows and the bars would be all the way up.

"What the hell?" Pulling his own orange antidote syringe, he plunged it into his upper thigh, then walked back to where Emma was standing. "Come closer," he said, then took a second syringe from his inside jacket pocket and did the same to her. Once done with the injections, he pulled his pistol from his waistband. "Get behind me, baby."

The airtight windows slowly opened, making a loud, hissing sound. It attracted the attention of the infected standing on the other side, some of whom turned and slowly walked toward it. Now the only barrier between the sick and the guests were the reinforced bars, which were about to rise as well.

Air rushed inside the laboratory. The infected

stuck their clawing, bloodied hands inside the barrier, grabbing a man standing near the window by his jacket. Pulling him closer to the bars, which were still in place, other infected stuck their fingers in his flesh, causing the now hysterically screaming man to panic, extending his hands towards the crowd inside the room, asking for help. A few guests helped him away from the hellish hands, trying to stop the bleeding from his neck and face. Others cowered in fear at the end of the room.

Shots rang from the back as the now-terrorized guests looked in their direction, shielding their ears with both hands as most instinctively knelt in reaction to the noise. The two dark-suited men now stood in front of the slowly opening door, shooting at the infected scientists who walked towards them. Some of them moved slowly while others ran, and all of them growled and moaned. They slid past the front door, walking into the corridor as a few guests followed them.

What the hell is going on? Do they think they'll shoot themselves out of here? Tomas kneeled, paying close attention to the unfolding scene.

As the bullets flew, they not only hit the infected but grazed many of the guests. The reinforcing bars began to rise, allowing the crazed scientists who hadn't followed the two men shooting their way out to crawl inside, grabbing and biting the guests and scientists who remained inside wherever they could. The room erupted in horrified screams as Tomas, who'd initially wanted to follow the two men, quickly changed his mind.

Pushing one of the guests out of his way while holding Emma's hand, he fired at one of the infected scientists who jumped through the window, now that the bars were clear of it, then another. As their bodies fell on the ground, convulsing, two more infected rushed in.

Seeing no way out, he looked back at the janitor's closet. "Baby, I don't have enough ammo to go through all of them. Come this way." Shooting an infected scientist who'd just bit a screaming victim's ear clean off his head, he led Emma to the back room, opened the door, and then slammed it shut as soon as they were inside. The infected scientists rushed, growling and clawing the door from the outside.

"We're stuck. What do we do now?" Thomas heard Emma's trembling voice ask in the dark.

)(

Miracle 87 headquarters conference room, 1600 hours

Three hours earlier.

"Look, all I'm saying is that if they'd relaxed those ethical rules a bit, we would have made leaps in the biopharmaceutical field by now. Leaps," Henry Hoffman, the BioBase executive, told Jennifer Ryan, the project manager. The other staff members around them raised their champagne glasses as more guests entered the room, adorned by a large banner that read:

Congratulations on your achievement, Team Miracle.

"Where is your lead scientist?" Henry asked Jennifer, "where is Emma?"

"She's down there at the corner," Jennifer pointed down the room, "she's not the limelight type of person, you know."

"So, what's next?" Henry asked Jennifer with a fake smile plastered on his face.

"Well, the testing phase is over, so we move to production now," she replied, looking at him and then shifting her gaze to the rest of her colleagues standing in the room.

Jennifer stepped onto a small podium next to the group of scientists and guests and hit her glass with a dessert spoon near the microphone. The sound echoed through the speakers placed all around the large conference hall.

"Ladies and gentlemen, we are gathered here today to finally celebrate the end of the testing rounds for the M87 experiment, also known as Miracle 87. It has been a long and hard eight years, but we finally can say that the modified Lentiviral vector on the eighty-seventh base pair has done the trick. We named the product Miracle 87 because we began our research at the eighty-seventh base pair, scanning up and down the DNA base-pairs until we made our breakthrough. A very special thank you to BioBase for providing us with the testing equipment, and for their support throughout this testing phase."

Placing the glass on a nearby table, she pointed at a group of men in suits as the entire room turned to face them, clapping in celebration.

Tomas, the head of security for Miracle 87 and Emma's husband, walked in the room, staying closer to the walls and observing the cheering crowd.

"Why are they here?" he whispered, approaching Emma, who was also standing at the edge of the room.

"Relax, they're helping us with the party," Emma replied, leaning toward him but still looking at the guests in the room clapping.

"Couldn't you find anyone else? You should know better than me that they would love to get their hands on your research."

She turned to face Tomas. "Would you relax and enjoy this?"

Closing his eyes and shaking his head in frustration, he adjusted the gun in his shoulder holster under his jacket.

"It's going to be OK, honey." She gently grabbed his other hand to calm him down a bit. "I'm sure the corporate office searched and investigated all of them."

Biting the inside of his lower lip, he continued to shake his head. "Baby, they investigated the three people that are standing here. My men tell me that there are at least another five walking around the lab that the mighty corporate office has given access to. Anyway, I took two antidote syringes from your desk this morning, and I'm keeping them."

"You're going to get me in trouble, Tom," she whispered, getting closer to him.

"This doesn't feel right, Emma." He looked around the hall as some of the scientists, wearing white lab coats, walked in through the conference room's wide-open door and approached the long table that held trays of food.

"Baby, you're in the civilian world now. Not everyone is evil here. Sometimes people help each other, you know?"

"I love how trusting you are; I really do. But you're talking about an ideal world, a world where I wouldn't need to exist, and unfortunately, we don't live in that—"

A distant boom penetrated the building, shaking the glasses and bottles. As the lights flickered, the guests gasped, looking around in panic.

Wasting no time, Tomas grabbed Emma's hand, heading for the hall through one of the emergency exit doors.

"Tomas, I can't leave the team," she objected as he pulled her out of the room.

Without saying a word, Tomas pulled out his ID card. He approached another door that led to a long corridor to the elevators. Opening it, he was confronted by a mob of scientists in lab coats with bloodshot eyes and bloodied faces rushing in and attacking others trying to run down the hall.

Faced with an impossible human wall, he pushed them inside one of the air-sealed laboratories where a fair amount of people were already hiding and pressed the Emergency room seal red button next to the door.

The now sealed and secured room, filled with guests and white-coated scientists, went dark for a moment before lighting up again as the sealing process set in, isolating its power and air feed from the grid.

He directed Emma to the end of the room, trying to regroup and figure out what to do next as the lights flickered again.

)(

Miracle 87 headquarters laboratory, three days earlier.

"That's a wrap, then. Let's mark the sequence and get this recorded." Owen raised his eyes from his microscope and looked over at Jeremy. "The libraries are compiled, and the strand works as it is, but you know it's not ready for production. Not for the purposes we mean it for, anyway."

"Look, the funds are depleted. The Health Department sent a letter to our corporate office telling them that if the results aren't in by Thursday, two days from now, we'll lose the contract," Jeremy replied.

"I know, I heard about that, but you're fully

aware that what we have so far is just the viral shell, which can easily absorb and recombine with pretty much any donor that comes in contact with it, including other viruses. That's why we do the experiments in a sterile lab, three stories down a concrete bunker," Owen replied, getting up from his chair and stretching his arms.

"Yeah, and they never tell us what other projects they have in there." Jeremy took a step toward the table where the rack holding the vials that they'd just compiled were. "Maybe BioBase would do a better job at managing these projects."

Sighing, Owen looked down while rubbing his nose. "Would you rather end up on the street? Because I assure you, once BioBase gets their hands on it, it will be game over. At this point, we have to do what's best for us."

"Maybe we will have a better chance if they managed these projects," Jeremy said, walking to the table so that only his back showed to Owen and shielding his hands as he grabbed an unsealed vial from the rack and placed it inside his right lab coat's pocket carefully, so as not to spill it. "I'm going to the cafeteria to get a coffee. Do you want anything?"

"I'm good. I'm almost finished with these new strains of the antidote Jennifer asked for last week," Owen said, sitting back down and resuming work.

Placing his ID card on the card reader, Jeremy opened the hermetically sealed vestibule door and closed it behind him. He took off his lab coat, hanging it on a hanger to his side while he transferred the vial to his pants pocket, then opened the outside door labeled in bold red letters:

Warning! M87 Biohazard! Do not handle or transfer any genetic material without proper packaging and authorization beyond this point.

He walked out into the corridor as a few scientists and lab technicians walked past him in front of a door bearing a similar bold red label:

Warning! ABLV Biohazard! Because there are multiple experiments conducted, do not handle or transfer any genetic material without proper packaging or authorization.

Stopped in front of the elevator, he put his hand inside his pocket to check the vial. Jeremy immediately felt his pocket was wet.

"Damn it," he mumbled, feeling the liquid touch his thigh through his pants as the elevator doors opened. He stepped inside, but more technicians entered just before the doors closed, chattering. Knowing that he was potentially contaminating all of them, he tried to shield the vial during the elevator ride by sealing it as best he could with his thumb.

Once on the ground floor, Jeremy checked on the vial. It was still intact, but it had leaked all over his hand. Wiping it on the inside of his pants pocket, he pulled his cell phone and dialed a number.

"I'm downstairs," he said as soon as Phil, the maintenance guy and his accomplice, picked up.

"OK, I'm coming," Phil said, and hung up.

About five seconds later, a man wearing a pair of gray pants, a yellow polo shirt, and a yellow hat opened the door. "Come in." He bladed his body to let Jeremy in, peeking his head out into the corridor to see if Jeremy was followed.

They walked through the dimly lit maintenance tunnels, which, as expected, twisted and turned, finally entering a room labeled *Maintenance Crew Only*. Jeremy pulled the vial out of his pocket as Phil opened a small cooler found of the round table in the middle of the room.

"Do you have a napkin there?" Jeremy asked Phil, placing the vial inside the cooler and closing it.

"Here, take these." Phil handed him a roll of paper towels he grabbed from the counter behind him. "There's a sink there, too, if you want to wash your hands."

"I'm fine, just hand this over, and let's get this done." The two shook hands as Phil opened the front door.

"OK, I'll be right back. There's pizza in the fridge next to the sink, and I have a special herbal cigarette to celebrate the payday," Phil said with a chuckle. He grabbed the cooler as Jeremy threw the paper towel he tore from the roll inside a garbage can next to him, coughing with his mouth closed to clear his sore throat.

Holding the cooler with both hands, Phil briskly

walked outside through the parking lot, heading to his car. He opened the back door and placed the cooler on the seat, then walked back in the building. Looking around to see if anyone saw him, Phil opened the building door. Feeling a little lightheaded, he took a deep breath before entering.

A man in a black suit walked up to his car, opened its door, and removed the cooler. He quickly slammed it shut and disappeared through the parked cars, looking past his shoulder to make sure no one was following him.

"Did you get it?" another black-suited man asked him as soon as he entered the car that screeched to a stop in front of him.

"Yes, get this to the lab ASAP." He placed the cooler on the back seat, then got into the front. "Let's go. We have two days to develop the antidote ourselves."

)(

Phil entered the building through the maintenance back door and walked to the crew lounge where Jeremy was sitting.

"All right baby, let's get this party started." He smiled and rubbed his hands together after closing the door behind him, then looked at Jeremy. "Hey, are you OK, man? You look a little pale."

"Yeah, I'm fine. It's probably excitement." Jeremy stood up. "Where's that joint? Let's party!"

The two men sat at the round table as Phil pulled a cigarette from his pocket and lit it up. Jeremy opened the fridge and pulled out the pizza box inside, taking a slice.

"Hey, you really don't look so good man," Phil asked him, exhaling smoke out of his lungs.

"It's probably the M87," Jeremy replied with his mouth full. "I'm not worried. If either of us gets infected, I can get the antidote from upstairs. Just have to wait for Owen leave."

The pain in the back of their throats intensified. Jeremy swallowed. Shivers ran down his body. He felt lightheaded and placed his head on the table. *This isn't feeling high. I'm feeling sick. There's no way the vector worked this quickly.*

"Hey, wow, dude, don't fall asleep here, you have to go upstairs. If my boss finds you here, I'll be in trouble," Phil coughed, nudging Jeremy. He got up, holding onto the chair to steady himself.

"Just don't go left!" Phil continued, "my boss is in his office today."

Jeremy looked around in a haze. The "special herbal" cigarette was doing its own damage as well. "I'll go, chill out." He opened the door and walked back toward the exit.

Halfway there, Jeremy felt as if he was going to

throw up and laid down in a fetal position behind a couple of rigid plastic containers, coughing as his entire body shivered.

)(

BioBase offices, 1300 hours, six hours prior to the incident.

"You all look sharp, I love it," Henry, the head of the BioBase security team said, closing the door and looking at the six men dressed in black suits, wearing white shirts and bowties.

He approached the rectangular table in the middle of the room and placed a grey, hard-shell briefcase on top of it. "I hope all of you know that you are the best of the best, and the most dependable Bio-Base employees." He unlatched the briefcase fasteners. "We have an excellent opportunity coming up to gain more contracts. However, the company currently holding them is being stubborn, even though they know full well they can't go any further with their research."

He opened the briefcase, revealing orange intramuscular syringes and aerosol spray bottles.

"Using these won't harm you, I promise," Henry continued, picking up one of the plain white aerosol canisters. "The gas contains the viral vector they're working on, and the orange intramuscular syringes contain an antiviral cocktail just in case there might be any other contaminants there. We don't know what other experiments they're conducting behind those closed doors."

"So, you're coming with us then?" Jack asked, taking a half step forward.

"Of course I am." Henry adjusted his cufflink. "I'll be upstairs with the rest of the guests. Now, once inside, we'll help them set up the party room. You," he pointed to Jack, "Leroy, and Kevin will carry three of these canisters each. You," he pointed to Jack, "will go to the maintenance area and release your aerosol canisters near the air filters."

Henry placed the aerosol canister on the table and picked up one of the orange intramuscular syringes, pointing it to Kevin. "You will ride the elevators a few times and release the vector there."

He took a half step toward Leroy. "Finally, you will release it in the corridors, near the sensors. That should set off the biohazard alarms indicating that they have a leak in their laboratories. The Health Department should investigate, shut them down, and we inherit their projects and grants."

"Aren't they losing this grant already?"

"As I said, we'll take them for everything. All the grants they hold."

"I have my doubts about this plan," Jack began, only to be interrupted by Henry.

"You're not here to think. Just release the aerosols and move out of the building. Not that hard of a concept."

Tightening his lips, Jack walked to the table and picked up one of the needles and three of the aerosol canisters, placing them inside his backpack.

)(

30 minutes prior to the incident

"That's the signal." Kevin put his cell phone inside his jacket pocket and faced Jack and Leroy. "You go by the elevator shaft and spray all of it. The movement should take it to every floor. Jack, you go by the air ventilation system, and I'll walk through the corridors and spray as much as I can."

The three men took their backpacks and walked in different directions as Jack pressed an ID card on a card reader in front of a door that read *Restricted Entry. Maintenance crew only.*

Pushing the door open, he turned on a flashlight and walked down the corridor, shining its light on the tubes above. *Ah, there it is.* Jack kept his light on a thick tube labeled *Air Ventilation.* Jack walked along that tube deep into the tunnel, illuminating the corridor in front of him occasionally to make sure he didn't trip on the wires and oxygen tanks, which were scattered throughout. Jack opened one canister and began to spray the odorless gas it contained, spreading the vector walking forward. Turning a corner, he shined his light to the side and saw two feet sticking out from behind a couple of boxes. A man wearing a blood-stained white lab coat was lying there, with blood and white foam coming out of his mouth.

Taken aback for a moment, Jack stopped spraying and hid the canister behind his back. "Hey, are you OK, man?" he asked. "Are you hurt?" He shined his light on the body, but the slumped man didn't respond. Afraid that there might be a misunderstanding, he reached and lifted the man's head, pressing his hand on his sweaty forehead.

The man opened his eyelids, revealing bloodshot eyes, and immediately lunged at Jack, biting his cheek off. Screaming, Jack pushed him away, reaching for his backpack as blood rushed out of his face. Hurriedly backtracking, he opened his bag and pulled out the orange intramuscular syringe as he looked in the direction of the lab technician getting up. *Oh, shit, what did I get myself into?*

He plunged the syringe into his thigh, injecting himself as the technician gained speed and rushed him again. Extending his hand to push him away, Jack ran past the crazed man, throwing some metal tubes and other maintenance equipment on the ground to slow the man down. Unzipping his backpack, he placed everything on the floor. "Screw this." He pulled a multi-tool knife from his left pocket, his hand coated with blood from his gushing cheek. Puncturing all the canisters, he ran down the corridor, hoping to find a door he could escape through. He tried two or three doors, feeling as if he was going around in circles, but at least the crazy lab technician wasn't following him anymore.

He finally reached what looked like the end of the maintenance corridor. He saw a few chairs and a TV, and on the side, there was one last door labeled "Office," which he pushed open only to see one of the maintenance workers slumped over a desk. "Oh shit, what the hell is going on here?" he whispered as the maintenance worker lifted his head.

"Who the fuck are you?" he said, yawning. "What the fuck happened to your face?"

"Oh, there's an, um, there is a crazy scientist guy running through the tunnels, man."

"What?" the maintenance worker exclaimed.

"Yeah, that guy took a chunk off my face," Jack said, coughing as he felt a pain on the back of his throat.

The maintenance worker reached for a white wired telephone on his desk. Jack hurriedly took two steps forward and yanked the wire out.

"Hey, what the hell are you doing?"

"You can't..." Jack coughed blood on the maintenance worker's face. "You can't call. I'm sorry."

"The hell I can't! Get out of this area. I don't care if the management wants to do surprise inspections, you guys are crazy."

Startled, they heard someone banging on the door. "Holy hell, what is it now?" The maintenance worker walked past Jack to the door and opened it, revealing the lab technician with his bloodied lab coat and face. He immediately lunged and bit the maintenance worker's nose off.

As the two rolled on the floor, one screaming, the other growling, Jack ran out of the office, backtracking the way he came and kicking pipes and any debris he could behind him.

)(

Meanwhile, upstairs.

"I sprayed the elevators," Kevin said as he approached Leroy, who was pushing a cart with speakers and supplies for the party. "I couldn't go to the lower levels; the elevators require a different card for it, and there are a lot of people still working on all floors."

"I know." Leroy looked around, holding onto the small cart with both his hands. "Let's get this over quickly. I have a date tonight."

"Well, I'm done. Where the hell is Jack?"

"I don't know. He went downstairs to the air pumps. He's probably lost in those maintenance tunnels."

Kevin pulled his phone out of his pocket as they briskly walked down the corridor toward the conference room where everyone was heading, dialing Jack. They approached the front door of the conference room, hearing a woman giving a speech inside.

"He's not picking up." He sighed and leaned on

the doorframe. "I really don't understand this guy."

Looking back toward the corridor, he noticed a few of the guests and laboratory technicians running to the elevator. Others rushed to the emergency exit doors as alarms ensued. At the same time, they saw Jack stumbling into the corridor with his bleeding cheek, dragging an oxygen tank.

"There he is. What in the world happened to his face?"

As the workers scattered in fear, a few security guards drew their weapons, ordering them to stop. Jack not only did not stop but lunged toward them. They, in turn, shot at him. Jack raised the tank to shield himself. *Boom!* A round went through the tank, which exploded, killing Jack and setting off the fire suppression system, which immediately began to shower the entire area.

)(

The screaming and growling continued for at least another hour after the fire suppression system was set off. Tomas and Emma waited patiently for a rescue service to show up at any moment. At least the first responders would have to show up, eventually the CDC. But no one made it to where they were. The couple now were stranded in the middle of ground zero of this new chimeric viral disease. Tomas cautiously opened the door. Darkness, silence, and half a foot of water on the floor greeted them.

"What do we do now?" Tomas whispered, pointing his gun at the open laboratory door. The floor was littered with floating dead bodies, papers, and other debris. Minding his footing, he walked slowly, sliding his feet against the underwater floor to make sure he didn't trip.

"I don't know," Emma replied, holding on to his jacket, "but based on how everyone got sick at the same time and we didn't, I'd say we have the antidote in our body."

"Yeah, that's great," Tomas replied, unimpressed. "Follow me. I'm heading for the stairs."

Emma turned on her phone to use it as a flashlight, illuminating the area as the couple headed for the stairs. They exchanged glances as they passed a bloodied poster:

"Be Ethical, Do the Right Thing."

#

"Oh my god, Adam," Irene muttered. "Where do you get all these stories from? Poor people, and for what, a little more money?"

Irene looked up at the crackling speakers as she heard Steve, the manufacturing expert for the mission, say, "Captain Deris, are you there?"

"Yes," Irene answered once she floated to the communications panel. "It's good to hear your voice,

Steve."

"I have a message from Adam."

"A message, huh?"

"Yeah, he says; It's about time we got you out of there and into a proper shower." Steve chuckled. "Please prepare for E.V.A. Your room has been empty for far too long."

"Is it now?" Irene chuckled as well, "where is he anyway?"

"He is on his way down to the planet with a team to scout and assess our landing site. We're making the final preparations to bring you here. You should see Eric and Violet outside the hatch at any moment."

"Please make sure to bring the data transport container. I'll try to salvage whatever data I have here," Irene said, peeking out of the round window. "I see them," she continued. "Hi, guys." She waved at the two who slowly approached the outside hatch, removing wires and clearing the way out.

"Will do, Irene. I'll be there in a few seconds, grabbing the data transport container now."

Irene floated over to the main computer and powered it down. She opened a compartment below the Captain's seat, revealing the cockpit mainframe. Making sure the power cords were utterly disconnected, Irene removed all the solid-state drives one by one, placing them inside a static-shielded shiny plastic bag. She secured the bag by zipping it up. Irene floated to the side panels and made sure all the meshes holding the packs in place were tightly fastened. She then moved to the side of the cabin and lifted a curtain, revealing the two E.V.A. suits behind it. Their boots were magnetically held on the ground, and their pants folded to their sides. She put her feet inside the boots on the right and began to roll up the white suit, zipping it as she went. Finally, pressing a button on both boots, she de-magnetized them and floated to the hatch.

"We're all here. Ready," Steve said on the radio.

Just before she put the helmet on, Irene reached out and placed the small book inside her E.V.A. suit. Then she screwed the helmet on, hearing the comforting hiss of the locking mechanism.

"I'm in the E.V.A. suit, ready."

"Okay, I will depressurize the cabin little by little," she heard Violet say.

"Go."

The muffled hiss intensified as the air rushed through the ventilation valve. Irene re-engaged her magnetic boots, which stuck to the floor. She grabbed the bag where the hard drives were stored and prepared for the hatch to open.

Since the crew members had removed the air and slowly decompressed the cockpit, nothing flew out when they opened the hatch. Holding a metal container, Steve floated inside the now-dark cockpit, illuminating it with his helmet lights. He opened the case, and Irene placed the hard drives in.

"Do you have everything?" Steve asked, facing Irene.

"I'd like to bring Adam's bag, but we can leave the rest here." She moved to the net and grabbed Adam's bag. "We're done here. Let's go."

Steve made way for Irene to exit and sealed the hatch once he went out behind her. The four astronauts formed a line as they floated to the central part of the ship. Now Irene could see the extent of the damage the asteroid impact had created.

"We are so lucky it didn't hit the reactor," she said.

"Yeah," Steve replied, "that's what the chief said as well."

The astronauts floated past the cryogenic preservation module as Violet, who was leading the line, turned and went around the section. The lights were on, and the engines now turned off, looked intact. Just behind them, the reactor section also looked good, with no scratches or dents as the four astronauts approached the entry-exit hatch lit by light blue small L.E.D lights, signifying that it was ready to receive. Next to it, the escape shuttle bays were completely open.

"Okay, we know the drill, two at a time," Violet said, holding on to a rail on the side of the hatch. "Irene, you first."

Irene went into the hatch accompanied by Steve, as Violet and Eric now magnetized their boots and stood on the little yellow and black striped metal ramps made especially for that reason on both sides of the entry point.

The decompression chamber lit red as the two astronauts magnetized their boots, which grounded them to the floor. By lifting his left heel, Steve activated the suit's walk mode. The electromagnets lined on the boot's sole weakened gradually, heel-to-toe allowing him to slowly walk to the side panel. He turned a red knob clockwise and pressed a couple of buttons to begin pressurizing the vestibule.

In a few minutes, the red lights flashed blue, then green. It signified that the vestibule was now completely pressurized, and it was safe for the astronauts to go into the preparation room and join the rest of the crew inside the Morning Star.

"Sit here," Stacy, the Morning Star's doctor, said once Irene removed her helmet and took in a deep breath. "Let me look at you."

She held Irene's head with both her hands and lowered her lower eyelids, tilting her head slightly. "Open your mouth, please," she directed Irene as Lucas, the second doctor, unzipped her suit and attached a pulse oximeter on her index finger.

"How do you feel, Irene?" he asked.

"I'm good, Lucas, I just need a shower." Irene got up, holding on to a rail above her head and shaking the suit off her leg.

"Can you walk?" Stacy asked, looking at Irene

getting up.

"Of course I can, Stacy, I was in zero-g only for a few days."

"Good." She faced Lucas. "Take Irene to the infirmary, get a full readout of her vitals. How about you, how are you doing?" she asked Steve, who gave her a thumb up as the vestibule door closed behind them.

"What about this?" Lucas picked up the small book that fell on the floor as Irene removed her suit.

"That comes with me," she replied, taking it from his hands.

"Okay, let's go." Lucas held Irene's arm, helping her walk out of the well-lit vestibule staging area to the corridor. After a short walk, they entered the infirmary, where a few beds were.

"Let me see your arm," he said. Irene rolled up her sleeve, and he placed a sphygmomanometer on her arm. After taking a reading, he took out his stethoscope. "Breathe normally for me, please."

"I'm fine, Lucas, can I take a shower now?" Irene asked after Lucas finished listening to her lungs.

"Irene, you know where they are. Take it easy on the hot water; we just fired up the boilers."

"Thank you." Irene left the room and walked through the single long corridor, which ran the length of Morning Star, and into the showers.

After a few minutes, she came out of the shower

room, walked to her room, and sank onto the bed. *Ah, finally, a bed.*

She picked up Adam's book and flipped the page only to hear a knock on her door.

"Come in," she answered, looking at Chief Helmsey as he opened the door.

"I'd like to welcome and congratulate you. You are a brave captain and kept your cool when the chips were down, as they say," he said, standing at the door. "I'll let you rest now. Again, welcome back on board the Morning Star."

"Wait, what about Adam?" she asked.

"He is with Team One. They left a little before your rescue mission. They should be back soon. I'll let you know. I took control of the vessel while both of you are away, and given the fact that you were stranded, I have decided that you need rest. That is an order, Captain." He smiled.

Helmsey left the room as Irene took a couple of pillows and placed them behind her back to get comfortable. After looking around for a few seconds, she realized that she was so excited to be back on board the Morning Star, that she wouldn't be able to get any sleep. So, she opened the book to the bookmark and began to read the next story.

THE EXPERIMENT

K eller kicked the wooden door in, as Crasher quickly stepped inside, illuminating the dark room with the bright L.E.D. lights on his ballistic shield. Their two support gunners, Nestor and Jones, hastily joined him, pointing their rifles with flashlights attached to the barrels. Even though the forest just outside the cabin was bright and the sun was high in the sky, inside was pitch dark. The short but ample room only held a wooden bed covered by a dirty blanket on the left and a small table with a metal coffee mug on the right. The SWAT team quickly occupied it. Nestor and Jones ran to their respective left and right sectors and reported, "Clear."

"The lab door is up ahead," Ericsson, the team

leader, said, entering the room as Keller announced "Clear" as well.

"Whoa." Nestor broke formation, walking to the dull grey metal door at the end of the small cabin. "It will take more than the ram to get this open, boss."

"Control, we have a second door here." Ericsson radioed in their status.

"Acknowledged, Team One, we have a passcode for you. Let me know when you're ready for it."

"All right team, line up, let's get this done," Ericsson said, looking at the team members who had slowly stacked themselves up against the concrete wall. They were led by Crasher, who was carrying a black heavy ballistic shield.

"We are ready when you are, Control," he said as the team stacked up.

"Do you see a keypad there?" he heard Control's voice ask in his earpiece.

"Yes," Ericsson replied, looking at the keypad on the left of the metallic doorframe.

"According to Intel, the passcode is six digits long. Let me know when you are ready."

Ericsson walked to the end of the narrow room, which, unlike the rest of the wooden walls, was a concrete plate with a visible metal door in it that was secured to the concrete by four pistons. The keypad with lit buttons was on its left side. "Ready."

"Zero, two, nine, three, three, eight," the female voice of Control slowly said.

The pneumatic pistons made a hissing sound and began to retract as soon as Ericsson input the code. Keller pushed the door open to his right, making room for Crasher, who went straight in as soon as the door opened enough to allow him to put the shield through. Nestor ran to his left, and Jones rushed to his right, both of their guns up and illuminating the dark laboratory inside. It had an operating table in the middle, and metal tables lined up along the walls littered with large vials held up by small scaffolds. Metal surgery scalpels and small hooks hung on the walls just in front of them.

Ericsson followed the formation, looking ahead at the room illuminated by flashlight beams.

"What did you say this raid was for?" Jones asked, pointing his rifle with its mounted flashlight at the surgery table in the middle of the lab.

"To secure the premises, that's all," Ericsson replied.

"There's no one here. It seems no one has been here in a while," Nestor added, slowly walking to the end of the room while pointing his rifle forward.

Keller passed his finger across the metal table next to him. It left a streak in the dust that had settled there. "That's weird."

"What's weird?" Ericsson asked.

"This was a sealed laboratory, right?"

"And?"

"Where is all this dust coming from?"

Ericsson looked at Keller, standing next to one of the metal tables that had flasks and Petri dishes on top of it. "Maybe they burned something."

"You're right." Crasher sniffed the heavy air. "It does smell like burned flesh inside here."

Ericsson turned his head to his shoulder, where he'd hooked his radio microphone. "Control. We might have a problem."

"What is it, Team One?"

"We breached the lab, but it's empty and... dusty?"

They all heard a new, male voice through their earpieces. "Team One, this is Doctor Hekse with the D.O.D., can you hear me okay?"

"Loud and clear," Ericsson replied. "Why are we talking to you?"

"Can you please describe to me what you see?"

"The room is about eight feet tall." Ericsson paused, looking to his right. "What have you got, Jones?" he asked the gunner, keeping the radio keyed in.

"I'd say twenty feet long and seven feet wide," Jones replied, shining his flashlight around.

"That sounds about right." Ericsson's voice echoed throughout the room. "There are metal tables along the walls, a sink at the end of the room, and a surgery table in the middle. At the very end, there are two empty metal cages."

"And dust," Crasher added, "lots of dust. Where is this stuff coming from?" He let go of the radio's button, picking the shield he had placed leaning on his feet with his other hand.

"Well, dust can come from anything, and at times, especially in closed areas, it could be as high as seventy percent...human skin... Team One, respirators on please."

"Shit, now he tells us?" Jones said, slinging his rifle to his back, removing his goggles, and reaching for the hazmat pouch.

"What the hell is that?" Crasher exclaimed, pointing out a pulsating cocoon in the corner of the room next to Nestor as he illuminated it with shield's L.E.D. lights.

"What the fuck!" Nestor turned around and pointed his rifle to it. The cocoon's pulsations quickened as soon as the lights hit its slimy outer shell, which began to expand, leaking fluids on the dirty ceramic tiles.

"Stop the investigation! Everyone get back to the exit, don't touch anything!" Ericsson screamed as a paw with four elongated claws ripped through the shell, spilling fluids.

"Boss, there's another one here," Jones said with an alarming voice from the end of the room, illuminating the second cocoon with his rifle's flashlight.

"Get back, retreat to the exit point, move!" Ericsson turned around and rushed through the door, followed by Keller as Crasher pointed his shield facing the back of the room toward Jones and Nestor.

Both gunners slowly retreated toward the door, walking backward on either side of the surgery table and looking at each other over their shoulders. As they reached the middle of the table, about four feet away from the cocoons, the one on the left burst, throwing slime and plasma everywhere as Nestor fired at it.

Crasher pointed his shield toward Nestor to illuminate his surroundings with its lights as a large, dog-like creature jumped out of the corner where the cocoon was. Screeching, it lunged at Nestor, who tried to shoot it midair. The beast took fire and fell on the ground, growling and making high-pitched noises at Nestor as he continued firing at it.

"Report!" Ericsson demanded on the radio as he heard the gunshots.

"The cocoons have some kind of a large dog inside..." Crasher began to report. Then more gunfire erupted inside the room.

"Team One, report," Ericsson heard Control say over the radio as the firing inside the lab intensified.

Nestor took another step back toward the door, looking at the rapidly expanding cocoon on his side as Jones raised his rifle to scan the room for any other threats.

"Guys, get in formation behind me," Crasher said, holding his shield with one hand. He pulled his pistol out of his thigh holster, pointing it over the top of the shield in the direction of the dark room.

"Is it just me or is it getting warmer here?" Jones asked, turning to walk backward while still pointing his rifle at the dog-like creature, which began to growl and convulse, turning around and clawing the floor with its paws.

"This thing isn't dead!" he exclaimed, reaching Crasher and placing his left hand on his shoulder to let him know that he was now in retreat formation.

"The one on my side..." Nestor began to speak as the cocoon made a popping and splashing sound.

As another slimy, greyish dog jumped out of the remains of the cocoon, as all the three fired in that direction. Nestor's right thigh gave in as one of the bullets ricocheted off the wall and went through him. He extended his right hand to the surgery table to break his fall as the creature rushed in to grab his leg and quickly drag him away.

Crusher and Jones stopped firing and moved to the left side of the table to see what had happened to him.

"Nestor, Nestor, are you okay?" Crasher called out as soon as they had a clear view of where he should be - but he wasn't there. There was only a streak of blood leading to the far corner of the room.

"Crasher, Nestor, Jones, what's happening inside

there?" they heard Ericsson ask over the radio.

"Boss, we have a problem..." Jones began to say, kneeling and following the blood streak with his rifle's flashlight. As soon as he completely knelt, one of the creatures darted forward, clawing his face and sending his helmet rolling to the floor. It then swiftly dragged him toward the dark end of the room.

As the body of Jones disappeared under the desk, Crasher heard growls coming from the end of the dark room. Pistol-first, he advanced in that direction, illuminating his way with his shield. As soon as he passed the table's corner, he saw the two creatures with short hind legs and long front legs, bloodied faces kneeling and ripping flesh and blood from the bodies of Nestor and Jones.

"No!" Crasher's blood boiled as he rapidly fired at them with his 9mm pistol.

Startled, the two creatures turned their attention to the lights emanating from the shield, and both lunged at it.

"Crasher, Nestor, Jones, report!" Ericsson screamed into the radio as he moved to head back in.

"Boss, we don't know what's happening there." Keller held up his hand. "I think it's best to just close the door and call for more men."

Ericsson's right eye twitched in anger as he pulled his arm away from Keller. "No one gets left behind."

He took Keller's rifle and checked the chamber. "Stay here and lock the door if I don't come out in three minutes."

Ericsson shouldered his rifle and turned its flashlight on, entering the metal door that led to where the rest of the team were. Keller pulled out his 9mm pistol and put his hand on his shoulder. "We're going in together."

As the two entered the laboratory, a black helicopter hovered in the forest above the cabin, releasing ropes that four soldiers repelled down. They quickly ran into the cabin and, without hesitating, closed the metal door as gunfire erupted inside the room.

The team was followed by Agent Winters, who wore a dark suit, and Doctor Hekse in a white lab coat. They entered the cabin and approached the soldiers.

"Entry is secure, sir," one of the soldiers reported to Agent Winters.

"Thank you, Captain," he replied. He turned around, facing the doctor. "Do you consider that a successful experiment?"

"Why did you send them there?" he asked. "I told you it works."

"You've promised a lot, Hekse, but all we have here is a room full of monsters."

"I told you that their cocoons could resist fire, and they did. I don't understand why you had to test it with these poor souls."

Agent Winters took a few steps toward the army captain. "Burn it."

"You know their cocoons are fire-resistant, right?" Professor Hekse followed Winters and the group of soldiers inside the cabin as the captain reached for the keypad on the side of the door and entered a code. The pistons extended slightly, pushing the metallic door forward as a muffled boom sounded inside the laboratory.

Winters turned around to face Professor Hekse. "Call the C.D.C., tell them we have a biohazard situation here."

Hekse looked at him with a regretful, almost scared face. "I don't think they'll be able to help with this."

"What do you suggest, then?"

"Bring the engineers, drop about two tons of cement on top, seal this entrance, and all airways that lead there."

"In hopes of what? From what you are describing, that would be useless."

"In hopes of cutting off oxygen, agent." Hekse arrogantly raised his voice. "As with all the improvised solutions I'm forced to make, Agent Winters, it's not ideal, but it could work. Maybe the lack of oxygen will slow their metabolism enough."

"Enough for what?"

"Enough so we can reenter and capture them, of

course."

"What about the rest of the facility?" Winters asked, rubbing his neck in frustration.

"The labs inside this facility are all isolated, with almost six-foot-wide concrete walls. They should be just fine the way they are."

The soldiers closed the cabin door and surrounded Hekse as Winters stepped away from the group, pulled his cell phone out of his pocket, and initiated a call.

"What's next?" the captain asked the professor.

"We're running another experiment on the other side of this complex." Hekse pointed in the direction of the forest. "Let's stay here for a moment." He pulled a few folded papers from his pocket and looked at them. "I want to be available should anything else go wrong."

Winters approached Hekse as the soldiers looked around, talking to each other. "You know who just called me?"

"How would I know that, Agent Winters?" Hekse folded the papers, placing them back inside his pocket.

"Project Louisiana called," Winters continued, "they say there's a flaw in your experiment design and would like to revise the security procedures."

"I told you, just like I told the scientists there, fire and bleach would be the best way to kill the virus. Obviously, someone somewhere didn't read the entire packet."

"Well, we have to deal with that now."

"I have to talk to the scientists inside. Look." Hekse took a step closer to Agent Winters. "I am a scientist, and the D.O.D. has asked me to perform experiments, great. They provide the equipment and pay for the outfit, also great!" He took another step. "These other technicians and scientists are not me and don't do things the way I would. They're picked by the D.O.D. They have to follow my instructions and realize that while these projects have a lot of potential, they're also dealing with dangerous stuff."

Winter's phone rang once again as Hekse tightened his lips. "I rest my case."

The agent answered. "Winters here," he said, turning away from Hekse, who crossed his arms in front of him in frustration.

"Thank you for the notification. I'll let him know," Winters said a moment later, turning back around after a few seconds.

"Was that call also meant for me?" Hekse asked as Winters placed the phone inside his pocket.

"Yes. Project Spark has initiated their test run."

(O)

Meanwhile, inside the adjoining experiment area, codename Spark.

Alerton, the lead technician, walked to the main control panel and checked the generator's temperature. "We need to go as close to zero degrees Kelvin as we can. Otherwise, we risk the magnets heating beyond control."

"Let's lower the power input. Did you call Hekse?" Irving, the electrical engineer, peeked past his station at Alerton, the project manager, as the rhythmic whooshing sound coming from the rapidly spinning magnets increased.

"If anything, we need to drain the power system," Emmers, the magnetic core engineer, replied from behind his panel located at the end of the room by the door.

"We talked about this, draining the power won't slow the magnets down." Irving raised his voice past the intensifying whirling sound that the generator was now producing.

The spinning generator began to glow as electrical arcs emanated from its core. Much like lightning, it crawled across the white walls and concrete floor looking for anything it could find to ground. The technicians reacted to this event by frantically adjusting dials and switches on the panels they were working on to contain the power discharges.

"The magnetic rings aren't responding," Irving said, turning knobs and looking at a display monitor on his station. "I think we should do what Emmers is saying and bring in the ground plate."

"What are you talking about?" Alerton exclaimed. "Just unplug the damn thing."

"I unplugged it ten seconds ago!" Emmers raised his voice past the whooshing sound from his station. "The generator is powering itself."

"Okay, let's drain some of this power, bring in the ground plate." Emmers lowered his voice, walking to Alerton's station and looking at the panel he was working on. As the technician flipped a couple of switches, a mechanical arm holding a sizeable round lead plate extended from the right side of the room, slowly moving opposite to the reactor.

"Ground plate is in position," one of the technicians shouted as the mechanical arm pressed the lead ground plate against the back wall of the laboratory near the reactor. It immediately attracted most of the electrical charges, which heated the plate and pushed it further against the wall. The now-red, glowing lead plate sunk into the concrete wall, cracking it. Emmers and Irving left their stations and briskly walked out of the room.

Alerton quickly went to the central console and inserted a key, opening a panel labeled Emergency Shutdown, which revealed a red button. Looking at the rapidly spinning magnet rings held by scaffolding on their sides, he pressed it, expecting the generator to slow down…but it didn't. The violent electrical arches emanating from the generator, which continued to spin, pushed the red glowing lead plate deeper into the concrete wall and cracked it further. He left the room, closing the door behind him, and hastily walked down the corridor to his office.

The lights in the entire laboratory flickered as he picked up the phone on his desk, pressing the number one and listening to the dial tone.

"This is Alerton, lead technician for project 'Sparkle,'" he said as soon as someone picked up. "I need to talk to Hekse."

The lights flickered one last time, then went out as the red emergency lights lit up. "Hello?" He spoke into the phone again before noticing that it was silent.

"Damn it!" He slammed the phone on his table.

"Alerton!" Irving called, just outside the open door to his office.

"I'm in here. What the hell happened to the lights?"

"Can't tell for sure, but my best guess is that those electrical arcs hit the power grid and shorted it." Irving walked through the office door, shining a flashlight at Alerton.

"Where is Emmers?" Alerton asked, shielding his eyes from the bright beam. "And put that down, will you?"

Irving lowered his flashlight. "I think he left the lab."

Alerton walked around his desk. "You know he can't do that, the surface doors lock up every time there is an emergency."

"Yeah, about that…he left via the air vent."

Sighing, Alerton took a step closer to Irving. "Did you get in touch with Hekse?"

"No, the lines are down."

"Let me try my cell." Irving put his hand inside his pocket, reaching for his cell phone.

"We're thirty feet underground inside a concrete bunker. You know it won't work."

"Argh," he exclaimed as a loud boom and more crackling sounds overtook the lab. Irving turned around, placing the phone in his pocket and illuminating the rest of the corridor with his flashlight.

"We have to leave the lab." Alerton joined Irving as they walked down the corridor.

"Not without turning off the generator first," Alerton said as the two reached the door.

"I wish that was an option, but it's not, and you know it," Irving replied, pushing the exit door and heading up the staircase that led to the air vent.

As the technician disappeared through the door, Alerton went back to the reactor room, noticing that the closer he got, the more pungent the smell of burning rubber got.

Ouch, the knob is hot. I can't open it, not without some gloves. His thought was interrupted by the gas-powered fire suppression system, which got triggered by the smoke as it forcefully pushed gas from the ceiling, beginning to remove air from the facility.

As the door burst in flames, the hinges holding it in place melted, and it fell on the ground. Taking a step back from the heat, Alerton peeked inside the lab to see what was happening with the reactor. The powerful electrical arcs had now pushed the lead concrete plate deep into the concrete wall, creating a tunnel.

The fire suppression system alarm was accompanied by red strobe lights that filled the entire laboratory. Yellow lights indicating the locations where oxygen masks were blinked in tandem as Alerton quickly ran to one of them, taking a mask from one of the wall containers and putting it on. "Fire suppression system is operational, evacuate the facility now," the female-voiced automated alarm system announced as more emergency lights illuminated the corridors.

Hekse is really not going to like this. Alerton ran back through the corridor and headed for the air vent. As the inert gas filled the laboratory, it pushed oxygen away, effectively suffocating the electrical fires that were about to overtake it. Alerton climbed inside the wide tube that led to the surface and looked up. *You have got to be kidding me.* The fire suppression system had sealed all the air vents.

Adjusting his oxygen mask, he walked to another yellow blinking station and grabbed another mask, which was attached to a small oxygen tank. By now, the fires were gone, and the only sound he could hear was the whirring of the magnetic rings of the generator. Extending his hands to feel the wall, he walked back to his office and turned on his laptop, which wasn't connected to the power grid, so he could find out how long the fire suppression system would keep the facility completely sealed before it let go—*eight more minutes. Okay, you got this.* He looked at his watch and walked to the corridor in the direction of the exit, only to hear a thunderous growling sound coming from the generator room.

What the hell was that?

#

"What a world. Full of monsters and threats. I'm sure that the professor meant well; however, the road to hell is, at times, paved with good intentions."

Irene picked up another sticky note from the margin before flipping the page.

"I hear her laughter every time I pass by the corridor, next to her room. I hear her playing the piano. I miss her. I want to go inside and say hi."

"John, it took us five years to convince her to stay inside."

"Time to let her out?"

"You didn't open the door, did you?"

Oh, Adam, are these future stories you are outlining here with these sticky notes? I have so many questions. Irene smiled faintly, placing the note back on the margin and closing the book.

She put her head on her pillow, looking at the small L.E.D. lights every three feet or so along the length of the ceiling, illuminated the room. There were also lights in the middle of each of the panels, dimly illuminating the floor. She rubbed her eyes with the pulpy part of her thumbs. *I cannot believe I'm tired again.* She closed her eyes and fell asleep.

#

The pulsating light emanating from the emergency white and red strobe lights located on the top of her room's entrance penetrated her eyelids. Irene opened her eyes, turned around, and looked at it as the high pitch general alarm sound followed.

She quickly got up, put her sneakers on, and headed for the control room wearing her captain's polo shirt.

Speed walking through the corridors past the other crew members, she turned to the control room where the chief and most of the crew were already chatting.

"What's going on?" Irene asked, fixing the collar of her shirt.

"It's Adam." The chief replied, as Irene entered the room, then shifting his eyes up at a monitor showing the outside of the Morning Star.

"What about Adam?"

"On its trip back, Team One was tasked to release

more communication satellites. They should come in handy when we're going to be on the surface," Helmsey said, looking at Irene. "Adam is performing an EVA to switch on and deploy a few satellites..." The chief got interrupted by Adam's voice coming through the speakers.

"There is a band of debris emerging from the horizon. You should be able to see it now if you have any cameras pointed that way."

Irene took a deep breath as if something stung her. *Is it back?*

"How can it be back?" Eric asked. "We just exchanged orbits with the debris. Calculations say it shouldn't pass by for another 20 days, give or take. There is no way it gained speed this quickly."

"Adam, how far are you from the Morning Star?" Irene asked Adam as the chief continued talking to the other members in the control room.

"I am on an EVA a few miles away from the Morning Star. I got separated from the shuttle. I think they're in trouble as well," Adam replied to Irene.

"Unless their orbit is not a circle, but elliptical," the crew member said to the chief.

"Still, based on the calculations Adam made, they shouldn't be here this soon."

"Adam's calculations might have been wrong."

"Anyone know the status of the shuttle?" Irene asked, looking around.

"That shuttle was hit by another asteroid. It's

gone, but the crew is making their way here," Helmsey responded as he looked at a monitor showing two astronauts entering an airlock.

"Fact is that we can's stay here," Eric added as more crew members gathered around the entrance of the control room.

"Maybe this is another cluster," Irene added. "Helsey 8K might have a broken ring. That would explain the sudden appearance."

"Something must've happened in between our transit and initial Hope's scans. Something not in the reports."

"Man, I don't know what it is, but I'd say you have about ten to fifteen minutes max to get out of there," Adam said, rejoining the conversation. "This band is growing and moving fast."

"Adam, get back inside here," the chief told him.

"No time for that," Irene interrupted.

"What?"

"We have no time for that. Adam said he is a few *miles* out. We have to fire the thrusters and move the vessel out of impact trajectory. If he comes close to us, he will be more in danger. Adam, please do your best to get out of the debris trajectory as you can."

"Irene, we can't afford to lose people like this."

"I know," she replied, looking at the direction of the cryogenic module where the embryos were. "But I can move the ship out of this orbit. We don't have time to wait for him."

Helmsey looked around the room as if to ask for a vote.

"We have no time for this," Irene continued. "I'm taking control of the ship on captain's and pilot's authority."

Taken aback by the sudden orders, the chief tightened his eyebrows." We can't leave him out there, Irene. His EVA suit has maybe another forty-five minutes of oxygen."

"I will get him myself, Chief. For now, I need all non-essential crew to go back in their respective chambers and pull out the emergency equipment." She looked around the room as the strobe lights illuminated the area red and blue. No one moved.

"I'll contact you when I'm in the engine room." Irene walked through the frozen-in-panic crew members.

"Make way!" she screamed at them as the chief walked to the panel and silenced the alarm. "Make a hole."

The chief looked around as Irene swiftly walked through the group standing by one of the doors.

"Alright, you heard the captain. Don't wait for my orders, I need four to stay here with me, the rest of you go to your rooms and brace for impact. Mark, Liam, make sure the cryogenic section is secure, and the emergency lockdown is in place," the chief ordered two crew members who were standing next to him.

Irene walked to the engine room, passing the cryogenic module. She picked up a wireless headset hanging on one of the chairs in front of the panels.

"Chief, can you hear me?"

"Loud and clear."

"Please open this channel; I need Adam here as well." She stopped in front of the main thruster panel and flipped switches, turning it on.

Three monitors slid up from their respective openings at the very end of the board. One displayed Morning Star's thruster status, the other Helsey 8K's orbit. The third monitor presented a series of boxes where Irene input the adjusted coordinates. As soon as she finished, the third screen showed the progress of the new path.

"Alright, coms are set up," the chief finally said as other members added their callsigns.

"Adam," Irene said.

"I'm here," Adam replied.

"We are going to move the craft out of the impact trajectory. I'm calculating the new orbit now. It seems we will move several thousand miles away from you, in a closer orbit to Helsey 8K."

Adam didn't respond, and the rest of the crew went silent as Irene continued. "Chief, have someone prepare an escape shuttle and leave it ready for me at the bay."

"How about we launch one now?"

"We can, but the more people we put out there, the more lives we risk."

"And what, risk the lives of both our pilots and the captain of the ship?"

"Chief, Adam and I are the best-suited crewmembers to go on a mission like this, and you know it," Irene said with a firm tone. "Sending anyone else out with space debris and asteroids flying around will not only endanger their lives but Adam's as well. I think we have proof enough with Team One barely making it here and losing the shuttle. Time is ticking."

"Control room copy," Chief's voice echoed in the radio speakers. "Violet, let's make that happen ASAP."

"Violet copy," Violet responded.

"Irene, are you sure about this?"

"Yes," Irene said as she continued her calculations of the new trajectory.

Adam's voice came through the speaker. "Oh, this band is huge. Some massive rocks are coming your way, Morning Star."

"Calculations complete," the computer confirmed. "New orbit pattern established. Thruster AL-3 malfunction. Manual operation suggested."

"I have the new thruster positions," Irene transmitted through the radio. "I need a team to get to the side thruster by the Airlock 3 and reposition it manually. It's thruster AL-3."

"Esther, Henry, you're up." The Chief continued coordinating crewmembers from the control room.

"This is Esther, Henry is prepping the suits. We will be on-site in 2 minutes."

"Come on, people. The clock is ticking." Irene got up from her chair and moved to the engine-firing panel.

"Adam, how much air you got left?"

"Uh, 32 minutes."

"Hang in there, baby," Irene said, setting a timer on her watch.

"Copy that," Adam replied.

Irene continued to work the system, looking at all the thruster indications in the monitor in front of her. All were green as she positioned them except one.

"Esther, what's your status?"

"She is in front of the airlock, exiting Morning Star now," Henry replied.

"Hurry up but be careful," Irene replied. "Chief, are you there?"

"Standing by," the chief replied.

"Which is ready?"

"Shuttle Eleven."

"Copy that." Irene looked at the screen in front of her. The thruster which Esther was adjusting showed movement in the wrong direction.

"Esther, are you by the thruster?"

"Correct," Esther replied.

"Ok, have you opened the manual control?"

"Correct."

"Ok. Turn the handle to twenty-eight degrees."

"Esther copy," she replied.

The thruster finally showed movement in the until it got in the right direction.

"All green," Irene confirmed. "Esther, move inside ASAP. I'm about to maneuver Morning Star manually."

"Esther copy," she said, followed by "ouch!" In a distressed voice.

"Esther, are you ok?"

"The debris is here," Esther replied. "I got hit, my suit is leaking air."

"Esther get back in; it's time to move," the chief said.

The sound of debris impacting the fuselage of Morningstar intensified as Irene waited for confirmation of Esther re-entry.

"Esther is inside," Henry finally confirmed. "We are inside the airlock."

"Everyone hold on," Irene said. "I am firing the thrusters." She pressed a button that fired the side thrusters, rotating the remaining fuselage of the Morning Star. As its fuselage moved, rocks began to hit it, and more alarms began to indicate hull breaches.

As the trajectory depicted in the monitor aligned with Irene's projection, she immediately fired the reverse thrusters located opposite the ones that just rotated the ship. The fuselage shook from the sudden push forward from the main engine as glasses, bottles, and other unsecured items fell on the floor.

"Orientation set, preparing to shift orbits," Irene decisively said, looking at the new orbit projection in the monitor above her head.

"Everyone, please wear your oxygen masks," the chief announced on the radio. "There are multiple hull breaches, and we are leaking air."

Irene engaged the main engine, which shifted Morning Star's orbit out of the debris band. The fuselage moved out of the incoming group of asteroids, which passed it at incredible speed.

Irene cut power to the main engine as the side thrusters engaged automatically, maintaining Morning Star's orientation as it exchanged orbits.

"New orbit achieved," Irene finally said. "Adam, how are you holding?" she asked as the sound of impacting rocks on the hull diminished and stopped.

The radio crackled in silence.

"Adam?"

"I think we either moved out of the radio range, or the debris is interfering with the radio signal," the chief observed.

Irene got up, holding on to one of the panels on the side of the engine room. "Chief, do we have a location for Adam?"

"We do. But he might have moved."

"Try to re-establish contact, please. I completed the orbit transition."

"We have multiple hull breaches," the chief continued, "wear your oxygen mask."

"Understood," Irene confirmed, reaching for the emergency apparatus compartment next to the hatch. She pulled an oxygen mask out of there and put it on. Irene continued to walk through the corridor following the pulsating white emergency strobe lights to the escape shuttle bay. Found shuttle eleven

"Chief, I'm launching, please open Bay Eleven."

The radio was silent, but the bay opened up. "Chief copy," he replied. "Be careful, Irene."

Irene moved the escape shuttle out of the bay.

"Which way, Chief?"

"Ok, Irene, I am plotting you to Adam's last location. We have this channel open and will continue to look for him. It's just that there is so much movement there right now."

"Got it." Irene looked at the screen in front of her. It showed a dot representing Adams's last location and the escape shuttle she was in. Once she cleared the vicinity of the Morning Star, she engaged her thrusters speeding toward Adam.

"Adam?" she continued to transmit as the radio got lively with the Morning Star crew members performing emergency repairs on the ship's body.

"Yeah. I'm here," Adam finally replied faintly through the static.

"Adam! Where are you?"

"I...I don't know Irene. I think I got hit probably by a stray meteorite. I'm leaking air." His voice got fainter. "And I'm spinning out of control."

"Chief. Can we triangulate this signal?"

"A little busy here, Irene, hold on. Please keep him talking."

"Adam, can you hear the Chief?"

"No, I can hear only you."

"You are out of range of the Morning Star. And that communications satellite you just deployed is not working."

"Ok," Adam replied. "I lost sight of the satellite, and I can no longer see the Morning Star."

"Continue talking to me. What's your oxygen status?"

"I can't tell, my gauge is not working," Adam replied.

"Keep him talking," the Chief continued, "the signal is too weak."

"I think we have a visibility issue," Irene added. "Adam says he can't see you."

"Line of sight, that's why we can't hear him, we are bouncing signals from you. I'm sorry this is going slow, we're having atmosphere issues here."

"Adam?" Irene sighed, looking down, biting her lip.

"Yes, Irene."

"Do you love me?"

"Of course, I do, Irene, what kind of question is that?"

"It's just that when you came to the escape pod, you seemed too cold and ordering."

"Is that what you think? Oh, Irene. It's not like that. Everything I do, I do it for you. I try to be as confident as I can. At times to impress you. "

"What do you mean?"

"It's not that I want to push you or order you around, Irene. I couldn't do half the things I do if it weren't for you. You have such an impact on me, physically and mentally. That gives me that extra juice and confidence to make things happen. At the airlock, I was trying to remain calm and collected for you."

"Well. You can drop that. You got me. And incidentally, you have the same effect on me as well. I hope you know that."

The radio crackled in silence once again as Adam didn't respond.

"Adam?" Irene asked, maneuvering the shuttle and increasing its speed. She checked the timer on her wrist: 17 minutes. *He should have plenty of O2 left.*

"Irene," she heard Violet's voice on the radio. "We've triangulated the signal; Adam should be within your sight. Look around."

Irene cut the main shuttle engine at the same time, engaging reverse thrusters. As the vessel came to a stop, she fired one of the side directional thrusters making a 180-degree turn in space.

"Come on, come on, come on," she whispered to herself. "Adam, can you hear me?" she said out loud on her radio's microphone. Nothing—static persisted.

The sun set over Helsey 8K's horizon, plunging the immediate area in darkness. She glanced briefly at it as the asteroid band continued to streak through the night above her.

She looked at the surface of Hesley 8K, hoping to see any sign of Adam. As darkness completely enveloped her, Irene noticed a blinking light in the distance.

"Adam?" she asked over the radio, pushing the flight stick forward, heading for the light. Hearing no response, she continued to get closer, realizing that it was Adam's distress beacon. His EVA suit was spinning out of control.

Irene hurriedly approached Adam. Matching his traveling speed and reversing the craft's direction, she put her helmet on and opened the rear cargo portion of the vessel. Backing up till Adam's EVA suit was inside the aircraft, she rapidly closed the door and pressed a button on the dashboard console, pressurizing the cabin.

"Cabin pressurized," the shuttle's computer finally announced as Irene wasted no time, she removed her helmet and rushed to Adam's EVA suit. The oxygen tanks he was wearing as a backpack had scratches, and one of them had a hole.

Adam! She twisted and removed his helmet only to feel his head laying limp in the suit.

"No, no, no, Adam!" She looked around for help, and the emergency health kit caught her eye. She rushed over, picked it up, and placed it on the floor next to her. Irene unzipped the hard-shell cover and flipped open the upper lid, revealing the resuscitation device inside. She pulled an adrenaline syringe from it and placed it on the floor next to Adam. Irene unlatched his chest piece, removing it. She then took a pair of shears and cut Adam's shirt off. Pulling the two electrodes from the kit, she attached them best she could to Adam's torso. She then took an oxygen mask and affixed it around Adam's mouth and nose. She tightened the mask's straps around Adam's head and connected wires to the electrodes, which in turn connected to the automated defibrillator.

"Analyzing," the kit's automated voice announced. "No heartbeat detected, use the adrenaline syringe immediately. Shock advised."

Pulling the cap with her teeth, Irene exposed the needle and plunged it in his chest, thrusting the hormone directly to his heart Irene pressed the shock button.

"Please stay clear," the device said as it delivered a shock to Adam's chest.

Adam convulsed as the oxygen mask, controlled by the defibrillator, pumped oxygen in and out of his lungs.

"Analyzing. Shock advised," the device said again.

Irene repeated the same motion, pressing the red shock button, and Adam convulsed again. Then the pulse monitor beeped once, indicating a heartbeat, then one more time.

"Proceeding with CPR," the kit finally said as the oxygen mask continued pumping air in and out his lungs in a breathing manner.

Irene continued to undo Adam's EVA suit, removing the upper half. She laid him on the floor, pushing aside the rest of the equipment she'd pulled from him. She made sure his resuscitation apparatus remained on his face as the heartbeat monitor showed an increase in his stable breathing.

Irene continued to remove the bottom half of the EVA suit, shifting Adam's body to the side. He reacted, moving his arm.

"Adam?" Irene said, turning him to face up as Adam coughed and swallowed, taking a deep breath.

She stared at him for a little while before Adam opened his eyes, looking at Irene.

"Are you here with me?"

"Ow," Adam growled through the oxygen mask on his face. "It feels as if I've been stabbed, what happened? How long was I out for?"

"I don't know." Irene let out a sigh, sitting on the floor. "I thought I lost you."

Adam was silent for a few seconds. "Yeah, I thought I was done."

"What happened to you?"

"I don't know. I know I lost oxygen pressure. Must've gotten hit by one of those rocks. It sent me rotating out of control. I think I passed out."

"Yeah. You did."

"And you saved me," Adam smiled, looking at Irene. "What would I do without you."

The radio crackled as the Morning Star tried to contact the shuttle.

Irene got up and sat in the pilot's seat. "Stay there for a little while, let me get us back. I think the Morning Star got hit a second time."

Irene engaged the thruster, heading back for the Morning Star, as indicated by her navigation. They approached the Morning Star, which was slowly rotating on its horizontal axis.

"Hm, I thought I engaged the automatic thrusters to keep orientation intact," Irene muttered to herself before transmitting. "Morning Star, shuttle eleven is inbound carrying two."

"Shuttle Eleven, Morning Star is on a thirty-degree rotation, match it. The bay is open. How's Adam?" the chief responded.

"Adam is awake and conscious," Irene said, maneuvering the shuttle to match the Morning Star's rotation. "How's the ship chief. How are the babies?"

"The boat is still holding air. We have a few injured members; otherwise, all is well. Babies are fine."

Taking a sigh of relief, Irene lined up with the rotating fuselage and entered the bay. As the doors closed behind them, the bay compartment began pressurizing.

The chief met Irene as soon as she opened the bay door. He knelt and looked in at Adam, who, at this point, was sitting against the panel opposite the entrance.

Lucas followed carefully, pulling Adam out of the back bay while Stacy attached additional monitoring electrodes to his body. Irene walked out of the shuttle, making room for the medics rushing in.

"How bad is it, Chief?"

"We have five minor injuries, all about to be discharged. In the beginning, we had eight breaches. Seven have been sealed, and the last one is confined in a room. We sealed that room to prevent air leaking. Engineers are out fixing it as we speak."

"Aw, easy!" Adam exclaimed as Stacy placed an electrode measuring sensor over where Irene had injected him with adrenaline.

"Sorry," she replied, continuing to measure his vitals.

Lucas finally got up. "Ok, blood oxygen levels are optimal, but your heart rate is elevated."

"I used the resuscitation kit," Irene said, adding, "Shocked him twice."

"I see the electrodes." Lucas approached her. "You saved his life, good job."

"You have my heart now," Adam said, sitting on the floor looking at Irene.

"I didn't have it before?"

Adam smiled. "It beats only for you now."

"I think these two love birds need a room," the chief said, poking fun at the exchange. "What do you prescribe, doctor?"

Stacy looked at the chief, then at Adam and Irene with a smile. "Both of you need to rest. Though I'd like to examine you in the med bay as soon as possible," she said to Adam as he put one knee on the floor, preparing to get up.

"Of course, Doc," Adam replied, extending his right leg and supporting himself with his left knee. He moved the rest of his EVA suit pants off.

Both doctors walked out of the shuttle bay as the chief approached Adam and Irene.

"We owe you our lives," he said as Irene helped Adam stand up on his feet. "We are lucky to have you."

"We are family here chief, you know it," Irene replied as she knelt, sliding Adam's hand over her shoulder and placing her other hand around his waist, helping him up. "We are all sacrificing something."

"Oh. Just before this asteroid band passed by, we were about to get a briefing from the scout mission. I postponed it pending repairs."

"We better begin formulating a plan to evacuate," Irene added. "Helsey 8K's orbit doesn't seem too friendly, at least not at present."

"I agree, but for the time being, the engineers are in control, patching the breaches. And they asked us to keep movement at minimal."

"You said the Morning Star is on a 30-degree rotation?" Irene stopped. "I can stabilize it if necessary."

"Engineers are already out. It's fine as is," the chief replied.

"Alright then, I'm going back to my room," Irene said, walking the direction of her room with Adam, who was now standing up on his own.

As the two slowly walked through the corridor, Stacy came out of the med bay entrance. "Adam, please come this way, I want to run one last test on your heart, lungs, and oxygen levels."

"More tests?" Adam replied, stopping. "I thought we were done when you placed those electrodes..." He looked at Stacy, who was staring at him with an unimpressed face. "Alright, let's do this." He walked her way.

"I'll be in my room," Irene told Adam as the latter walked into the med bay.

"I'll see you there," Adam replied.

Irene entered her room to find pretty much everything thrown around. She cleaned the place as best she could and finally picked up Adam's book from the floor and placed it on the small table next to her. She laid on her bed, staring at the ceiling lights. *I can't sleep.* She got up and sat on her bed. Irene adjusted her pillow, picked the book from her side and flipped the pages, finding the bookmark.

WAR

The curved concrete bunker ceiling vibrated under the pressure of the massive explosion above ground. It sprinkled the soldiers inside with dust and dirt as the lightbulb hanging above them, the only light source illuminating the area, flickered and turned off.

Recovering from the violent and frightening rumble of the blast, some of the soldiers lit their surroundings by throwing green chem lights on the floor. One of them approached Emmers, the technician, who was setting up the beacon. Most of the platoon resumed adjusting their facemask filters. Others put their helmets back on their heads, and a few cowered, covering their heads.

"We don't have time for this!" Ingersoll, the platoon commander, screamed through his mask at the cowering soldiers. "Up! Up! Everyone get up!"

As the soldiers began to get up, brushing dirt from their uniforms, Larry placed the tripod of his M204 heavy machine gun to face the only way out of the bunker, its door. The radio buzzed with chatter as Control began to talk back and forth with the approaching bomber pilots.

"Any platoons still inside the hive?"

"Echo Platoon is still installing the beacon," the comms technician replied.

The radio went silent as Control kept the airwave clear for any other platoons that could be operating inside the hive.

"Echo," Control resumed, "you are the last remaining platoon. Please be advised that 'Firestorm' is pending your final transmission."

Emmers faced Ingersoll, speaking through his facemask. Everyone heard screeches, and insect screams just outside the concrete fortified bunker door. "I'm ready whenever you are."

The platoon commander shifted his gaze to look at the rest of the soldiers as the overgrown insects continued to scratch and hit the front door.

One of the soldiers approached it, placing his hand on it. "They're just outside. I don't think they've softened them enough."

"We have to make it topside." Ingersoll looked at Larry, who was lying on the floor, gripping his weapon. "Larry, how are you doing?"

"Locked and loaded, baby!" Larry released his weapon's slide, chambering the first round.

"Everyone!" Ingersoll yelled, "pay attention here. Once Emmers activates the beacon, we'll likely have a few minutes to exfiltrate before they rain hell on this place, so listen up! We'll open the front door..."

"Are you crazy!" a soldier from the back of the room screamed. "This bunker can take the explosions —"

"Shut the fuck up!" Ingersoll interrupted the soldier. "We will open the door! Stay out of the initial M204 fire cone, and once we have a corridor, we will exit *to* the corridor and create a three-hundred-and-sixty-degree field of fire. From that point, we will proceed to the left, the *left*! Do you understand? The exit is *left*!"

He looked at the soldiers, who stared at him through their air purifier masks without saying a word, then turned facing Emmers. "Do it."

Emmers knelt beside the beacon device he'd just installed and flipped a switch. It indicated it was operational by three blinking red lights on top of it.

Ingersoll walked close to the comms technician, who had the radio and grabbed the mic. "Control, the beacon is live."

A few seconds passed by as Ingersoll awaited confirmation from Control that the beacon was received.

"Strong beacon signal received, Echo Platoon, time to the final drop T minus five minutes. The outside targets have been softened, get out now."

"Everyone!" Ingersoll announced one last time, "We make our way out as a team! Watch the corners and pay attention to the platoon members around you. Let's go!"

In one motion, he twisted the locking mechanism, opening the fortified door. Immediately, giant bug tentacles pushed it back, flinging him at the soldiers who had their weapons pointed toward the door. The mutated creatures began to run inside the room as Larry opened fire, bullets ricocheting against the concrete walls and hitting everything, even his fellow soldiers.

"Team, go out and form the 360!" Ingersoll ordered the platoon as he noticed a break in the bug wave.

Two soldiers hastily moved out into the corridor. They opened fire with flamethrowers as they continued to walk in opposite directions down the hall, where more of the oversized insects crawled. The rest of the team followed closely, supporting them with machinegun fire. Larry unfolded his tripod and set up behind the flamethrower on the right to relieve him and make room for the team to escape through the hole they'd made earlier when they breached the hive, which once was a laboratory.

"M204 ready and set up to fire!" Larry screamed to the flamethrower operator in front of him once he'd reloaded his weapon. "Back up and retreat!" The flamethrower operator stopped shooting and took a step to his left as Larry held his weapon ready to fire.

Screeches echoed in the corridor, which was filling with bug carcasses, announcing that danger was still lurking. Larry fired at the enormous approaching insects as the rest of the team widened the distance between him and them, clearing more mutant bugs coming from the space between the wall's breach hole and the team of flamethrowers and Larry.

Two tentacles extended from one of the corridors and struck one of the soldiers in the stomach, penetrating just below the armor he was wearing. Then the rest of the overgrown bug appeared around the corner, legs first. The screaming soldier dropped his weapon and fell on the ground as the team of flamethrowers turned and fired at the orange insect, which looked like a giant assassin bug.

Larry continued to fire at the insects rushing through the corridor. Noticing that the flamethrower team was no longer beside him, he got up to join them, still firing as more insects crawled behind, effectively separating him from the rest of the escaping platoon.

As the flamethrower team battled the new threat, Larry took a few steps back, only to stop in his tracks as the oversized insects overpowered the team. Larry saw no other way to get around them but to continue down the corridor.

"Damn it," he mumbled, shooting at the insects in short bursts. He knew that the nearest and only exit to get outside the laboratory was through that breach the team had infiltrated. He continued past a new corridor and made a right turn, only to face more insects. These didn't move as fast, just hung from the ceiling—they looked like supergiant water bugs. He didn't fire at them, just continued walking down the same corridor intending to make the next right turn.

Approaching a corridor intersection, Larry noticed more bugs that, just like the others, seemed dormant. *What the hell is happening here?* He slowly crept along the wall, stepping over dead bodies of scientists that littered the floor. Feeling a sudden weakness, he paused at the intersection to adjust his air purifier mask. Across from him were large windows. The ceiling was illuminated by a green light that seemed to waver. Peeking around the corner, he decided to check out where the light was coming from, only to see that it was a large pool swarming with jellyfish-looking creatures.

Suddenly the creatures, in unison, spewed green gas which rose up and above the pool. Hearing movement behind him, Larry kneeled and turned around to see menacing orange assassin bugs, slowly moving along the corridor's floor and ceiling. They ignored him —instead, they rammed the glass as hard as they could. Larry slowly moved out of their way and headed to the end of the corridor intersection, noticing there was one corridor where no bugs went in. Crawling now, he moved deeper into that corridor. He stopped next to an open, double-sided door to reload his weapon from the ammo pouch. Breathing was getting harder. *My filter is going. I have to get out.* He turned on his flashlight and shined it down the corridor, seeing a sign. *Spinoloricus cinziae experiments, do not enter.*

"Yeah, tell me where to exit, not where *not* to go." He shouldered his weapon and continued down the corridor, his flashlight beam becoming greener and greener. He passed a second set of doors as the air grew almost unbreathable. Realizing that he couldn't continue further, Larry backtracked to the doors and entered an office to regroup and hopefully find a map of the place.

∧

The first thing the platoon members noticed when jumping out of the wall they had breached was the green sky. "This is new." Ingersoll approached the platoon, which was waiting for the last members to exit the hive.

"They're changing our atmosphere to suit them," a civilian wearing a bloodied lab coat standing next to him said, holding his air purifier mask to his face with both hands.

"Who the hell are you?"

"My name is Professor Oake—" The radio got lively again, interrupting him, this time with a countdown.

"All right, we have completed two objectives, apparently." Ingersoll raised his voice to be heard through his air purifier. "Let's clear the area!" He motioned the platoon to continue moving down the hill.

As everyone hurriedly ran away from the hive that oversized insects began to emerge from, airplanes flew overhead. They were closely followed by massive, fiery explosions sending debris and insects that had caught fire flying everywhere as the team took cover behind some large boulders that littered the hillside.

"What the hell was that?"

"That would be our air force."

"Already? We are not even out of the hive complex yet."

"Stop talking and move out of the fire zone!" Ingersoll screamed, looking back at the opening where faint screeches came from deep inside.

The platoon continued running. Some soldiers tumbled, and others helped them up by grabbing them by their shoulders as they all continued to move as far as they could. Mutant insects exited from the open hole created by the airstrike and rushed to attack the retreating soldiers.

As the rumbling sound of the supersonic bombers intensified in the distance, the radio continued with the final countdown: "Five, four, three, two, one..."

"What the hell, man, we are still in the danger

zone!" The platoon scattered as the ground shook from the booming explosions unleashed from above, while giant spiderwebs shot up in the sky from somewhere deep in the hive.

The second wave of bombers swooped in as the bombs from the first wave impacted their targets, tearing the hive apart as they exploded deep inside the reinforced laboratory walls.

Some of the aircraft got caught in the webs, plunging into the facility themselves. One of them swung in the direction of the fleeing platoon and crashed in the hill, tangled by the white stringy substance.

"Where is he going?" A soldier pointed to the scientist scurrying away from the platoon.

"Don't stop!" another screamed. "Keep running!"

The platoon reached the bottom of the hill, where the laboratory once operated and ran through a shallow creek. Once the second wave passed, silence permeated the battlefield, broken only by delayed ordinance explosions and insect screeches, which now were far in the distance.

"Don't stop running!" Ingersoll turned around to see a few soldiers slowing down to catch their breath. "The nukes are coming. We're still in the death ring, keep moving!"

"Fuck, man!" another screamed before he resumed jogging, breathing hard through his air filter.

The platoon continued to run, reaching the small

forest where they'd landed at the beginning of the assault. Running through the trees, they heard the final rumble of the supersonic stealth bombers. "This is it, don't stop, don't look back!"

As the supersonic sound faded away, the platoon reached the protective trenches they'd dug in the hours before the assault began. The soldiers lifted the heavy lead covers designed to protect them from the initial blast, though they were assured that they would be well outside the death range of the nukes.

∧

12 hours later,

Delta Forward Operating Base.

"Look, I'm not saying that the ordinances didn't have any effect, only that the beacon is still pulsing. It might be that they missed that specific room," the army general said, pacing in front of the screen with a projection of a topographic map of the area they'd recently bombed.

"Yeah, it might be a thousand different things. That doesn't change the fact that the beacon, the target of three bombing runs, is still pulsing. We need to get back there and figure it out," another ranking officer replied, looking at him.

"The area is highly irradiated. We can't right

now."

"We don't know if the bombing had a good effect."

"Satellite shows minimal movement."

"Where is Professor Oakenisht?"

"We don't know. He escaped and made contact with one of the assaulting platoons," one of the members of the intelligence-gathering unit standing by the entrance of the large tent replied.

"Let's hope he took the hard drive with him."

"Sir," a soldier said as he walked in the conference tent. "We have intensifying movement in the hive. Bugs are still alive and well there."

"What?"

"Red-eye satellite moved in position a few minutes ago. There's movement in and around the hive, and the gas release hasn't slowed down at all."

The general shifted his gaze to the other officials sitting at the table as the soldier closed the fabric door behind him and left the tent.

"I'm taking that as a negative result on the bombing run."

"Then we need a different approach," one of the military advisors said.

As everyone turned to him, he got up from his chair. "May I?" he asked the uniformed general.

"Who are you?" the general asked without moving.

"My name is Ian Teryman, lead bioengineer at LifeCorp...or at least I was, till last month."

"Who the hell brought you here?" the general sighed in frustration.

One of the military officers sitting around the table raised his hand. "The Biowarfare unit brought him in as an advisor and specialist."

"Very well then, let's hear from the bio guy." The general lifted his hands and took a seat, crossing his arms.

"Look, this situation should have been considered before we began to work on biologically engineering small insects. These bugs that you're fighting aren't the real problem. Inside the lab where these experiments were taking place, there was a considerable amount of Spinoloricus cinziae colonies. For those who don't know what I'm talking about, these are anaerobic creatures, microscopic. Thanks to this disaster that you call experimentation, they not only changed their DNA structure, but now they're actively changing the atmosphere to fit them. The green gas that's coming out is not a sign of green algae. It's the opposite. That's basically CO_2 mixed with spores. They are releasing it, that's what the DNA modification did."

Getting up from his chair, he looked around the room again. "I'm sure you think that the giant bugs are your problem, and they might be, for the moment. But they're not the reason the atmosphere is changing. The last platoon that got even near enough to the complex, you know, where the real tinkering was taking place only made it around the outer perimeter, not even close to where these colonies are. The fact that Spinoloricus cinziae are anaerobic *water* creatures should tell you that radiation impact will be diminished. Now, analysis of the gasses they're emitting suggests that there might rapid evolution going on, possibly with other creatures there. The large bugs on the outside will see the effects of those gasses soon. And your men should bring in oxygen tanks instead of air purifiers. There won't be any air inside there."

"Professor Oakenisht told us—"

"The professor thinks that the damage is coming from the bug mutation. It's not, he's wrong, I'm right."

The general got up and walked closer to the scientist. "We've authorized eight other bombing runs on that complex. Look at me straight in the eye and tell me eight more runs of that kind won't have an effect.

"They'll cause a lot of damage, but if you let more nukes go, you will only prevent our ground troops from reaching the colony pools where this atmosphere-changing gas is coming from."

"Thank you for your input. Now, do we have any news from the professor?"

Another advisor got up from his chair. "Last we had contact with him, he was with Echo Platoon at the edge of 'danger close.'"

"I'm sorry, you keep on asking about him, but

what do you think he can contribute?" Ian asked arrogantly as all his remarks were being ignored.

"He made this mess. We believe he can fix it," the general replied.

"Oakenisht is a chemist. I followed his research closely when we worked together in the CDC just before his project became classified. He sees the world as pure chemical reactions, but nature doesn't think so. In theory, the base markers he developed trigger many mutations. I believe this issue we have spawns from a trigger in the steroid hormone receptors…"

"You're speaking alien to me, sir," the general interrupted Ian again. "I need to know how to stop this. I don't need a biology lesson."

"Well, from what I'm seeing, mutations seem to happen pretty spontaneously inside there. I'd wait till they slow down a bit."

"Yeah, that's what Oakenisht said."

"Nuclear weapons are the most destructive weapons we have in our arsenal." One of the panel members finally interrupted the exchange. "They not only have the ability to damage targets physically but chemically, via radiation as well."

"Sir, I know you're itching to press that red button, but you're dealing with evolution here, not war. Nature has its ways of adapting." Ian looked toward the round table where the panel member was sitting. "I'm not sure any of our weapons will be of much use in this case. This statement is twice true when it comes to nuclear weapons."

"Yeah, but the longer we wait, the more they change and mutate, isn't that what you said?"

"Yes, and with you polluting the area, you're making it harder for us to get in there, collect samples, and solve this scientifically before we destroy the entire planet." Ian looked at all the rest of the members of the panel.

"Ah, so you're volunteering for the next mission?" the general asked.

"Oh, no, I'm a lab technician, I'm not a warrior."

"You don't need to be a warrior. I'll embed you with the next package, Frank Platoon. You wanted to collect a sample. I'm willing to put you in the middle of the action."

A group of soldiers wearing facemasks entered the room, interrupting the debate. "We must evacuate the area. There's a plume of that green gas heading our way."

As all the members of the panel got up and headed for the door, the general approached the scientist. "It seems you're our man now."

#

Irene closed the book and laid her head on her pillow. Looking at the metal plates on the ceiling, she sighed. *It's scary not to be the top of the food chain. I guess we'll have to deal with some of that on the surface of Helsey 8K.* She closed her eyes and placed the book on her chest, falling asleep.

#

Her first thought was to reach and unbuckle herself from the harness. Looking down at the bedsheets, she smiled. "Ah, gravity." Irene stretched her arms and legs out as far as she could and got off the bed. She walked to the side panel and pressed a button, sliding open the closet door, revealing her clothes. She got dressed and headed out of her room wearing a pair of rubber sneakers.

She walked to the rear of the ship and opened the reactor room gate, revealing the engine compartment. Not seeing anyone there, she inspected the interior and looked at the monitors, which displayed the engine's status—all normal. Irene turned around and closed the engine compartment door behind her. Next, she approached the reactor monitors, *thirty-five percent power* —all readings within the norm.

She stepped out of the engine-reactor section and pressed the lock button on the outside wall, which closed the large lead and concrete door that separated living quarters from the reactor and engines. Taking a few more steps, she entered the corridor, looking at the monitors on the top of each escape shuttle bay. They were all open. Placing one hand on the metal hatch,

Irene leaned forward to check the interior of the escape pod on her left.

"Already inspecting?" She heard Chief Helmsey's voice behind her.

"Force of habit, I guess, Chief." Irene turned her head, looking at him.

"The boat is fine. Well, except it has a few extra holes and no head now."

Irene straightened her back and made eye contact with Elmsey narrowing her eyes.

"Come on, Captain, loosen up," he said, cracking a smile sensing the tension. "Come, let's go to the situation room. We are doing the briefing we suspended when the second pass occurred."

"That's some good news."

"I was on my way to wake you up."

"Let's go then. I want to hear what they have to say."

The two walked through the narrow corridor between the living quarters and the infirmary. The situation room was located at the end of it. Entering, they saw most of the twenty-three-member crew gathered, some sitting, others standing.

"Okay, I found Irene inspecting the ship; we're all here. Tell us what you found, Gary."

"Very well." Gary got up and inserted a memory card into a slot on the table, which displayed images he'd taken of the surface. "There is excellent vegetation on the surface, and the air is breathable. We should be able to establish a colony down there, no problem. The water, however, is full of organisms I don't recognize. We're testing it in the infirmary as we speak, so, boil everything before consumption." He switched images. "I've pinpointed an area with good vegetation on this river bend, and plenty of the raw materials we will need to build our first colony."

"We should adhere to the standard procedure and send only the necessary personnel down first," the chief intervened. "I don't want to risk lives."

"That would be what the book says; however, we don't know if we're still on the asteroid belt orbit. At this moment, more lives are at risk if we stay here."

"Even with this new orbit change?" Helmsey asked.

"Look, Chief." Irene got up so she could see everyone in the room. "I would love to manually maneuver the Morning Star forever. But the fact is that we have no cockpit, our scans are unreliable at best, and we will eventually run out of supplies. We have to go down to the surface."

"She's right," Adam added, entering the room. "We are done here."

"Adam, it's good to see you are quickly recovering," the chief said, looking at Adam as the rest of the room filled with murmurs.

"Thank Irene." Adam looked at where Irene was

standing as the latter smiled. "But I think the real question here is 'Are we *ready* to go down to the surface?'"

"What do you mean?"

"We are all experts in our fields here, engineers, pilots, doctors, so on, right?" Adam walked to the middle of the room, looking at the crewmembers. "Your ship's captain and pilots, the experts of space navigation, are telling you that we are done up here. We have reached our limits." He placed both hands on the table where the chief had placed the escape shuttle keys. "We now need to know if we are ready to go down to the surface, to deal with weather, structures, safety, all of that."

"How about that, Gary?" Helmsey turned to face him.

"We haven't had much time to track weather patterns," Gary said. "I can say that right now, it's clear over our landing zone. As far as housing goes, I'll defer comments to the engineers."

"Steve?" Helmsey looked around for him.

"Look." Steve got up. "We can use our escape shuttles as housing until we find suitable materials we can build with. Though I see plenty of forests down there, building housing will take some time. That's all I can add right now."

"All in all, my recommendation of evacuation stands," Irene added.

Helmsey finally got up, standing next to Adam and Irene as Gary and Steve got up as well. He turned to look around at all the crew members in the room. "All comments are noted," he said, "and this is the decision based on those comments. All of those who are considered to be nonessential up here onboard the Morning Star are to begin the evacuation process. You are our essentials down on the surface, and that's where we need you. The rest will remain here for a little longer so we can at least salvage some of this equipment."

Irene raised her hand. "I agree with that decision."

Adam did the same. "I agree too."

Helmsey looked around the room as all crew-members raised their hands almost unanimously.

"Agreed then, we will begin evacuation procedures as soon as we formulate a coherent plan through-and-through. That is all, the meeting is concluded."

Everyone got up, heading for the exits as the room filled with chatter. Irene looked over at the chief. "Let me know if you need me. I'll be in my room."

"I'll begin scheduling escape shuttles for departure and notify teams. Would you like to go down with the first wave?"

"No, Chief. The captain is the last to leave the ship. An ancient, otherworldly tradition, as far as we are concerned, but it is a tradition nonetheless."

"I respect that." Helmsey smiled. "You can go get some very well-deserved rest, and I will let you know when the last wave evacuates."

"Sounds good to me."

"Adam, I know Stacy discharged you. How do you feel?" Helmsey asked Adam as he passed by.

"I'm good Chief, what do you need?"

"I need you, and you too, Henry, to check on the Shuttle Three release mechanism. It's giving off a warning light."

"You got it, Chief," Adam answered as both he and Irene turned around.

"I'm still reading your book," Irene told Adam once they reached the end of the short corridor, "even with all that's happening. I'm enjoying it."

"I'm happy you are." Adam took a step closer to her, touching her hair.

She smiled, looking at him. "At some point, I'd love to sit and talk about it."

"When we get on the surface," Adam replied, leaning forward and kissing Irene lightly on her lips.

Biting her lower lip, Irene looked at Adam and said, "We definitely will."

As Adam disappeared past the corner, Irene turned around and walked to her room. She picked up the book and laid on her bed, flipping it to where the bookmark was.

ELLIE

"**M**iss Farang, can you wait here for a moment?" Professor Hutch asked Ellie as she passed by his desk, together with the other students who were exiting the auditorium. "I want to ask you something regarding your last exam."

Adjusting the shoulder strap of her bookbag, Ellie sighed, then stopped and approached the rectangular desk as the other students walked by her.

He pulled a small booklet out of a pile, opening it. "You know, you started the semester with promisingly good grades. You are now barely passing. What happened?" Hutch asked once the auditorium was empty.

"I'm trying my best, Professor," she replied. "I'm having a little trouble sleeping lately."

"That's what you told me last month," he said. "You also told me that you were going to the doctor to get it checked."

"I did," Ellie replied, looking down. "The doctor prescribed me something, but I don't think it's working."

"Well, I asked Dr. Forester, the head of the Psychology Department, to talk to you—if you agree, of course."

Ellie brought her hand to her mouth. "Do I have to?"

"You don't," the professor quickly said. "I'm just trying to help you, Ellie. I can see that something is bothering you, and we have some of the best professionals in all fields here on campus."

Ellie rubbed her eyes with both her hands and brought them on top of her head, pulling her dark hair back from her face and revealing pale skin and dark circles around her eyes. The professor got up from his chair and walked around the table. "What do you say?"

"Fine, professor," Ellie finally ceded.

"Excellent," he replied. "Dr. Forester's office is in this building, on the third floor, Room 303A. I'll call her and tell her that you're going up."

"Can I have my exam now?"

"I am only doing this for your wellbeing Ellie," Hutch repeated his earlier statement as he handed the exam to her. "Dr. Forester, too. We're lucky she agreed to see you."

Ellie picked up her exam with a sigh looking at the *F* grade circled in red on top of the booklet. She walked out of the auditorium toward the staircase to the third floor. The heavy fireproof door fell back to its original position, eliminating most of the noise coming from the hall.

Halfway up the first set of stairs, the dreadfully familiar whispers began to accompany the echoing sound of her footsteps. The hints got louder and louder, and she quickened her pace. Reaching the third-floor entrance, Ellie opened the door, letting the noise wash the whispers out.

Unlike the first floor, this wing of the building had very few students walking around. Looking up at the small room numbers printed on the doorframes, Ellie continued down the corridor until she found it.

"Three-oh-three-a," she murmured, knocking on the door and waiting for someone to come to open it. No one came, and after waiting for a minute, she twisted the knob, slowly pushing the door open only to realize that this door led to a waiting room, which was currently empty. She walked inside and took a seat on the chair closest to her.

Sitting on the black folding chair, Ellie brought both hands to her knees as she looked at the inspirational quote pictures hanging on the walls. The one directly in front of her was a large picture of a beautiful white sailboat with red sails with a calm blue ocean in the background. *Only you can make your dreams come true.* And in true college fashion, next to it, there was a pinboard with notes and schedules.

On her left, about three chairs away was a dull glass door with the obligatory *Dr. Emily Forester, Psychology* label. Chatter and occasional squeaking of sneakers against tiles came from the door leading to the corridor, on the right, as students rushed to their classes.

Sighing, Ellie placed her bookbag on her lap as if it was a big imaginary shield that kept everyone from approaching and asking questions. Questions of which she had grown very tired of lately: *Are you sleeping well, are you eating enough? Ugh, it's like Grandma has asked everyone to annoy me.*

The door opened, and a middle-aged woman wearing a purple knee-high skirt and a black shirt with purple accent lines came out, holding a clipboard.

"Ellie?" She took a step forward.

"That's me." Ellie got up. "And you are?"

"My name is Doctor Forester. I'm the college's psychologist. You can call me Emily." She extended her hand to Ellie's. "Professor Huck sounded a little concerned with your grades, especially this semester."

Ellie just stared at the doctor as a student hurriedly exited the room, holding a few books under his arm and looking down.

"Okay, I'm here. So, what do we do now?" Ellie peeked around the doctor to see if there was anyone else inside the room.

The doctor invited her inside her office. "Anything you want, Ellie. Tell me what's bothering you. Maybe I can help."

"I don't think anyone can help me, doctor," she said as she took a few steps inside Emily's office, looking around. On the left of it was a rectangular desk with a big ergonomic chair, and above it, there was a framed diploma. All she could read from it was the word *psychology*. There was a brown couch on her right and a chair immediately next to it. Behind the sofa was a big window with open blinds, illuminating the entire room with sunlight.

"Why do you say that, Ellie? Some so many people care about you, and I'm sure they are willing to help you any way they can. Including me." Dr. Forester carefully closed the glass door, which completely muffled the noise coming from the corridor. "Please, have a seat."

Ellie walked and sat on the couch, looking up at her as she placed her book bag on top of her knees. "Can I ask you a question, doctor?"

"Of course, you can ask me anything."

"Do you have a special room in your head, a place where you stash your deepest secrets?"

"I don't understand, Ellie. Can you tell me more about this?"

"You know, a secret, like that time when you hid candy from your sister and ate it knowing that she was looking for it, or when you broke that pencil and put it back on the table without telling anyone?"

"Well, Ellie, we all have that little room inside our heads. That's just for us."

"How can I let you in my special room when I know nothing about yours, Doctor?" Ellie looked at Emily with a tight-lipped smile.

Emily sat and adjusted the chair to be at Ellie's eye level. "What do you want to know, Ellie?"

"Whatever you choose to share, Doctor."

"Well, if you must know, when I was in college, I once inadvertently copied one answer in a test."

Ellie chuckled. "Aha. So even doctors cheat."

"Let this be our secret, ok?" Emily slightly smiled, bringing her hand in front of her looking at Elie's every move, noticing her pale skin and wandering eyes, which had dark circles under them.

She quickly changed subjects. "So, tell me, Ellie, what is bothering you so much that your grades are suffering?"

"I can't stay asleep. I've been to several other doctors, and they prescribed sleeping pills, which I'm taking, but I still can't get much sleep." Ellie gripped her bookbag even tighter, swallowing.

Looking at Ellie's defensive posture, the doctor

placed her hand on her arm. "Ellie, you're safe here. We can stop this interview anytime you want. I don't want to upset you."

"I think it's because of scary dreams, but I can't remember any of that when I wake up," Ellie continued, looking at Emily, who was nodding her head. "I have a sinking feeling, but I think that's because of the lack of sleep."

"So, you do fall asleep." Emily tried to clarify the situation.

"I do, but I can't *stay* asleep."

"You said something about medications? Can you show me what pills you got, if any?"

Ellie pulled a bottle of pills from her bookbag and handed it to the doctor, then placed the bookbag back on her knees.

"I trust you are taking these as prescribed," the doctor said, looking at the label on the bottle before raising her head to look at Ellie, who nodded.

"And you still can't sleep for long sessions?" She raised her eyebrows in surprise. "I'm sorry for saying this, but that's very unusual. These are some serious sleeping pills."

"Look, doctor." Ellie reached out and took the bottle of pills from her hand. "I only agreed to see you because I don't know what to do anymore." She placed the pill bottle inside her bag. "My mother was recently admitted to the psychiatric ward, my father is home once a month, if that, and my older sister has moved out. I'm home alone, and I can't sleep. I can't focus in class. And at times, I think I see things that aren't there."

"Help me understand here a little bit, Ellie. When did all of this exactly begin to happen?"

"Around the time my mom got admitted to the hospital."

"Why did your mother get admitted there?"

"She had trouble sleeping most of her life, and six months before her being admitted, she got diagnosed with schizophrenia. The doctors prescribed pills and treatments, but nothing worked. My dad finally had to get her somewhere where she could get better care, at least for a little while."

"And you say your symptoms began *after* she left? Do you miss your mother? Are you scared to be home alone, Ellie?" Dr. Forester asked as she looked at Ellie.

"It all began a couple of days after everyone left the house." Ellie bowed her head, hiding her gaze. "Of course, I miss my mother, Doctor. But the reason I can't fall asleep isn't that—well, partly. But it's mostly the whispers and shadows that come out when I close my eyes, or when I stand in a silent room, or I am alone. I have nightmares of shadows reaching for me. At times I can feel them on my skin. I hear whispers." She swallowed. "That wakes me up."

Ellie sighed and sunk on the couch. "The other doctor examined me and prescribed me the pills. When I went back to her telling her that I still couldn't sleep, she just gave me more pills and didn't ask me anything."

"Went back? How long has this been going on?"

"Uh, about six months now." Ellie looked up at the bare white wall in front of her, where a framed ink-blot image was hanging. "Give or take a week. I'm just not sure anymore."

"Six months?" Emily stood up from her chair. "Professor Huck told me its only been a couple of weeks."

"I coped with it for a while, but lately, it has gotten worse." Ellie sighed.

"Ok," Emily replied. "I can see some effects of sleep deprivation in you. I know the other doctor tried to address it by prescribing you sleep medication, but some individuals have a high tolerance to certain substances, and simply raising the dosage won't work at times. It certainly is not working with you."

Gripping the bookbag even tighter, Ellie looked at Emily, shaking her head as though to confirm that raising the dosage was not working.

"It seems to me that we might have to change the approach to this problem. Have you tried hypnosis?"

"No, the other psychologist said it wouldn't help." Ellie swallowed.

"We can always try," the doctor replied.

"Anything that would help me, Emily," Ellie said, letting go of the bookbag. "I swear I'm not crazy."

"I know," the doctor replied, touching her forearm. "Of course, you aren't. You're a strong young woman for enduring all of this and still functioning. How about we try a short session and see where that takes us, what do you say?"

Ellie breathed a sigh of relief. "If you think that it will help, then let's do it."

"Good," Emily replied. "Give me a moment." She got up, opened the office door, and walked to the front door, locking it. Ellie followed her every move. "I don't want anyone distracting us," the doctor said, slightly smiling as she noticed her stare.

Ellie laid on the couch as Emily closed the glass door, stepped to her desk, and turned on the lamp. Turning on another light on the wall next to it, Emily then closed the window blinds, dimming the room considerably. The doctor took a brass metronome from her desk and placed it on top of the small table next to the couch where both Ellie and she could see it.

The rhythmic clicking of the metronome filled the room as the doctor sat back on her chair, adjusting it, so she had a good view of Ellie.

"What do we do now, doctor?" Ellie rested her head on the little pillow on the couch's armrest.

"Try to relax and focus on the sound," Emily said. "You're safe here."

"Okay," Ellie replied, looking at the ceiling.

Both doctor and patient continued to stay quiet,

listening to the metronome as Ellie's eyes eclipsed, and her arms relaxed, falling on her sides.

"You feel safe here, Ellie," Emily softly said, noticing that Ellie took a deep breath.

"I feel safe here, Doctor," she replied with her eyes closed.

"I can pull you out any time, there is no need to be scared," Emily reassured Ellie, leaning forward and watching her eyes move under her eyelids. "Tell me, what do you see, Ellie?"

"I'm home. I feel safe here," she said with a faint smile.

"That's good. Home is a safe place to be. What's around you?"

"Oh, it's dark here. I can hear the TV in the living room, but I know I'm alone."

"Where is this room of yours?"

"Oh, my rooms are upstairs."

"Care to describe them for me?"

"Well, my room is nothing special, really, just a bed, my study desk, and a lamp on the side of it. I have a few Metallica posters on the wall above my bed and one on my door. The closet is generally shut, but I put my skateboard there, and the clothes I don't use."

Emily reached to her table and took up a notepad and a pencil, scribbling everything Ellie was saying. "How about this other room you told me about?

Where's the entrance to that?"

"Oh, that room. There is no door to that room, at least no one can see it. It's on the wall behind my bed."

"Is it open now?"

"Yes, it is." Ellie sighed. "It's dark here as well. I like it here," she continued, smiling with her eyes closed. "No one can find me."

"What's inside this room, Ellie?" Emily asked.

"Oh, I'm not sure I can tell you, Doctor. They might not like it if I tell others about them."

"Who are 'they,' Ellie?"

"Well, hanging on the wall, there are three candles that light up the entire place," Ellie said. "Skely generally stands upright, but at times when he comes in, he knocks it down on the floor and makes a mess, which I have to clean."

"Who is Skely?"

"Oh, Skely is the skeleton next to the candelabrum, he's cool."

"Okay," Emily said, writing it all down. "What else is inside this room?"

Suddenly the lights in the studio flickered as shadows enveloped the walls, extending up from the floor until they slowly touched the ceiling.

"You shouldn't be here, Doctor. I like you, but you shouldn't be here."

Emily's eyes and mouth opened wide in awe, watching the flickering lights as the sound of the metronome got fainter, as though there was something in between her and it. The shadows morphed into faces and hands, which crept along the walls, dimming the lights passing in front of them.

Shivers ran down her spine as she pulled her chair closer to the couch where Ellie was lying. "Okay, Ellie, when I count to three, you come back to me. Ready? One, two, three." She snapped her fingers as Ellie suddenly gripped her bookbag, holding it tight to her chest as she opened her eyes. The shadows quickly disappeared, and the metronome sound returned.

The rhythmic clicks of the metronome persisted as Emily looked around, trying to come to terms with what she just experienced. Ellie stared at the ceiling, then slowly faced the doctor.

"Ellie, sweetie, you don't need a psychologist, you need an exorcist," Emily said, passing her left hand over her right forearm to calm her goosebumps.

"What happened?" Ellie stood up from the couch. "What did I say, Doctor?"

The room slightly warmed up as Emily got up and walked to the window, opening the blinds and letting the sunlight in again. She took the metronome, stopped it, and placed it back on her table as Ellie stood there in silence, watching the doctor turning off the lamps and open the door.

"You didn't say anything, Ellie," Emily replied,

staring at the floor, avoiding eye contact with her.

Ellie got up from the couch as the room warmed up a little more. "What do I do now, Doctor?"

"I will have to consult with a colleague of mine and try to find a cure for your ailment," she replied, looking at her with worried eyes. "If you need help with anything, don't hesitate to call me. At any time of the day." She handed her a business card.

Ellie walked out of the office, looking around with a confused, blank stare as the doctor picked up her phone and dialed Professor Hutch.

"How is she?" he asked as soon as he picked up the phone.

"Listen to me carefully, what's happening to Ellie is not only in her head. Her other doctor is just medicating her, but I think there's something more sinister at play here," Emily said, watching the front door to her office finally swing closed.

"Give me a minute," Hutch replied. "I'm coming up."

A few minutes passed, and the door opened. "I have never heard that statement from you before," Hutch said, closing the door behind him. He held a cup of coffee on his hand. "I've got to hear this one."

"Is Ellie still outside?"

"Yeah, I passed her by the corridor." Hutch took a sip.

"I stand behind my statement. Her subconscious

is all over the place, and something strange happened inside this room during the interview."

"What was it?"

"I don't know how to describe it." She looked suspiciously at the walls. "But she needs a priest or a paranormal investigator. The entire room got cold, like a refrigerator, and the walls got dark."

"I am officially stunned," the professor replied, looking at his visibly-shaken colleague. "I never thought you of all people would advise anyone to consult a paranormal investigator."

"I'm at a loss for advice on this one."

"Well, I know a couple of former students who might help."

"Hutch, she's not a test subject."

"Would you rather just watch her go down the drain? Because based on her pattern of behavior, that's where she'll end up."

Sighing, Emily headed for the corridor. "As I said, I can't help her. If you can, then you should."

"Let me make a couple of phone calls," Hutch said as he pulled out his cellphone. "I'll let you know."

"You absolutely have to," Emily said, turning her back on him. "I have a class to teach in five minutes. I will talk to you later." She grabbed a couple of books from her desk and, together with Hutch, walked out of her office. Emily turned left as Hutch turned right, toward where he last saw Ellie.

And there she was, next to the staircase, staring at the floor as if she didn't know what to do.

"Ellie." Professor Hutch put the phone inside his pocket. "I spoke with Dr. Forester, and I think I might have a way to help with your condition. I have a few friends that could help you. Would you like me to give them a call?"

Ellie didn't say anything, just gawked at the professor, swallowing. Feeling the distress she was in, Huck took a step closer. "Look, grades can be taken care of, don't worry about that. I'll talk to the professors here..."

"No, please," Ellie begged, "please don't tell anyone about this, they'll think I'm crazy. I assure you, Professor, I am *not* crazy."

"I didn't mean that Ellie, God no. I meant to say that you are having difficulties in life, that's all. Anyway, that's beside the point. What do you say I call one of my former students? He runs a paranormal investigation company; he can try to at least shed some light on whatever is going on."

"I know there's something strange happening to me, Professor. I...I just... I want to go home." She sighed, looking away.

"Okay, as you wish. Here, take my number." Huck reached in his pocket, pulling out a business card and handing it to Ellie. "You can call me any time if you change your mind."

Ellie took the card and placed it inside her

pocket, then adjusted her bookbag shoulder straps and walked away.

Entering the same staircase as before, the whispers crept up again, this time a lot louder, as if they were a foot away. She tried to keep calm, briskly going downstairs and opening the double doors that led to the lobby. By the time she walked outside, though, she could barely hear above the whispers.

"I can't do this," she muttered, reaching in her pocket for her phone. She stopped and pulled Professor Hutch's card out and dialed the numbers.

"Hello," she heard him say.

"Professor Hutch, it's Ellie."

"Hi Ellie, is everything okay?"

Ellie crossed her arms in front of her. "How soon can you get the paranormal guys to come?"

"I don't know. I have yet to call them."

"Can you please call them?" Ellie continued walking as a few students looked at her, overhearing the conversation.

"Sure, I'll let you know."

Ending the call, she pulled out a pair of dark sunglasses and put them on before walking to the bus stop.

))((

Six hours later, Ellie Farang's residence.

"Hi Ellie," a young man in his late twenties wearing a black polo shirt and khaki pants greeted her as soon as she opened the front door. "My name is Robert. This is Mike." He bladed his body, revealing a few more people behind him. "She's Sondra, and this is Dr. Ericsson. Professor Hutch…"

"I know, he just called me," Ellie interrupted him. "Please come in." She opened the door as everyone walked inside. Mike and Sondra walked in holding black pelican boxes, the ones that professionals usually carried equipment around in.

As Mike, Robert, and Sondra continued to bring in equipment, Dr. Ericsson placed her purse on the table in the living room, looking around.

"Dr. Forester is a very good friend of mine," she said as she approached Ellie. "She asked me to try to help you. And I will."

"Thank you, Doctor," Ellie replied, looking at the paranormal team standing by the door.

"Can we install our equipment around?" Sondra finally asked as Mike brought in the last of the boxes.

"Can we?" Dr. Ericsson asked Ellie.

"Of course," Ellie replied, looking at the team members who silently opened the boxes, revealing small cameras and sensors. They walked around the room, placing them on the desks and turning them on. She followed Robert and Sondra with her eyes as they went upstairs, placing a few sensors along the staircase.

"We've invited a priest as well, recommended by Emily. He's on his way. Meanwhile, shall we begin?" Dr. Ericsson pointed to the couch in the living room, asking Ellie to have a seat there.

"Before you start, where is your room, Ellie?" Mike asked Ellie, who pointed to the direction of her room upstairs as she and the doctor walked to the couch.

"How much longer to get that baseline?" Mike asked Sondra, who was looking at a tablet standing in the middle of the living room.

"Did you finish placing the rest of the sensors?" Sondra asked.

"Yes, Robert went upstairs and placed the rest of the equipment."

"One more minute," she replied without taking her eyes from the tablet. "You can start in the meanwhile, don't wait for me."

"We're good, Dr. Ericsson." Robert walked near the couch. "You may begin the session."

"Very well," she replied. "Hit those lights and dim the room, please." Sitting in front of Ellie, Dr. Ericsson brought the chair closer to the couch. "Are you ready, Ellie?"

"Yes, I am," she responded, looking as the doctor pulled out a pendulum. Steadying the silver-engrained enclosure holding a white tetrahedron crystal, Sondra adjusted herself on the seat.

"Just focus on the pendulum," she heard the doctor's soothing voice say in the dark room. Lying on the couch, Ellie looked up at the shadows of the team members walking around, holding up the devices they brought with them to detect any energy fluctuations that spirits might cause if they happened to pass in front of them.

Ellie got the same sensation of weakness she'd felt in Dr. Forester's office, which wasn't surprising given the fact that she hadn't had much sleep for the past five days.

"You feel safe here, Ellie," Dr. Ericsson said again as she lay on the couch.

"I feel safe here, doctor."

"Good," the doctor replied. "Let's stay here for a while. Tell me what you see, if you see something."

"I am home, the lights are on, the fireplace crackling. It feels as if there is a storm outside, but I feel safe here."

"That's good, Ellie. There's an entire team here to help you with your troubles. Also, we called Dr. Forester and a priest. Now, what else do you see?"

"Nothing. I'm walking upstairs to my room. That's where I feel the safest, especially when Mom and Dad fight downstairs."

"Are they in the house now?" the psychologist asked Ellie, looking at one of the team members walking around with his device. He looked back at her, shaking his head as if to say "nothing."

"No..." Ellie dragged the word out. "But I feel as if they're down there. I feel the tension."

"I'm sorry if that upsets you, Ellie." The doctor touched her hand. "I'm here, and I can pull you out any time you wish. For now, why don't you tell me about your room?"

"There is nothing special here, just my posters, table, and..." Ellie dragged her word again.

"What else is there, Ellie?"

"The door is open here. I think I'd like for you to bring me out now," Ellie said, her eyes racing under her eyelids.

"Let's continue a little longer." The doctor looked at the paranormal investigators, who all headed upstairs, following their beeping devices.

"As I told Doctor Forester, I like you, Doctor, but Skely is on the floor, and that means only one thing. *He* is out here somewhere."

"Who is Skely? Who..." the doctor began to ask, but the dim room got darker and darker. Objects and picture frames began to shake, some of them falling on the floor.

"We got activity upstairs," Mike said, standing on the staircase. "More than I've ever seen."

"Tell me, Ellie, who else is here?"

"HE is here."

"Who is HE, Ellie?"

"I can go inside that room now and look who is inside." Goosebumps erupted over Ellies' body. "It's freezing here."

"Inside where, Ellie?"

"Inside the room." Ellie walked through the dark of her mind closer to the open door in the wall. Jumping over her bed, she entered. Three feet above the floor in front of her, a candelabrum's quivering light tinted the inside yellow. Three thick candles burned halfway down on top of a desk on her right formed a triangle around a big open book. The chair, usually in front of the desk, laid on the floor. Next to it, the skeleton was drenched in blood, its skull missing. Stepping over it, Ellie grabbed one of the lit candles from the desk and continued deeper.

Her ankle almost gave in as she took another step. She looked down only to realize that she was no longer walking on tiles, but bedrock. A similar shaky yellow light ahead let her know that there was more to this room than she could see. After a few more steps, Ellie found herself walking down a narrow, rocky passage.

Something caught her eye, and Ellie brought the candle in front of her to illuminate it. "What are you doing all the way inside here?" She bent over, grabbing Skely's skull. Instinctively she turned around to show Dr. Ericsson what she found. *What am I doing?* She realized that she could no longer hear her guiding voice. In fact, she heard nothing at all, not even her footsteps.

The passage got narrower as Ellie continued to move toward the candlelight in the distance. She held Skely's skull and the candle with one hand, and with the other, she felt her way forward.

Momentarily she turned around to see that the apartment behind her had disappeared in the gloom. A gust of wind passed through the passage, nearly extinguishing all the candles. The whispers returned. Panicking, she bladed her body, moving toward the candle at the end of this narrow passage. *These whispers are different.* She could discern what they say.

"Stay with us, Farang." She felt the wind of the whisper behind her left ear. "Stay with us, and we will make sure no one stands in your way."

"Stay with us, Ellie." Another voice felt as if it was coming from something hovering above her head.

"Doctor?" Her voice sounded as if she was inside a soundproof room. Total silence enveloped her as Ellie continued to move toward the light at the end of the passage, which seemed to get further away as she progressed.

The shadows grew longer and more profound as whispers filled the living room. Dr. Ericsson looked at the investigators, who were having a tough time with their instruments. "Ellie, can you hear me?" she asked– Ellie didn't respond.

Ghostly apparitions slowly morphed into

human-like figures. Others were not—they had multiple hands, strange heads, and frightful eyes. One large, amorphic shadow slowly moved down the stairs and stopped hovering over the doctor. As Robert tried to go through it, it flung him against the wall. He banged his head and remained motionless on the floor.

"Robert!" Sondra screamed, rushing to him only to be flung the other way and meet the same fate.

The front doorbell rang. Dr. Ericsson tried to get up, only to be forced down by the massive shadow, which now formed defined horns on his head and deep red eyes. *Okay, we're done here.* "Ellie, if you can hear me, I will count to three. On my..." She suddenly felt as she couldn't move her tongue.

Dr. Forester opened the front door and demanded, "What is going on here?"

Looking at Forester with scared eyes, the doctor pointed at Ellie on the couch just before the red-eyed, horned creature ripped her tongue out. Blood rushed out of her mouth as Dr. Forester took a step inside, the priest behind her. His presence disturbed all the shadows, some of which blew the windows out as they escaped.

Holding a bible in his hand, the priest began to chant as Dr. Forester knelt beside Ellie. "Three, two, one..." She couldn't finish the countdown, her tongue pressing against her throat as the priest pulled out a small bottle of holy water and began to spray it around the vicinity.

Suddenly Ellie felt a warmth behind her. The

cold walls of the narrow passage widened and, as though they were made of smoke, vanished in front of her eyes, replaced by a dark mist.

She looked down and saw her feet, wearing socks...*white socks, I remember these.* Suddenly the haze surrounding her widened. She noticed the priest and Dr. Forester, who was holding her hands against her throat, choking. The front door of her house was wide open. Dark ghostly figures leaking out onto the front porch of the house extended like a carpet to welcome her into the world. She got up from the couch, holding the creepy skull and candle in her hand. The warm feeling of safety enveloped her. All the whispers momentarily disappeared; outside noise came to her ears muffled. The priest tried spraying Ellie with holy water, but the shadow moving behind her knocked him down.

Ellie turned around to see who knocked the priest down. Red eyes penetrating out of a shadowy figure, stared at her.

"Stay with us, and we will make sure no one stands in your way," it whispered loudly as fainter whispers echoed its call.

She lifted her head and looked around the room. One of the shadows had its hand inside Emily's mouth. In turn, Emily was trying to get it out. Another was on top of the priest, pinning him on the floor. The rest of the shadows were still flowing downstairs.

She made eye contact with Emily. "Let her go," Ellie commanded. As more shadowy figures filled the room and surrounded her like a black fog, some growled at the priest as the shadow let Emily fall on the floor with a thud. Ellie slowly walked outside following the dark carpet, which extended in front of her. The front door of the house violently closed.

#

Irene closed the book as she sat on her bed, looking at her shadow. *Hm, I wonder if her subconscious spilled out on the real world. Is it looking for someone?*

She left the book on top of her bed and headed out of her room to the kitchen area. *Maybe I can find some coffee here.* The engineers had restored all power to most things, including the corridor lighting. She entered the food pantry room to see Violet and Stacy talking.

"Hi Irene," Stacy greeted her. "How are you feeling?"

"Pretty good considering all," Irene replied, smiling. "How about you?"

"Anxious," Stacy replied, "though I could say the same for pretty much everyone on board."

Irene changed subjects. "Is there any coffee here?"

"The food processor is up and running," Violet said. "I just got some myself."

Irene walked to the processor and pressed a few buttons on the menu to select coffee.

"Irene, can I ask you something?" Violet asked, taking a step closer to her.

"Sure." Irene picked up a plastic cup, placing it under the food processor.

"How are you so calm with everything that is going on?"

"What do you mean?" Irene asked, looking at coffee dripping in the cup.

"Gary was pretty shaken when the escape shuttle got hit by the debris. He hid it fairly well during the briefing. You and Adam, on the other hand, have been in situations like this for the past three days, and none of it seems to faze you."

Irene looked at Violet, then at Stacy. "I am doing everything I can to ensure we are safe. Sure, accidents happen, but the important thing is to move forward."

"Is that book interesting?" Stacy asked Irene, changing the conversation subject.

"What book?" Irene looked at the coffee cup, which was almost full.

"You had it with you when you got rescued, re-member?"

"Ah, yes." Irene beamed, reaching out and picking up the hot cup of coffee. "I actually like it," she paused for a moment, "a lot."

"Is that how you're doing it? How you're keeping your stress level in check?" Stacy smiled.

"It is working for me." Irene took a sip from the cup. "You should try it as well."

"That's one way to deal with it," Violet said. "Let's hope we bring the digital library down with us."

"We will," Irene said. "Maybe you should try to read something out of it right now. Hopefully, reading will have the same effect on you as it has on me."

Violet raised her right eyebrow. "That's a pretty good idea."

"Well, I'll talk to you later," Irene said. She walked out into the corridor heading for her room. Closing the door behind her and placing the hot cup of coffee on her table, Irene picked the book with a smile. She looked at Adam's name on the cover. *Yeah, I have my personal stress reliever right here.*

THE MISSING 32

An Imprint Legacy story

"**G**ood morning Haytown! We have yet another beautiful day, one of the last days of summer here. Temperatures are expected to rise above..." The voice of the reporter coming from the radio filled the small bedroom, illuminated by two large windows. Squinting, the man sighed, took a deep breath, and rolled his body sideways in bed to see where the sound of this report was coming from.

Noticing the radio alarm clock on top of a wooden dresser, he moved to the corner of the bed, placing his hands on it to help himself sit up. Feeling light-headed, he grabbed the mattress and closed his eyes, trying to stabilize himself.

"... Now we bring you an update on the crisis that struck Haytown three days ago, the missing thirty-two," the reporter on the radio continued as the man took a deep breath and pushed himself off the bed. He closed his eyes as a throbbing headache prevented him from even remembering his name. His hands stuck to the bedsheets. *Is this mud?* He looked at them. *Why do I have mud on my hands, and why did I go to bed without washing myself?*

Without getting up, he raised his right foot and looked at his boot, then pants. "That's my uniform. My uniform." He got up, whispering to himself, trying to make sense of the words he was articulating. He then looked at the shirt he was wearing, which was brown. A patch that said "Haytown Sheriff's Office" was on each sleeve. Raising an eyebrow in suspicion, he looked at the gun-belt. *Did I fall asleep with all this shit on? Man, I hope I didn't drink that much last night, and who's house is this?* He unsnapped his revolver from the deep-brown leather holster and placed it next to his hip as he extended his left hand.

"Anyone here?" he said out loud, taking a step toward the door.

The bedroom he'd woken up in was located at the end of a narrow corridor. Its walls were made of ordinary sheetrock covered with a wavy patterned wallpaper. He placed his left hand on the door and looked down the narrow passage. On his left, about five feet away from him, there was an open door through which he could see a bathroom sink. He took a quick peek in and continued walking toward what looked like the living room. There was a dresser, wood stove, and a couch in it. There were three windows in the room, one on each side of the front door and one on his left. All of them had mud on the metal mesh screens.

He opened the front door and walked outside, finding that he was in a small house in the middle of the woods. It was sunny and warm indeed—however, the immediate area was shrouded in an eerie silence. Satisfied that he was alone, he holstered his weapon, looking at the wet mud on his hand.

I haven't been here for too long. This stuff is still wet. He walked back to the bathroom to wash his hands. Stopping in front of the sink, he looked at his reflection in the mirror. There was dirty, dry saliva all around his mouth and a scrape on his left cheek. His brown eyes were bloodshot, and his hair was disheveled and had more mud in it. The white undershirt that stuck out of his brown uniform shirt was dirty and had some red stains, which made him check himself for any cuts or wounds. His knuckles were bloody.

I really don't know where I am or what this place is. After looking at the reflection of his nametag, he turned on the faucet, letting the water rushed out. *Carter.* He finished washing his hands, grabbed a green towel from a hanger on the wall just behind him, and dried them off. *"Carter, Sheriff Carter,"* echoed in his ears.

As he walked back to the living room, he tried to remember how he got to this place. He reached for his cell phone and dialed the last number he had called three days ago, labeled *Work*.

A woman picked up after the phone rang twice.

"Sheriff Carter? My god, where have you

been?" she asked with a trembling worried voice.

"What are you talking about?"

"You left the station house three days ago and vanished without a trace! We sent a car to your house but didn't find you. There's an active search out for you right now. Let me connect you to the agent in charge."

"What are you talking about?" Carter responded before he heard a thud over the speaker.

Not even ten seconds later, she picked up again. "Where are you, Chief?"

~ ~ ~

Haytown's police station was in the center of the town on Main Street. Next to it, there was a large parking lot which was empty most of the time. But at present, the lot's entrance was blocked by one of Haytown's sheriff cars, and inside there were black SUVs bearing government license plates, as well as a big bus parked on the side. On the sidewalk, next to the adjoining office building, there was a group of people sitting. Some of them lay on the ground next to what appeared to be a shrine.

The blue and white police SUV stopped in front of the station next to a row of black suburban trucks. Carter, accompanied by Aaron, his deputy, got out and walked in the station to be greeted by his secretary, Jennine.

"My God, what have you been doing these past three days?" she asked, looking at Carter's muddy, dirty uniform.

"Can you please find one of those clean uniforms I have in my office, Jennine?" Carter asked her, stumbling past the front gate. "I'll be in the shower." He turned to Aaron. "Bring my uniform there for me, please."

"Boss, the medics want to examine you."

"Sure, I just need a shower first," Carter said, closing the bathroom door where the showers were.

Several Emergency Medical Technicians walked in the station carrying red duffle bags shortly after.

"Where is he?" one of them asked.

"In the shower," Jennine answered, walking in the room with Carter's uniform.

"We'll wait out here for him." The technicians put their bags down as the doctor walked into the station.

A few minutes later, Carter walked out of the shower, adjusting his pants and shirt, entering his office. The medical team entered the room after a few seconds. They pulled out their instruments, measuring his blood pressure and heart rate.

"Sheriff Carter, all the tests and measurements are within the norm. Just a little malnutrition, dehydration, and a good amount of exposure to the elements," the doctor said, inspecting the clipboard he held, walking closer to Carter. "You got some scratches on your back as well."

"Thank you, sir," Carter answered. Adjusting his shirt, he got up from his chair as a black-suited FBI agent opened the office door.

"Please sign this form for me. We've been asked to disclose these findings to the National Guard's medical team," the doctor continued, ignoring the FBI agent and handing Carter the clipboard.

"Sheriff Carter, it's good to finally see you. My name is Agent Klebond, with the Federal Bureau of Investigations." Klebond closed the door behind himself, then took a step into the office. "We were brought in to help stabilize the town after the governor declared a state of emergency." He unbuttoned his jacket. "After you and all the kids went missing."

"I have no idea what you're talking about," Carter replied, signing the form and handing the clipboard back to the doctor, who left the room.

"Yeah, about that, do you remember anything that can help us out?"

"Read me in. Tell me, what did I miss?" Carter looked at the agent as he removed his jacket, placing it on top of the wooden chair next to him. "Maybe that will jog my memory."

"That's the thing. You are part of the investigation now. Several eyewitnesses place you on the sidelines of the baseball field where the incident took place and after, following the crowd. I want to know what's in your head. Reading you in would contaminate that information. If you want to help, you can start by telling me what you did for the past three days."

"I don't know." Carter wore his black socks and uniform shoes, tying the shoelaces.

"Think!"

"I remember waking up in that bed—your men are probably checking it out right now. I washed my hands and walked out of there, and once I saw where I was, I called in. That's all I remember. I don't even know about this baseball field thing, what is it?"

"You were supposed to keep an eye on the game."

"What game?"

Jennine knocked on the door then opened it. "Carter, there's someone here to see you."

"Can it wait? We're in the middle of something here," Klebond replied, looking at Jennine.

"Who is it?" Carter asked before Trish, his ex-wife, barged in the office and slapped him across the face.

Carter clenched his teeth, holding himself back as Jennine walked out of the office, closing the door behind her. "Trish, now's not the time for this..."

"She's missing," Trish whispered through her teeth, holding back her tears.

"Who's missing?"

"You had one job, and you failed, you miserable piece of shit!" Trish raised her hand to slap Carter again, as Klebond held her hand.

"Ma'am, we are aware of the situation," he began to tell her, only to be stopped by Carter, who grabbed his wrist, making eye contact with Klebond as if to ask him to let it go.

"Agent, I need a minute with my ex-wife if you don't mind."

Klebond sighed and let go of her hand. "I'll give you two a little space." He left the office as well.

"I don't know what you are talking about," Carter said as soon as Klebond closed the door.

"As always, you and your excuses." Trish took a step closer to Carter. "But for once, you have to be a father as well. You have to find our daughter..."

"I don't remember a damn thing, Trish!" Carter interrupted her. "This is the first I've heard Sam is missing."

The medical technicians, accompanied by his deputy Aaron, interrupted their conversation by loudly knocking on and then immediately opening the door, barging into the office.

Carter rolled his eyes in annoyance. "What now?"

"The National Guard's doctor released his report regarding you," the medic replied, followed by Aaron saying, "Boss, the people want to talk to you. They're all gathered by the shrine."

Trish sighed, looking at Klebond, who was staring at everyone inside the office from the glass door. Head in hands, she stormed out of the office sobbing.

"The military doctor seems to think your memories will come back, but there's no timeframe," the medic continued as Klebond walked into the office. "It could be hours, days, months, or years."

"And he couldn't be here to elaborate on that?"

"Look, man," the medic replied, "I'm just passing on the information, okay."

"Is there any way to speed that process?" Klebond intervened.

"Well, this is all in the mind," the medic replied, looking at him as Carter sat in a nearby chair, placing his head on his hands. "Hypnotherapy has worked in the past."

"Hypno..." Carter sighed, rolling his eyes.

"You're showing symptoms of selective amnesia, common with high-stress situations. I would recommend you rest," the medic said. "I know everyone in town has had a tough time coping with life lately, but *you* need to recoup before we try anything else."

Carter sighed. "I'll take that." He got up from his chair, heading for the door, followed by Aaron.

"Carter." Klebond followed the sheriff as well. "I'm sure I don't need to tell you that you can't leave town."

"Are you serious right now?" Carter looked at Klebond, tightening up his fist. "Get out of my way."

Carter walked out of the office building. It was a bright summer day, and apart from the unusually high military-uniformed presence, everything seemed quiet. The makeshift shrine across the sidewalk had lots of burnt and burning candles on the ground, where loved ones had placed countless pictures of children and people, undoubtedly the missing ones. He stopped for a moment, scratching his rough beard and trying to recognize the faces. Feeling a lump in his stomach, he realized that he knew everyone.

"What are you doing about this?" he heard a voice from behind ask him. "It's been three days since Jerry went missing."

Turning around, he saw Elizabeth, a nurse and a mother of one of the children, looking at him with tearful eyes. "You have to help us."

"I'm still recovering, Liz," he began, only to be interrupted by another parent.

"We told our stories to the man in the suit, wrote up all our accounts—those of us who saw something, anyway. Yet they keep telling us to just sit tight? I want to go out and look for my daughter!"

"I understand that, but you also know how this works. We don't want to all go out and leave the town empty," Carter said, taking a deep breath to calm his nerves. A few more parents gathered. "What if they come back? What if something happens to you?" He continued speaking, slightly raising his voice. "We have the situation under control, look around. There are so many people helping. We *will* find them."

"It's easy for you to say," a man said as he made his way to the front of the group facing Carter.

"Don't be too quick to judge," Elizabeth told the man.

"No, I haven't slept in days. I'm going crazy. I need answers!" The man's voice broke as he struggled to hold back his tears.

"Boss." Aaron tapped him on his shoulder. "I fueled your cruiser."

"Thanks, Aaron."

"I parked it around the building; here are the keys." Aaron handed Carter a pair of car keys.

A man wearing a black suit with a white shirt underneath, much like Klebond's, approached the crowd and walked closer to Carter. "My name is Agent Simple," he introduced himself. "We've arranged a meeting with one of our psychologists."

Carter sighed and turned around to face him. "I'm not doing any of that, Agent Simple."

"This will greatly help our investigation..." Simple continued as Carter stared at him. Swallowing, he turned around, facing the office building after breaking the intense stare with Simple.

"What's wrong with him?" the man asked Liz, who looked at Carter.

"His daughter is missing as well," Liz told the man, who went silent immediately, his lips trembling. "He just got back to town like the others. That's why I told you don't be too quick to speak."

"Liz, my life is destroyed. I miss my daughter." The man broke down, crying on her shoulder.

"I'm sure they'll find them. The best thing we can do right now is to remain calm."

As Carter walked away from the crowd and entered his vehicle, Klebond approached Simple and said, "Follow him."

~~~

Carter pulled out of the parking spot in front of the station and drove out of the city center. After a few minutes, he saw the baseball field on his right in the distance. Happy laughter and children's playing voices echoed in his mind. His head started spinning, and his vision blurred. Carter slowed down and pulled over next to the highway sign indicating that the next exit would be the way to go to the field. The inside voices persisted.

Closing his eyes, he placed his head on the steering wheel. "What the hell is happening to me!" Carter looked up at the sign after a few moments.

"You had one job!" His ex-wife's voice shook him out of his state.

Sighing, Carter adjusted himself in the seat and put the car in drive. He exited the roadway heading for the baseball field.

Halfway there, he slowed down at the sight of a national guard armored vehicle blocking the road.

"The field is closed," a soldier informed him, approaching the marked sheriff's vehicle.

"I know," Carter replied, "I just need to check on a piece of evidence the guys at the office need." Carter raised his identification card together with his shield.

The soldier took his credentials and entered his armored car. He emerged after a few minutes. "The feds confirmed your ID. Make it quick, please." He handed Carter his credentials back.

Carter continued to drive down the dirt road

leading to the field's parking area. Crime scene tape and big highway construction cones blocked the way inside. He parked behind a yellow school bus, got out of his car, and walked around to the front door. He entered the bus—no one there, only children's bookbags. He felt a lump in his stomach, remembering that he last saw Samantha, his daughter, inside that bus.

"Koler," he murmured, "where is…" He turned his head as if to ask the deputy standing next to him and stopped once he realized he was alone.

Sighing, he got off the bus and continued walking toward the field's front entrance. Raising the yellow plastic tape, Carter continued inside the arena. The chain-link fence door leading to the bleachers made a squeaking sound as he opened it. Carter stopped; goosebumps erupted over his body. Bleachers on his right side, field on his left, and the heat of the sun beating his head, he walked through the dirt path stopping in front of the dugout. There were helmets on the ground, soda cans, papers that looked as if they were stuck where someone had run over them. He looked out at the field —the bases were covered by dirt wind had brought in.

A black SUV pulled in behind Carter's cruiser. Agent Simple dialed Klebond's number on his phone. "He's by the field," he said as soon as Klebond picked up.

"I know. National Guard notified me. Keep an eye on him, but let him do his thing."

Simple hung up the phone and reached inside a backpack on his passenger's seat, pulling a pair of binoculars out.

A cloud covered the sunlight. It brought shade to the area where Carter was, and, for a moment, his vision blurred. Squinting, he looked up in the sky in its direction.

Images of a slow-moving craft casting a shadow that covered the entire field flashed before his eyes. In his visions of the area, people were now standing, some pointing up to the triangular-shaped craft, some cowering. He couldn't hear anything, though people seemed to be speaking, some of them pointing to their ears as a loud, pulsating rumble blanketed the area.

#

Irene stopped reading as a yellow note was in between the pages.

"Time. Ran. Out.

Or perhaps it slowed down.

Drastically!

Seconds turned to minutes.

Minutes feel as if they're hours.

A day – an eternity.

Next week?

Might as well be another universe.

Time. Ran. Out.

Or perhaps it slowed down.

I'll talk to you tomorrow."

Whoa, Adam, where does this belong? Irene looked up at the coffee cup on the table. Picking it, she took a sip, looking down at the note. She placed the cup back on the table and the sticky in between the previous pages and resumed reading.

#

Sunlight hit Carter again as the small white cloud moved away in the otherwise clear blue sky, shaking the visions out of him.

Walking on the field, he bent down and picked up a glove on top of the second base, noticing lots of footprints in the dirt leading to the right side of the field. He followed them to a corner of the chain-link fence surrounding the arena. Carter stopped and looked at an opening in it. It was pulled up about two feet high, creating a passage, and the ground under it was wet. Kneeling, he crawled through, doing his best not to touch the muddy soil and get it on his pants. "Mud," he muttered, remembering how he had it all over his hands and uniform when he woke up. Once on the other side, he continued, following footprints which let through the woods.

Agent Simple left his vehicle and trailed Carter from a distance.

Carter stepped over a fallen tree trunk. He lifted his head to see where the tree had fallen from, noticing more trunks and branches on the ground. Some of them were pressed against the ground so hard they were broken in several points. Yet the path marked by footprints and the occasional dirty pieces of clothing was evident.

Carter continued to saunter on, following the path, and found himself in the middle of a second field. Fallen, crushed trees were pressed against the ground in what appeared to be a triangular manner. Almost as if something large and imposingly heavy had landed there, pushing fifteen-foot tall trees out of its way as if they were grass. There were three significant square impressions on the ground. *Landing gear? Support beams?*

The footprints were harder to see here. Pieces of trees and branches littered the place, but here and there, he could see a paper soda cup, t-shirt, or shoe. The footprints ended abruptly. As if a ramp had extended there.

"Why here?" Carter murmured. "Of all the directions. They all came this way." He looked around, realizing where he was. About a quarter-mile from this location was the cabin where he woke up from.

He brought his injured fists up. Opening his palms, he looked around again as if to ask the surroundings for an answer.

"There's no way I was here by myself with no backup." He looked back at the trail he'd come from. "Who else was here with me?"

~~~

Simple stopped by the fence, following Carter with his eyes. He called Klebond again. "It's Simple. The sheriff went directly to the abduction site."

"I think the scene might have jogged his memory a bit," Klebond replied.

"What do you want me to do?"

"Let's have a chat with him now. I'm walking to you. I'll be there in about thirty seconds."

"Understood." Simple pressed *end call* on his phone, putting the device inside his pocket. He went through the same fence opening and walked toward the abduction site. He walked along the path, stepping over tree trunks where Carter was.

"The cabin you woke up is about a half a mile that way." Simple pointed toward the forest.

Carter turned his head and looked at him. "I should've known you people were in on this."

"In on what?"

"Why don't you tell me what happened? Why do you people insist on making me suffer?"

"I already told you, this is not about you, Sheriff Carter, this is about solving this abduction case."

"My daughter was inside that bus." Carter looked at Agent Simple. "You think I don't want this case solved?"

"Then help us, Sheriff."

"You think I'm intentionally withholding information?" Carter closed in on Agent Simple. "What the hell is wrong with you?"

Agent Klebond entered the field of fallen trees. "Then tell us where you were for the past three days."

"I don't remember that!" Carter raised his voice, looking at Klebond. "I can only tell you what I know and what I've recalled." Carter looked around. "I recalled a triangular craft hovering over the field. I followed the footprints. It's a little perplexing that everyone rushed here."

"Almost like they were led here by someone they trusted, wouldn't you say?" Klebond took a step closer to the two looking at Carter.

"What's your name again, Agent?" Carter asked Klebond.

"Klebond."

"Agent Klebond, will you tell me why you keep asking accusatory questions?"

"Sheriff Carter," Klebond answered, "you are the last person to turn up since the event. Pretty much everyone else we recovered remembered almost everything, but not you. What are you hiding?"

"I'm not hiding anything; I'm telling you as much as I know," Carter replied, lifting his fists up. "I can assume I fist-fought someone." Carter drew his revolver with the barrel pointing to the ground and opened the cylinder, inspecting it. He pushed the cylinder back in its place, holstering his weapon, and checked his reserve ammunition pouch. "I fired about six rounds," he added, looking around as to check the surroundings for bullet holes.

"Yeah, we found some spent shells here. Anything else?" Klebond asked.

"This just dawned on me as I was here, but I know I'm not alone when I attend these games. There's generally someone else with me. I just don't remember where Koler, my deputy, was during all this."

"What about him?"

"I last remember seeing him by the bus when the children got off," Carter replied, tightening his eyebrows. "How about you? Are you going to tell me anything you know? What the hell is going on, and how many are missing? Who is back, is my daughter back?"

"Sheriff, we've found about twelve of the initial missing thirty-two. We haven't told the media. After your exchange with your ex-wife in your office today, I double-checked, and yes, we have a young girl called Samantha Carter in custody. They're all at the edge of the town, inside a few trailers we have set up."

"Why haven't you told anyone?"

"Carter, this is a mass abduction. And your story matches with pretty much everyone else's—a craft hovered in the sky, and what appeared to be people came out, rounding children up. Some ran out in the fields, or into the woods, and others are still missing. We're still finding people, like yourself."

"What, like alien abduction?" Carter's mood lightened as he realized that his daughter was safe. He looked at Klebond and Simple, who maintained a somber attitude.

"I want to see her." Carter cleared his throat, looking toward the direction where he'd parked his car.

"Before we do that, you have to sign a non-disclosure agreement. What you learned here, and what you are about to see, are top secret."

"Fine."

The three walked back to where they parked.

"Get in my car." Klebond pointed to a black SUV parked near Carter's cruiser.

"Let's go to the farm," he told Simple, who put the car in drive as soon as Carter got in his vehicle.

The black SUV sped down Main Street past the shrine and the Sheriff's office, made a left on Pine Street past the hardware store, and just like that, exited the town. They drove for about twenty minutes on the highway through the forest and out to some fields. The SUV turned left onto a dirt road toward another National Guard armored vehicle.

A soldier lifted his hand, signaling them to stop. As the car came to a halt, Klebond pulled his FBI badge. The soldier took it in his hand and entered the vehicle. He reemerged a few moments later, signaling the operator on the driver's seat to clear the way. The black SUV stopped in front of at least seven trailers parked next to each other. Another soldier approached the car.

"Can I help you, agents?"

"We're looking for Carter," Klebond replied.

"C, Carter," the soldier repeated, pulling out a clipboard. "Ah, yes, Trailer Three."

"Thank you," Klebond said, opening the door and walking toward the trailer that had a number three on its side.

Carter quickly walked to the door and pulled on it. "It's locked. What the hell is going on?"

"They're being held under quarantine. Some of them are really shaken up." The soldier walked closer and placed an electronic key card on top of a card reader, and the door opened with a buzz and a click.

Carter opened the door and entered. "Sam! Samantha!" he called, and the voice of a six-year-old girl echoed from the back, "Daddy!"

Barely able to hold his tears, Carter's voice trembled as he said, "Come here, baby!" Samantha ran to his arms.

Carter pulled his daughter and looked her over to check for any wounds. "How are you baby, oh I'm so sorry I couldn't get to you sooner."

"I'm okay, daddy," she replied with a squeaky voice. "There are plenty of figurines here."

Klebond stepped inside the well-lit trailer full of beds and food trays and toys. He looked at Carter and Samantha talking as the other children raised their heads from their toys.

"Carter, we have to go," Klebond whispered in his ear. "She'll be in good hands for another few days. I need you to verify something for me." He looked at Carter as the latter hugged his daughter.

With a sigh, Carter turned his head and kissed Sam on her cheek. "Daddy has to go, baby girl, but I will come back, that I promise, even if it's the last thing I do in the world."

"Okay Daddy," Sam replied, smiling.

The three exited the trailer as the national guard soldier closed the door back up. "As we were looking for contacts, we asked the few adults that escaped the ordeal to help us identify those we rescued. We can account for everyone with one exception. Your deputy, Koler. He doesn't seem to have any next of kin."

"Koler, he moved here about three years ago, bought the Minil property on the other side of the town. They'd moved out."

"Why so?"

"Ah, old man Minil got too old to work the property, I guess."

"So, he was alone when he moved in, your deputy."

"I'm not sure off the top of my head," Carter replied as the four approached another, smaller trailer. "You know my memory is all over the place. Why so concerned with my deputy?"

"We just couldn't find anyone to notify, that's all. In a town where everyone knows everyone, it struck us as a bit strange."

The soldier walked up the ramp and scanned his keycard, unlocking the door. As the three entered the room, the soldier remained outside, closing the door behind them.

Inside there was a small bed, a few chairs, a TV hanging from one of the walls, and Koler, sitting and eating a sandwich, watching a show.

"Hey boss!" He got up as soon as Carter entered the trailer. "Man, it's good to see you. They're not telling us anything. How's everyone?"

"Everyone's good, Koler, how are you holding up?"

"I've been here for like three days." Koler placed his sandwich on a paper plate on the folding table in the middle of the trailer. Wiping his hands, he adjusted his uniform and took a step toward them. "Are you here to get me out?"

"Not yet," Carter replied, looking at Koler's blond hair. As the latter turned his head to check out Klebond. "The feds are still investigating. This is out of my hands. Where were you when the kids got abducted? I only remember you by the bus."

"I took Cruiser Forty-Five and parked by the outfield. Then I saw the craft landing. I've never seen anything like that, boss." Koler faced Carter.

Carter looked at his uniform, which was as dirty and muddy as his own when he'd woke up.

"They didn't give you anything to change with?" Carter turned his head to face Klebond.

"We will," Klebond said, reaching and knocking on the door as the soldier opened it from the outside.

"I just got briefed on what happened, and I'm working on getting all of you out," Carter said as he got Klebond's message to get out. "Sit tight for now."

"Sure thing, boss." Koler went back to the table as the three exited the trailer.

"We've separated the children from the rest of the adults, with a couple of exceptions, especially if kids and adults knew each other. As I said, almost everyone here knows each other." Klebond chuckled. "Everyone has passed through regression therapy, and most accounts match. We'll release everyone later today or first thing tomorrow."

"You know I got slapped by my ex-wife because she thought my daughter was missing, right?"

"There are still twelve missing children and adults," Klebond replied with an ominous tone. "You mentioned something dark above you, covering the sky. Can you tell me anything else?"

"No." Carter's face changed as he looked at Klebond. "I remember fighting, people, I remember firing my weapon. What do you think is going on, Agent?"

"I already told you, we still have twelve missings. We have a mass abduction in our hands."

Carter raised one side of his mouth in contempt. "You know that's..." He stopped talking as Klebond put his sunglasses covering his eyes. "Nuts," he finished the sentence, whispering to himself. The three walked to the edge of the camp where their car was parked.

"You'll be the first one to know when we will release everyone, Sheriff." Klebond turned, facing Carter. "That way, you can arrange for a press conference, and we can funnel the media information."

~~~

In two days, the Federal Bureau of Investigation closed their file on this mass abduction and turned over the case to the State of Indiana. As the farm base closed and the found children and adults began to trickle back in Haytown, many families moved away. Neighboring towns avoided that area, forcing the Indiana Authorities to consider closing Haytown and remove its zip code.

~~~

Washington, D.C. Two weeks later.

"Kriss, do you have a minute?" Simple opened the glass door of his office, following Klebond as he walked past.

"What is it, Steve?"

"You know, I was filing the Haytown case, and I noticed something peculiar."

"Do tell." Klebond stopped and walked back to Simple.

"Remember Sheriff Carter? He showed us his revolver, telling us that he likely exchanged fire with someone. That matched the six spent shells we found in the field."

"So?"

"Well, I was reading the report regarding the deputy who was found by the edge of the forest, and it says, gun full, no rounds fired."

"Maybe he didn't have time to fire?"

"He was found in the same state as Carter, disheveled. Like he fought with someone."

"That is curious. Do you still have his contact information?"

"Koler, I do, but it's invalid. Most families moved on from—" he lifted the folder "—Haytown. I tried tracing him. Can't find him."

Ten thousand miles away, somewhere in the middle of the Russian tundra.

Light leaked from the opening doors, illuminating the snowflakes and creating a bright band on the snowy ground. As the doors opened completely, three small humanoid creatures with slim necks and large heads walked out, accompanied by tall men. They escorted the group of children and adults, about twelve of them, to an underground entrance that led beneath the snow.

Watching the scene from farther away was a man wearing a black suit, white shirt, black tie, and a fedora hat. He placed his hand on his hat to keep it from flying away in the wind.

Koler approached him, still wearing the sheriff's deputy uniform. "That's all we could take, the rest escaped."

"That's okay, Hans. This is good enough for the

moment."

"Klebond was there," Koler said, unfazed that the fedora-wearing man called him by another name.

"Then, you need to disappear for a little while."

The small crowd of children and adults quickly vanished through the closing doors of the underground entrance. The fedora-wearing man and Koler, who he called Hans, walked inside the craft the group had come out of. It rapidly raised its ramp and flew up, disappearing in the dark, snowy sky

#

"Oh, the deception!" Irene flipped the page, revealing the next title.

THIS IS NOT A
BEDTIME STORY

The bright sun's rays warmed the afternoon air as the green field leading to the Gata's house filled with the sound of screaming children. It wasn't an unusual occurrence, since the children often played rough, especially when it was such a beautiful day outside.

#

Irene heard the front doorbell chime and took

her eyes from the book. "Come in." She placed the bookmark on the page, closing it.

The door retracted into the wall revealing Adam holding two trays, one in each hand. "I am here to provide food!" he exclaimed, smiling.

"My hero," Irene laughed, placing the book on her bed. Sliding off and taking a step toward him, Irene grabbed one of the trays, making sure Adam didn't lose his balance. "I thought you'd be busy with maintenance."

"Yeah." Adam looked around the room for somewhere to place his tray. "I am *that* good." He stopped. "Nah, I'm kidding, it was just a broken LED light."

"Hold on." Irene continued to laugh, holding her tray in her hand. "Let me extend the table." She walked to the wall on her right and, pressing a button, released a panel that extended the table she'd placed the cup of coffee on. Irene put her tray there, then walked next to her bed and opened a narrow closet, pulling two folding chairs out. "Here's one for you." Irene handed Adam a chair.

Irene took the cover off a small bowl of vegetables, smelling the steam. "Finally, something other than protein bars." She dipped a piece of bread in the soup, taking a bite from it.

"All you've done since you got back is lock yourself away in your room. Got me a little worried." Adam sipped water from a cup he picked up from the tray, watching Irene chow down on the food.

"Well, the accident and realizing that our journey is finally over got me down a little bit," Irene said after swallowing. "I must admit that your book has helped fend off that stress."

"*My* book helped you fend off stress?" Adam laughed. "Did you read the same book I gave you?"

"Oh, you say that like you don't know it." Irene got up and picked the book from the bed. "How you kept this a secret is beyond me," she said, looking at it.

Adam took a bite from his slice of bread. "You knew I was writing a short story book." He chuckled, looking at Irene. "As for everyone else, it took a lot of after-hours writing."

"What happens now?" Irene asked.

"About what?"

"The trip is over. We're here."

"We'll settle down in a wooden house by the prairie, and I'll raise chickens." Adam chuckled.

"And babies," Irene said, looking at him.

"I have to admit, that's a scarier prospect than doing a spacewalk after an asteroid impacts the Morning Star."

They both laughed as the front doorbell chime rang. "Come in," Irene said, still laughing

"Adam, we're prepping the shuttles for tomorrow's launch, we need you," the chief said, entering the room looking at the two. "What are you two laughing about?" he asked, instinctively smiling.

"Babies."

"Already?" He chuckled. "Alrighty then. You need some space?" he asked, winking at Adam and Irene.

"Not now," Irene replied with a giggle. "For god's sake, Chief."

Adam got up from his chair, collecting his food tray. He lightly kissed Irene on her lips. "I'll see you later, honey."

Irene folded the chairs up, stored them, and retracted the table with a smile plastered on her face as Adam and the chief walked to the door. "Do you guys need help?" she asked.

"We're doing this in zero-g," the chief replied, turning back to look at her, "outside of the Morning Star. Those crates are too heavy to move inside. You can double-check the cryo-chambers if you want."

"I'll be right there," Irene said as Adam and the chief continued walking down the corridor.

She opened her dresser and put on her captain's uniform, then exited her room, heading straight for the direction where the escape pods were. The corridor was now blocked by the heavy door separating the shuttle bay pods, as the crewmembers on the other side of it had opened the outer bay doors.

The shuttles carried crews of three and were designed to transport supplies from the Morning Star to the ground. As such, they weren't too big or imposing. The team could quickly release the clamps holding them inside. And that's what they had done.

All twelve shuttles were lined up outside the Morning Star, tethered to its body. They were being loaded with supplies and equipment the colonists were going to need once they landed on Helsey 8K. Irene looked at the monitors as the crew slowly installed the resource crates.

The cryogenic pod control panels were around the corner to her left, the only way the corridor led to. As soon as she walked in front of them, the Morning Star's body shook slightly. The transport shuttles that were ready and loaded were being brought back inside.

Irene approached the main control panel and typed her password. The widescreen above her head lit up with small green lights; each one indicated the status of individual embryos within. In silence, she inspected the screen's contents. *All green, excellent.*

"Doing one last check?" she heard a crewmember say from behind her.

"Yep," Irene replied, still looking at the screen.

"Well, what's the word captain, all green?" the crewmember asked. "We're getting ready to open the other side of the shuttle.

"All green," Irene lifted her head, looking at the crewmember who held his EVA helmet in his hand.

"Excellent," he said. "Now I'm going to need you to leave this area. We need to move some more supplies from here.

"Of course," Irene turned the screen off. She walked back to the corridor junction, where a few more crewmembers wearing EVA suits were standing. They sealed off the rest of the ship, opening the outer doors.

Having nothing else to do, Irene walked back to

her room. She sat on the table where her bowl of soup was, grabbed the book, and opened it, placing it next to her. *Where was I?* "Ah, yes, the NOT bedtime story," she chuckled. "Let's read a bedtime story that's not a bedtime story."

#

Alma, who was hanging the laundry to dry in her backyard, looked at the direction of the screams. They intensified as the children got closer.

"Mom, Mom, we saw the shadows again," Lenore, her eight-year-old daughter, said as she tugged Alma's white dress, trying to catch her breath.

"Are you sure, little one? It's broad daylight. The shadows never come out during the day." Alma took a large wet bedsheet and hung it on the string, placing one peg on to hold it in place.

"I swear, Mom, we all saw them." Lenore pointed to the two boys who ran up with her. "The Elert boy took his father's horse and ran to the castle to tell the king."

Alma's smile quickly faded as she realized that the children had indeed seen something and weren't just playing another game.

"Go inside and tell your father." She turned to face the boys. "You two go to your homes and do the same."

As the boys left the backyard, Alma followed Lenore inside the house. The sunny sky was getting progressively darker, and the wind intensified.

"Is this true?" Ylark, Alma's husband, and Lenore's father asked her as soon as Alma entered the wooden house.

"I'm not sure, but the kids are scared. Lenore said that the Elert boy went to the castle to tell the king that the dark is coming." Alma closed the door behind her. "You know there have been some strange deaths around the village these past two days. All of their families swear that this is the shadow's doing. We should leave."

"The Elert boy?" Ylark repeated. "Don't they live by the river at the far edge of the village?"

"Yes, they do." Alma opened the dresser next to her, pulled a sheet out, and placed some clothes and food inside. "Remember, his father died three days ago, by the cliff."

"Ah, they said he got too drunk and fell over. The Elert boy is just grieving."

"He might be grieving—" she pulled the sheet to make a small bag and tied a knot on top, placing it by her feet on the floor "—but five deaths by that cliff in three days is too much."

"Now that you mention it, our neighbors, the Picids, took their horse-drawn carriage when they left home this morning. They only do that when they leave for a long time, usually when they go to the castle."

Dark clouds brought by the stormy winds cast a shadow over the village. The animals must have felt that something sinister was approaching, and began to make loud sounds. "We should go too," Alma said.

"You go, my love. I will stay here to protect our house." Ylark reached for his sword by the door.

"Ylark, no." Alma took a step toward him and placed her hand on his shoulder. "We need you."

"And we all need a house and our livestock." He bent and peeked through the window, looking at the disturbed cows mooing in the backyard. "What's got to them?" He opened the door and walked outside. The winds, which had now reached the village, were slamming fence gates, picking up dirt from the road, and carrying all of it up in the dark sky.

Covering his mouth with his hand, Ylark looked at the enormous vortex above the village as a nearby barn suddenly shifted and slammed into his house, shaking it off its foundations. "Alma!" Ylark ran in her direction as his wife, holding Lenore, fell out of the window while the house's roof disconnected, flying up in the sky.

Running toward his terrified family, Ylark looked up at the dark clouds in disbelief as a massive scythe made of shadows swept through the house, nearly hitting them. "This way!" He grabbed Alma's arm and rushed to escape the weapon of death incarnate unleashed upon the village. Shrieks, screams, and growls increased as other villagers ran in all directions trying to escape the vortex while the Gata family ran to the forest.

Ommin himself walked the dirt road between the village houses, one slow step after the other. His black sandals seemed to hover just above the dirt, supported by a foggy veil of the souls he had enslaved.

Wearing a black robe with a large hood covering his face, the only other things visible were his nearly skeletal white hands, which held the large, black-bladed scythe over his head. Screams of the scared villagers filled the vicinity as he began to chant his spell, intensifying the winds as his red-eyed, ghostly soldiers circled the village, looking for more souls to trap.

{~~}

The sun was setting on the horizon, light yielding to darkness as the horsemen riding with Siluis, the king of Ediral, stopped on top of the hill, steadying their horses as they looked at the valley.

"It looks calm," Dimos, the army captain, said, slowly trotting his horse to stand next to the king.

"Do you think that the villagers are right on this one?" Siluis asked, looking over his silver pauldron at the approaching captain.

"Ommin has been trying to invade Ediral ever since we freed it. He will try again," Dimos said leaning forward in his saddle

Dismounting, the horsemen, all in heavy battle armor, tied their steeds to nearby trees as the rest of the army slowly approached.

"We will make camp here, Captain," Siluis said, looking down the green valley below at the village of Elhinoy. Its villagers had left it in a hurry after being terrorized for three consecutive nights by the shadow monsters sent by the dark Lord Ommin, though some had refused to leave their homes, vowing to protect their land.

Dimos left his steed with one of his soldiers and walked near the rest of the army, slowly gathering and dismounting their horses. "Set the tents up here and send the scouts out so we can see what else is going on around these woods," he ordered the other captains who joined him. Everyone began to run back and forth from the horse-drawn wagons, which slowly caught up with the rest of the defending army. The base of the hill became lively with soldiers moving supplies and tents, setting up camp as the white carriage carrying Artigas the wizard slowly approached.

"My king," she greeted Siluis, kneeling as the king approached the carriage. "I know you don't like disturbing news, especially of a battle that might soon take place, but I have sworn to stand by your side and help you. This," she pointed to the valley, "is it. It's the end of the prophecy."

Siluis touched her shoulder to signal her to get up. "Why do you speak of despair on the eve of what could be our finest battle?"

"My king, I haven't felt this kind of darkness since we liberated the kingdom, and you rescued me," Artigas said as she looked at the valley below, swallowing.

"What do you see, mage?"

Artigas reached and lowered the hood of her green cloak, revealing her blonde hair as she walked to the edge of the hill. "I see darkness and corrupted men. They will try their hardest to kill you and rule your land. I see death, my Lord."

{~~}

The full moon slowly rose over the valley, illuminating the trees and casting long shadows as the wind picked up, disturbing the torch flames.

"I hear their whispers in the air," Artigas said as she turned her head, looking at Siluis as the hunter's moon brightened the night sky. "Ommin's scythe is cresting."

Screams pierced the silence as shadows reached the village below.

"Captain, have you sent any scouts down to the village?"

"Yes, my lord."

"What do they say?"

"None have yet returned, my lord."

Feeling that something was amiss, Siluis looked at Dimos. "Mobilize the men. The time for battle is fast approaching. Get me my horse."

The sound of clanging armor and steel overtook the hill face as men and women prepared for battle. Five horsemen hurriedly headed downhill to the village as a loud shriek, accompanied by increasingly higher winds, approached the army. Shadowy figures with bright red eyes and long, articulated claws burst through the army camp and inside the tents, toppling fires and tearing soldiers apart. Some of them flew over the field, diving down and overtaking soldiers' bodies, turning them against one another as Artigas, the mage, approached Siluis. "My king, you have to go!"

As a few soldiers hurriedly brought Siluis his sword and armor, he faced Artigas and asked, "Do you remember what you told me the night when I rescued you, mage?"

"I do." Artigas bowed her head.

"You told me it's all for nothing. You," Siluis raised his sword and pointed in her direction, "told me that if I was to save even a shred of myself, I would have to battle my own fears. Well, mage, the greatest fear I have is being unable to protect my family and my kingdom."

"Then retreat, my king." Artigas kneeled, putting her hands together and begging, "The castle walls should provide you with some protection. Your allies are coming. I made sure of that."

"They will be too late; they always have been. No one wants to face Ommin. No, my beloved mage, I thank you for your concern, but if I am to die, I will do so here on the battlefield, not cowering inside my castle walls." Siluis took a step back and swung his sword in the wind. "Will you fight alongside me, Artigas?" he asked, facing soldiers battling the dark monsters in the distance.

"It would be my honor to die alongside you, my lord," Artigas said, looking up at Siluis.

"Then come, get up, join me, and we will win this battle!" He approached Artigas, inserting his sword inside his scabbard and touching her shoulder, making sure she got up with him. "We will win!"

Siluis mounted his horse, unsheathing his sword again. Abruptly squeezing his steed's abdomen, he rushed toward a group of soldiers fighting to keep one of their fellows from being dragged away by a few shadow monsters.

He hit one of them with his sword, which the wizard herself had forged, slicing it in two as the army regrouped and organized defenses against this surprise attack. A few soldiers, led by Dimos, joined him with torches and long swords, pushing the soldiers that Ommin's monsters had possessed away. The rest of the men began to reorganize, donning armor and grabbing swords as they formed up shoulder to shoulder. By now, the moon was high in the sky, and Ommin himself walked over the village carrying his scythe, destroying and burning everything in his path. Swinging his weapon, he cut down the villagers who were trying to escape the burning inferno, which had once been their homes.

{~~}

Ylark ran through the forest, holding on to Alma and Lenore as the winds picked up again. At this point, he could hear screams and the clanking of swords in the distance.

"There seem to be more people over there. King's army, perhaps?"

"Let me go check what's going on there. You two stay here." Ylark headed toward the noise.

"Mom, I'm scared," Lenore said, tugging Alma's

hand and looking at her father as he disappeared past the forest trees.

"It's okay, baby, Father will make sure we are okay." Alma kneeled next to a tree, looking as Ylark approaching the soldiers. The winds were now unbearably strong, snapping branches and bringing fiery debris wherever it blew.

The soldiers moved toward Ylark, who emerged from the dark forest alone. "Reveal yourself or face death!"

"I escaped from the village," he screamed so that they could hear his voice. Just then, a dark shadow flew directly into his stomach, taking control of his body, which convulsed for a moment before growling at the soldiers.

"No, Ylark!" Alma ran in his direction, shouting at the soldiers, who pointed their swords at him. "He is my husband; he is a good man!"

Frozen in fear, Lenore cowered behind the tree, watching her mother run to protect her father. As the trees behind her caught fire, she grabbed the bag made from bedsheets and crawled away from them.

The possessed body of Ylark lunged at the king as Alma continued to run toward them. "He is a good man. Please don't harm my husband!"

Ommin lifted his scythe, waving it in the dark and creating a whirlwind of flying shadows, smoke, and burnt debris. His arms appeared from under his robe, pushing the violent air funnel toward the army camp and swallowing everything in its path—soldiers, swords, and tents. Standing on the edge of the hill where Siluis was fighting shadows and pushing away the possessed soldiers, it sent the whirlwind of steel and fire crashing down on him. The winds stopped, dropping everyone and everything on the ground as the king, who was still sitting on his steed, held the hilt of a weapon which had penetrated his abdomen, thrust in by the force of the wind.

The evil whispers filling the air got louder and closer as the wizard again approached the king, who slumped over as the scattered soldiers began to re-form their defensive formation. She reached inside the saddlebag where she knew he held a toy that the queen always snuck in, to remind him that even though he was fighting alongside his men, there was a family that loved him waiting for him back in the castle. Pulling out the small cloth bear, she took a few steps back as Siluis's horse walked in circles, spooked by the shriek-ing, flying shadows circling the army like vultures.

Steadying the king's horse, she placed the toy on the ground and began to chant, extending one hand toward the king and the other on top of the fabric bear. Her tune intensified, and her hands began to glow with a faint blue light. It passed from the king to the toy, which inflated as if the incantation Artigas was performing gave it life. The bright glow attracted the attention of the dark shadows overhead, promptly fol-lowed by the army, which rushed to protect the king.

A red glowing fire arrow pierced the night sky, shot by the first soldier who arrived and saw the king in distress. It signified, "Protect the King." The entire army stopped their fighting and converged on where it originated as the shadow monsters savagely tore into the valiant men and women rushing to aid their king. Screams, fire, and growls surrounded Siluis, now standing amid bravery. Fighting with all his might and slashing the dark shadowy monsters, the injured king glowed.

"Your time has come, Siluis! Die!" The dark lord of evil, Ommin, swept the formation with its scythe, instantly sucking away the life force of everyone that was in the vicinity.

The king fell lifelessly from his horse, as did all the men who had tried to protect him from harm.

"You have to save the queen and the prince now," Artigas screamed to Dimos, placing the toy inside his saddlebag. "I will hold them back as long as I can. Go, don't look back!" She slapped the horse's haunch.

Turning around, Artigas placed her hand on Siluis' chest and picked up his sword. She pointed it to the dark sky as the shadows circled, shrieking, and moaning. The possessed soldiers walked toward her as well. She began to chant again, louder and louder before Ommin swung his scythe, penetrating her chest and releasing a bright bluish light which overtook the entire hill and valley at once, scattering the evil shadow monsters as the possessed soldiers fell to the ground.

"Go, protect the castle!" she screamed one last time to the soldiers near her just before her body vanished in the dark.

{~~}

"Milady," Dimos greeted Queen Arcinigeas, dismounting his horse in a hurry and kneeling in front of her as the castle guards hurriedly closed the large wooden gate. The loud shrieks signaling that the monsters were not too far behind spooked the horse, who reared up on his two hind feet, causing the saddlebag to open and the stuffed toy to fall on the cobblestone.

"Please get up, Captain," Arcinigeas said as she walked towards him. "Tell me, what news do you have from the battlefield?"

"My queen, the battle has come closer than we thought possible. The forces of the dark are pushing harder this time—they are outside the castle walls. Ommin himself is coming." Dimos got up, steadying himself.

She took a step closer to him. "What about Siluis? What about the king?"

"Milady, the king is..." Dimos began to say just as Caelestis, the young prince, walked in the hall behind his mother.

"The King is what?" Arcinigeas asked, before noticing the captain's gaze shifted to her right side. Turning around, she faced the child. "Caelestis, my son, please go upstairs, it's not safe here for you."

"I want to see Father!" the young prince exclaimed as a loud rumble rocked the large wooden front door.

"Here." Dimos knelt once again, picking up the stuffed toy from the floor. "The king asked me to give you this. He said it would keep you safe."

Caelestis took the bear and hugged it as the rumble rocked the castle walls again, sending rocks crashing down around them.

"Please take him to safety," Arcinigeas said to one of the guards. As they hurriedly walked away, she faced the captain again, who was now staring at her with his eyebrows raised. He swallowed in fear of how the queen was going to react to what he was about to say.

The guards who were hurriedly taking Caelestis to safety turned the corner just as Arcinigeas's cry of "No!" permeated the halls. They surrounded the prince and hastily brought him to the most fortified room in the castle. Before they had time to open it, though, dark and shadowy monsters attacked them, ripping through their armor and sending blood splattering on the walls as candles and torches fell to the ground. The last surviving soldier pushed Caelestis inside the room and locked the door from the outside.

Hugging the toy and trembling from fear, the young prince walked toward the only lit area, the fireplace. A strong gust of wind extinguished the flame, leaving the small room very dimly illuminated by two candles standing in the window's candelabrum. Ommin emerged from the dark pit of the fireplace, slowly growing and hissing at the frightened child. Darkness overtook the walls. His demonic form became defined gradually, illuminated by the quivering candlelight.

"Now that I have you, Caelestis, son of Siluis, heir of light and sky, I will rule this kingdom with darkness!" Holding his scythe of death by the snaith, Ommin hit the floor with its lower handle.

The cry of the dead souls under his sandals intensified.

The stuffed bear, the captain, had handed to the child in the front yard, suddenly came to life in his hands. The toy, which was facing out as Caelestis tightly hugged it, slowly wiggled in his arm, turned around and faced the child, who was frozen by fear. Extending his paw, the bear touched Caelestis on his forehead, just as his father, the king, would do every time he left for battle.

"Father?" Caelestis cried in desperation, breathing shallowly as a tear ran down his cheek. "Help me."

Bending down, Ommin swiftly protracted his sharp claws to finish the cowering frightened prince as the stuffed bear jumped out of his arms and stood between the monster and the child. With his paws pointing toward the monster, he yelled with an unusual but familiar voice,

"Stop!"

Angered, Ommin raised and swung its death scythe to hit it. A screaming whirlwind of souls filled the room. It nearly extinguished the remaining candles. But the stuffed bear jumped out of the path at the last moment.

Ommin snatched the toy midair with his claws. He wanted to tear it apart.

Another one of its shadow soldiers crawled on the ceiling, hissing and reaching for the prince, who sobbed as the scene unfolded in front of his eyes. Finally, grabbing the toy, Ommin brought it close to his gaping mouth.

"Father!" the prince exclaimed, as the other monster was now just above him.

The toy glowed bluish-white as it burned bright through Ommin's dark claws. With a whimper and a loud cry, the dark lord let it go on the floor. Its light cleared the dead souls' fog off the ground it fell upon. The toy bear then jumped to the ceiling, dragging the other monster to the ground as it whimpered, vanishing under its glow. A third monster joined the battle, coming out of the fireplace, but by now, the toy was glowing brighter. It threw one of the monsters against the wall and stretched out its paws as a bright beam of light emanated from them, obliterating it.

Seeing this, Ommin and his remaining red-eyed monsters rushed to get the boy. One crawled and stood behind his back, and the other growled, showing Caelestis his teeth. The stuffed bear jumped over the child's shoulder and hit one with the light emanating from his paw, causing it to disintegrate and shatter. It then jumped up to the ceiling, swung along the hanging candelabrum, and hit Ommin on his head with both paws. Unable to defend against the sudden reaction, Ommin's body glowed from inside out, exploding in pieces all over the room.

The room finally quieted as the fire lit up again in the fireplace, and the fog dissipated. Ommin was no longer present, and the fireplace regained its brightness.

"Mother?" Caelestis walked to the door holding the toy, which still glowed, illuminating his way. The door promptly opened as if the glow commanded it, ripping out the large wooden beam holding it in place from the outside and revealing the corridor, littered with bodies, swords, and torches. He walked to the room where he last saw his mother. Some straggling shadow monsters rushed to maim him, only to disintegrate in the light emanating from the bear, which now slowly spread to Caelestis himself.

Holding the living toy with his right hand, Caelestis, the heir of light and sky, walked into the front yard of the castle, the king's bright glow shielding him from the monsters who were still trying to harm him. He stopped in front of his mother, Queen Arcinigeas, who lay dead on the cobblestones facing the child. The light enveloped all the bloodied bodies in the vicinity, giving them life. As the queen slowly opened her eyes and looked at Caelestis, a young girl, Lenore, slid past the slightly open castle gate. She stood inside the front yard, shivering, and tightly holding the now-dirty and bloodied cloth bag which had all her belongings.

\#

"From darkness to light, Caelestis will be an amazing king." Irene placed her bookmark and closed the book. Sighing, she took a sip of water and set the cup back on the table.

She got up from the chair and, holding the book with her left hand, went out in the corridor. Crewmembers were walking about wrapping up the preparations for the evacuation. She closed her door and walked to the control room, where the chief, Adam, and a few more crewmembers were standing over the planning desk.

"Shuttles Three and Eleven are finally stocked, and the cryogenic pod is tethered to number Two." Adam pointed to the diagram displayed on the screen below it.

"So, we can plot the launch sequence now?" the chief asked.

"Sure," Adam said. "We all know our places."

"That sounds good," the chief replied. "Anyone else here has any other suggestions?" He raised his head, looking around the room. "Hi, Irene."

"I see the preparations are almost wrapped up," Irene said, walking to the desk. "Hi Chief," she greeted the chief. "I have nothing else; I mean, I checked the cryogenic pods. Green across the board."

"Yeah, I saw the login when I did my final check so I could unlock the mechanism holding it in place." The chief nodded. "Then, it's set. I'll make an announcement informing everyone to check their shuttle pod arrangements. We'll elaborate more tomorrow just before individual launches."

He walked to the control panel and picked up the microphone. "This is a general information message for the entire crew of the Morning Star. As you all know by now, we will begin the controlled evacuation procedure in ten hours. Everyone should refresh their memory as to what shuttle pod they will take down. More information will be available in eight hours during breakfast. Chief out." He hooked the microphone in its place. "I'm going to get a cup of coffee. See you all in eight hours. I'd try to get some sleep if I were you," he said, looking around.

As some crew members passed by the door where Irene was standing, Adam stopped in front of her. "I'm going to get some sleep."

"And I still have one more story to go," Irene replied, smiling slightly.

"Okay." Adam smiled, lightly kissed her on her lips, and followed the rest of the crew as everyone walked to their rooms.

Irene sat in one of the empty chairs in the control room. She placed her feet on the desk and opened the book again.

HANSEL

HB2957RA, Hansel

"This is not petrified wood." Lucas pointed to the fossil he placed on the table. His voice echoed through the large hall. "This fossil is, in fact, a fragment of a petrified bone, a radius to be exact—a human radius. For you members of the panel that are not familiar with human anatomy, this bone would be part of your forearm."

"That is preposterous!" one of the members shouted. "You two go out to the outer limits of the colony. Without permission, I might add. Collect some sticks and stones and start assigning them names of body parts. We have flown reconnaissance missions all over this planet, and we haven't found any life forms in over thirty years. Now you say there are fossilized bones?"

"Not just fossilized, petrified. Whoever this radius belonged to got buried underground quickly. And the volcanic process, which we see it all over this specific cave entrance, overtook and petrified it."

"Look," Kaia added, "we can try to find out more about this. Give us permission, and a couple of vehicles."

"We don't have time for this," Kaia's mother, Una, said as she looked at both standing in front of the semi-circular-shaped table the council used as a meeting panel. "All resources we have are engaged with maintenance or other schedules."

"Okay," Kaia replied, looking at her, then around the table at all the members. "How about this—let me run a constructive DNA test on them to see if they indeed are human. No resources needed for that."

The council members looked around at each other, chattering as Lucas shifted his gaze toward Kaia. "What the hell are you doing? We already know they're human," he whispered.

"*They* don't," Kaia whispered back, looking at the panel. "Perhaps if we make them understand that there were once others here, possibly before we landed, the council might be a little more receptive."

"And what if they are?" one of the councilmembers interrupted this whispering chatter. His voice echoed in the room.

"Excuse me?" Lucas raised his head, looking at their direction.

"What if they are human remains? What difference does that make for us?" Engel, the head of the council, replied. "They are not colonists; all our deceased have proper burial places within the perimeter."

"What difference..." Lucas lowered his head, raising his eyebrows in surprise. "There seems to have been a major cataclysm here. I think it would be wise to explore this event and figure out what happened here before we establish a colony on this planet, that's all I'm saying."

"The colony has been established, boy," Engel replied. "Besides, how did you come up with that?"

"Petrified bone fragments are not a smoking gun, but I am sure I will be able to find more evidence inside that cave."

"We've heard your argument and will consider it in our internal meeting. Meanwhile, we strongly recommend you stick to your assignments, scout the surface, and do not venture inside caves or cave openings unless accompanied by a proper team. This hearing is now over," Una concluded. They all got up from their chairs as Chairman Engel, not just the head of the council, but a professor in the colony's school, walked over to the couple. "I need to talk to you, both of you."

Accompanied by Engel, Kaia and Lucas exited the room, walking through the long, narrow metallic corridor connecting the council room with the rest of the structure, which once was used as an atmosphere processor.

"Look," he said, closing the door. "I think I am speaking to responsible adults here, right?" Engel looked at Kaia and Lucas. "At the very least, I'm assuming I am talking to a couple of brilliant ones. Right?" He continued walking around his table, which faced the door. "The truth is, we know that we are not the first ones to land here. Hansel has an enormous amount of gold just under the surface, concentrated in one place," Engel said. "We are still evaluating what exactly happened with the local population, which seems to be extinct. Past that, this news is of no substance to the colony. It could even spread panic." He placed both hands on the table, facing the two youths who stood by the door. "And it's not a priority."

"You mean to tell me that the council knew about this and still created a colony on a planet that might just become uninhabitable for reasons we don't understand? That's reckless."

"We learned about that from the drone reports. After we landed," he replied, facing the couple standing in front of him as he reached for a phone on his table. "We are here now. There is no going back for at least a few decades. Not until the second wave of colonists arrives. Speculating with unverified information and opinions will only complicate things rather than inform our members. We can't have that."

Just before he could grab the phone, someone knocked on the door.

"Come in," the councilmember reluctantly said, looking at the door past Kaia and Lucas.

"Chairman Engel," Una said once she opened the room. "I need to talk to my daughter." Una stepped inside his office.

"Ah, Una. I was just about to call you."

The two didn't say anything as Kaia moved closer to her mother. Una closed the door of Engel's office.

"Kaia, I didn't appreciate the tone with which you addressed the council today."

"What does my tone have to do with it..."

"Kaia," Una interrupted, making eye contact with her.

"Professor Engel, we're sorry," Kaia said with a sigh.

"Thank you for that apology, Kaia." Una looked at her, and she lowered her head, staring at the floor as if she had done something wrong.

"Oh, stop it." Engel chuckled, walking around the table, shaking Una's hand. "These two are brilliant. They have a bright future ahead of them." He put his hand on Luca's shoulder, looking at Kaia, who still avoided eye contact.

"Well, thank you, Professor Engel," Una replied, smiling. "They certainly are brilliant in their own way, but we have to go now."

"Absolutely." The councilmember swallowed. The two youths, accompanied by Una, turned around and headed for the exit.

"Thank you for your help," Una told Engel, closing the door.

Engel looked out of the glass door and followed

them with his eyes as the three turned a corner and disappeared. He pulled his communicator and dialed a number in a hurry. "We have to talk."

The three continued walking to the spiral staircase, past metal structures illuminated by sizable square LED lights. Their white light penetrated everywhere in the assembly, which had no windows.

"I have to finish the meeting. You two, go home. I am serious."

"Okay, Mom," Kaia replied as Una headed up the spiral staircase, and they continued down to the ground floor, exiting the structure.

~O~

"This way." Lucas grabbed Kaia's hand once out.

Kaia stopped, pulling her hand free. "I don't think we should go back there."

"Come on, baby. I want to see what's past the edge of that canyon. Maybe there's more inside that cave as well."

"Didn't you hear my mom?" Kaia lowered her voice to almost a whisper as one of the maintenance members walked past them, entering the structure. As soon as he disappeared past the door, she continued, "I'm sure they're calling your parents as well."

"And?" Lucas replied defiantly.

"The council seemed pretty serious about this; I

think we hit a chord with this one."

"I don't trust that councilmember, what's his name...Engel. He seemed to hide something."

"I don't think he knows what happened here. Massive amount of gold in one place? Petrified human-oid, if not actual human bones? And there's something else."

"Did I miss something?"

"I, ahem." Kaia cleared her voice, looking down to hide her eyes from Lucas. "I felt something else in that cave. I felt as if I had been there before."

"Oh no, Kaia, don't tell me that you're losing it under pressure."

"I don't think I am, I mean... I don't know, but the visit to the canyon's edge has to wait till tomorrow. I want to go home."

"Fine." Lucas took a step closer. "I'll see you to-morrow." He kissed Kaia on her cheek.

"Tomorrow." Kaia smiled.

~O~

Una walked back to the meeting room as the councilmembers were exiting. "The meeting is over," Engel said as he approached her, "but we need to talk."

"Yes, we do," Una replied, following Engel as the two separated from the group, which continued to walk outside the structure.

"You need to keep that child of yours in check," Engel said as soon as they re-entered his office.

"I believe her," Una replied, looking at him defiantly.

"And that's great. I'm happy for both of you. I hope it strengthens the bond you two have," Engel replied sarcastically. "I just think they should moderate their claims."

"What's wrong with revealing that there used to be intelligent life here?"

"Look, Una." Engel sighed. "We are light-years from help, here on our own. Revealing that there once was intelligent life here would get misinterpreted by the colonists," he continued before Una could intervene. "And before you tell me that people will understand, let me tell you that when it comes to life or death situations, people act irrationally."

"No one is talking about life and death here, Engel."

"It's implied. You're presenting me with fossilized humanoid or human bones. That implies that they existed here and died."

"Can you at least check her claims, see if she is right in any way?" Una asked, narrowing her eyes. "That way, we can interpret information correctly and calmly tell everyone."

"Fine, I'll send someone to check this out," Engel replied with a sigh. "I trust your feelings and visions, and it seems your daughter might have the same gift as well. But please, in the future, come to me *before* a full council meeting is called." He extended his hand.

"Agreed," Una said, shaking Engel's hand.

~O~

Hansel is in the Milky Way, too far for one single ship to get there. Instead, we laid a system of beacons and supplies with automated drones. We followed the proverbial breadcrumbs all the way here. The rest is history, for me, at least. My name is Kaia, and I was born on Hansel.

I have had dreams of another world for I'd say forever. It might be Earth, but I have never seen it. The colonists are here, the atmosphere processors are set, and Hansel is my home now, home to a thriving human colony.

Separated from our mothership, together with three thousand and five hundred other colonists, we were dropped off on to Hansel to, among other things, run the atmosphere processors that were already placed here by the drones over fifty years before we arrived. At full capacity, these behemoth structures ran an electrical current through the oceans already on Hansel, creating oxygen and jumpstarting the ozone-oxygen cycle, which by our scientist's estimations, should have happened already as a matter of natural course. Somehow, we didn't know why it wasn't happening. Fifty years later, the atmosphere formed. The processors now serve as housing for the colonists.

~O~

"Kaia, help me set up the table, sweetie," Una said, hearing the front door open and close.

Kaia took her muddy shoes and jacket off. She walked to the cabinet, pulling out two plates and plastic glasses.

Her mother brought a tray with food as Kaia poured water in two cups. She placed them on the table next to the plates. Her mother put some food there and brought in a couple of forks and knives. They sat at the table and began to eat.

"Mom, can I ask you something?" Kaia said.

Her mother looked up, "Uh-oh. What's with that look? Is this about today's meeting?"

"You know the stories Grandma used to tell about her grandpa? Remember the one about how he used to say he had visions about the end of the world?"

"You are talking about Grandpa Baishan."

"The explorer."

"Yes, what about him?"

"Remember how Grandma used to say that he spoke with ancestors?"

"Oh baby, those were different times. On a different planet, too, I might add. But what's this about?"

"I had a strange experience today during our scouting mission. I had this feeling all over my body like I was in the presence of someone I knew."

Her mother didn't say anything, just stared at Kaia as she continued, "I felt deep pain and regret."

"What is this about? Do you want me to enroll you in something else?"

"No, mom, you know I love exploring. I want to be where I am."

"You know Grandpa Baishan drove himself crazy with that."

"About Grandpa...you never told me, but what was it about the visions that drove him insane?"

"Oh, Kaia." Her mother placed her utensils on her plate. "Grandpa Baishan was a great man and an explorer. He, uh, he also used to drink a lot." She looked at Kaia, who took a sip of water from her glass. "That's what they, um, that's what they used to do down on Earth around those times. During the last of his discoveries, in a cave in some desert, I don't remember the name now, he claimed to have touched a bone, or a skull—I am not sure, Grandma never mentioned it specifically. Through it, he claimed to have seen how the world was going to end. He claimed that we had to take better care of the planet. And this was during a time where that concept was foreign on Earth. I mean, we call him grandpa, but it's more like grand-grand-grandpa. What he experienced on Earth was before the World Wars there even began. They moved around in horse and carriages."

"Seen how?" Kaia asked, narrowing her eyes.

"A vision, perhaps. I am not sure. Anyway, I never

met him, but the stories passed down to the family don't describe him as the articles in the newspapers do. He was a caring and loving man. He fathered seven children. I don't believe he was crazy. Others from our family, who became explorers, experienced the same—remember Aunt Kelsea. What do you mean you think you experienced something like they did?"

"I think I had a vision as I touched the bone we presented to the council today."

Una swallowed and continued to look at Kaia.

"We didn't go too deep into the cave. We just dug a little by the entrance, and I felt a connection as soon as I touched the petrified bone, without even knowing it was a bone. Shivers ran down my spine. It was as if I was there. I don't know how to explain," Kaia said, taking a sip of water from her cup.

"I know this is hard for you to understand, Kaia, but we can't begin talking to the colony or the council about this. Not until we have all the facts. Which we don't. Besides, the drones haven't picked up anything out of the ordinary."

"Drones can only see so much, Mom, and you know it." Kaia placed the cup back on the table.

"Well, you two have to stay within the perimeter." Una sank her fork in a steamed baby carrot.

"Mom, I want to go there again, there's something there."

"Kaia, this is not open for discussion. Let me talk to the panel and see if we can send some equipment there to find out what this is. If indeed a catastrophe happened here, the area outside the perimeter is dangerous."

Kaia crossed her arms. "Ugh, why do I even bother telling you things?"

"Kaia, I worry about you, that's why I am doing this," Una said once her mouth was free of food.

"I am nineteen years old, mom. I can make my own decisions."

"And we have mechanisms in place to help you with your decisions. Don't go out there by yourself until we sort this out. I mean it."

Kaia tightened her lips and did not say anything else. They finished eating the rest of their meal in silence.

~O~

As night slowly enveloped the colony, the automated light system kicked in, illuminating the muddy streets and houses built alongside them. Because the atmosphere on Hansel was relatively new, the temperatures dropped sharply during the nights regardless of the season. So, no one went out during the night, unless they were inside vehicles.

Having nowhere to go during this period, once they finished their meal, Kaia gathered the plates and placed them in the sink to wash them. Her grandmother's kachina doll grabbed her attention. Drying her hands, she turned around as Una sat on the couch in the living room, picking up her tablet.

Kaia approached her mother, drying her hands with a white towel. "Is there a story behind that doll?"

Una raised her head as Kaia placed the towel on the table and picked the doll up.

"That's Sunface. It represents warmth and shelter for the old and a bright future and playfulness for the young." She sighed, placing the tablet on the small coffee table in front of the couch, getting up. "It's doing its job a little too well," she chuckled, looking at Kaia.

"Oh, ha, ha." Kaia laughed ironically

"It has been part of our line forever, as far as I remember, at least."

"It reminds me of Great Grandma."

"You've never met her."

"I know, but I feel her every time I hold it."

Una swallowed, looking at Kaia, holding the doll. "So do I," she whispered to herself, going back to the couch and grabbing her tablet.

Holding the wooden doll adorned with feathers and leather straps, Kaia headed for her room. Her footsteps disturbed the silence that fell in the house.

She closed the metal door and sat on her bed on the right. Passing her fingers through the black feathers of the doll, she looked at its round wooden face. A black line ran along the diameter of its head, horizontally splitting it. That line, adorned by smaller white lines, separated the forehead, which in turn was divided in two by a similar vertical line in the middle going up. The left side was blue, the right side red, with sun-like rays emanating from the center outwards. The eyes, represented by two thick, horizontal black lines, seemed to always smile. Its mouth, a triangle of the same color, had two lines on both sides going down to what she understood to be its chin. Its face was yellow. Black feathers radiated out of the head. Its body was covered by white fur. The doll held a feather with its left hand and a blue leather strap in its right.

With a sigh, Kaia placed the doll on the table in front of her and laid on the bed, resting her eyes and thinking about the day she'd had.

A few minutes later, Una knocked on the door. "Come in," Kaia answered with her eyes closed.

Una walked inside Kaia's room and took the chair located in front of her table, sitting on it. "Do you feel like talking about this, Kaia?"

Kaia stood up on the bed and sighed in annoyance. "We hike daily in a new direction just to supplement the drone scouts. And you know they've flown all over Hansel. Cataloging plants and insects," she said, slightly tilting her head. "Hansel is made of deserts and forests with a large ice cap that covers most of the north pole. So the council says."

Una listened in silence as Kaia continued.

"I volunteered as soon as they announced that scouting missions were available. For me, it's like a calling. Drones can take pictures from above. They can't scout as I do. And I know that worries you. But every time we go out, I am conscientious of where and how far we go. You used to tell me stories about Grandfather." Kaia looked down and put her hands together, interlocking her fingers. "Then you stopped telling me stories about him."

Una faintly smiled. "My great-great-great-grand-father helped discover artifacts on Earth. Though his name didn't make it into the history books, the family knew. The story passed down was of him, Baishan, telling my great-great-great-grandmother that his father had told him where to go. He claimed he saw him, or a ghost of him."

"That's what I felt when I touched that rock before Lucas realized that was petrified bone. I felt déjà vu, like I'd lived on Hansel before. Though I know I haven't," Kaia said, straightening her back and lifting her eyes in excitement.

"That's what keeps me going, mom," she continued, "that déjà vu feeling like in those stories. They sound eerily like you're talking about me on Hansel, not my great-great-grandfather on Earth."

"Grandma used to say we are made of stardust, and she wasn't wrong," Una said, looking at the Sunface doll on the table. "Your great-great-grandfather was a born explorer, just like his father before him. As I got older, the stories got more serious. She told me how my great-grandfather would tell my great-grandmother on Earth that he had visions of another world, that if we didn't take care of our home planet, we were doomed."

Una reached to the table, grabbed the doll. "This was before we on Earth, and by *we*, I mean my grand-mother's generation, realized that global warming was slowly eating the planet. The closer they got to their departure day, my grandmother told her, the louder these visions of disaster got."

Una got up and faced the door, hiding her face

from Kaia. "She thought it was just anxiety, and that the visions would go away once they left. And they did, the visions stopped. She kept our line's story alive by telling everything to my mother, just as my mother did with me. I remember my mother telling me about her mother. She said to her that before she left home, my grandfather told her, *remember where you came from, you are now part of the universe, child.*

"I know you've wondered if I have experienced anything. Yes, I have. You have to understand that not everyone understands what we're going through."

"Before we came to today's meeting, we put the artifact through an x-ray machine. It confirmed my feeling that people, as in humans, once lived here on this planet," Kaia said, looking at her mother.

"You have to promise me that you won't go back out," Una said as she turned around and looked at Kaia.

"Mom..."

"Promise."

"I promise I won't do anything stupid."

"Thank you." Una put the doll on the table. "I have work to do, goodnight Kaia."

"Goodnight, Mom."

~O~

Hansel orbits a star, much like the one Earth rotates—at least that's what they tell us. Though I am told a day was roughly twenty-four hours on Earth, it's thirty here. Hansel is so much bigger than Earth. Every morning as the sun rises over the colony, it removes frigid air with wind. Colonists and workers go out after the winds have died out. And this day was no exception. Once the winds died, my phone rang. It was Lucas.

"Come on!" His excited voice brought a smile on Kaia's face.

"Lucas, I really don't feel like going to the site today."

"I promise this will be the last time. I promise," Lucas responded. "I'm by your front door, wear your hiking shoes."

Kaia put her shoes on and grabbed the water bottle she usually brought out on hikes. She went downstairs, where Lucas was waiting.

"Lucas, going back to that site is not a good idea. You heard the councilmember and my mom saying they were going to send people there."

"Yeah, maybe they'll help us."

"With what?" she asked Lucas. "Engel's people are there to likely destroy it, not help *us*."

"All the more reason to go there," Lucas replied, grabbing her hand. "Let's go."

The two took one of the transport vehicles the colony used to bus workers to and from facilities. That dropped them close to where their school was. From there, they commenced their hike to the site where they'd discovered the petrified bone.

Approaching it, they noticed tire tracks and foot-prints on the ground.

"It feels as if someone cleared this out. I remember a cave here, not—" Lucas paused for a moment looking around "—this. What is this anyway?"

"Looks like an office entrance now. I can see broken pieces of metal shelves down there, and chairs," Kaia answered, shining her flashlight inside the cave.

The two continued inside the cave, past a few pieces of equipment clearly brought in by maintenance workers from the colony. They walked through a corridor, which ended with a big thick door that had been forced open. Sliding past it, the two found themselves inside what appeared to be a records room. Pretty much, everything was destroyed. The smell of wet dirt penetrated their nostrils, and Kaia sneezed.

"Bless you. Look here." Lucas pointed with his flashlight to an empty space where the square indentation of an object that had been there previously was noticeable.

Kaia kneeled, touching the ground. "Looks like they took stuff from here."

"I want to continue walking further," Lucas said, looking around.

"We don't know where this tunnel leads." Kaia got up, lighting the tunnel walls with her flashlight.

"Let's go in for just a bit more." Lucas ambled, making sure he didn't trip in a hole or debris.

~O~

Meanwhile, at the council's headquarters.

The mission supervisor began his presentation as a few of his crew wheeled in a piece of equipment resembling a server tower. "We found evidence that there was life here. And not just plant or animal, but actual humanoid life. Down a cave, some of our scouts found."

"This doesn't look very old."

"No, it doesn't. In fact, I would say, based on the rust, some of our technicians say this is likely about a couple of hundred years old. Well-preserved, I might add."

"I have two questions for you," Una said. "What is it that you are presenting us with, and where are its makers?"

"Our cryptologists are close to decrypting some of these writings. I must admit, this specific piece of technology does seem eerily like ours. It's like a server tower, complete with spinning hard drives. Powered by electric."

"Maybe a crashed drone?"

"It's not ours," another member said. "All drones are accounted for. We know where all the processors landed, and all other technology we brought is used and recycled. That is not ours."

~O~

At the site.

Kaia and Lucas stopped by one of the walls where a few scattered bones were lying. "These don't seem that old, and they look as if they're human. What do you think?" Kaia reached out, touching one of them sticking from the dirt.

Immediately, it was as if someone had put on a hologram in front of her eyes. The room was dimly illuminated. Red strobe lights flashed as bright monitors showed images she couldn't discern. People appeared around her, coughing and kneeling from the smoke coming out of some pieces of equipment, which were on fire. More people gathered around. An alarm filled the room.

"What's going on outside?" someone asked, coughing as smoke slowly filled the room.

"The tectonic plates are shifting. The cities of Eilein and Kolars have completely folded."

"What are you talking about, folded?"

"The tectonic plates reversed, they flipped upside down. The cities that were on top are all buried. They're on the bottom now." The man extended his hand with his palm up and flipping it, so the palm faced down.

"What? Is that happening everywhere?"

"I don't know what's happening with this last volcano. The external feed is cut."

"Then we need to go out."

"And go where, exactly? The planet is destroying itself."

"Anywhere but this hole, I refuse to die here!"

A few people left and moved toward the other side of the room, out of Kaia's field of view as the man still standing in front continued, "They won't go very far; the shifting of the tectonic plates is creating volcanoes. My suspicion is that the second cataclysmic wave is yet to come."

"There's more?"

"No one listens; everyone talks! We've known and warned everyone about this for decades. I won't get into it now. It is too late. The global conveyor belt halted a few cycles ago, and coupled with the earthquakes it spawned, and now volcanoes? It seems the planet is getting rid of us."

"This can't end this way. There must be another way!"

"We stay here. At this point, there is no going out, but we must survive. For the good of our species."

Someone collapsed next to them as water penetrated the cave. Feeling as if she was drowning, Kaia let go of the bone. Everything around her darkened again.

"Kaia! Are you okay?" Lucas rushed to help Kaia, who let out a scream, then took deep breaths.

"I'm fine," she replied, falling to her knees and placing one hand to support her on the floor, the other one to her chest as though to make sure she could still breathe. "I'm fine."

"It seemed as if you were having a seizure." Lucas swallowed, rubbing her back and feeling her shivering.

"I'm fine." Kaia finally snapped out of it, looking at the direction of the back of the cave where she'd seen water rushing in her vision.

Kaia walked down the tunnel until they reached an ending. She could feel air coming through the back end of the cave. With a kick, it collapsed, revealing another way out of the cave. They made their way out just as a team of engineers from the colony approached its entrance. Walking down through the forest, they heard the machine rumble.

"What are they doing here?"

"I don't know...it seems they're sealing the cave entrance."

"I have to go see my mother."

"What? Now? What happened in the cave?"

"Nothing, Lucas, but I think the council sent them here to close the cave entrance. Remember what Engel said? He didn't seem very happy we found this one. I have to tell my mother, at least she must know." Kaia looked at Lucas as the crew bulldozed the cave entrance.

"Why are they doing that? We can learn so much from these caves."

"Unless the council wants to bury this information."

"I still don't get it. There was a human presence here, and something cataclysmic happened. The more we know, the more we can learn."

"That is, unless they already know. Besides, the council doesn't seem to be interested in what happened here. They're more interested in what the colony *can* do and how we can harvest resources."

The two made eye contact before Kaia took off through the forest, heading for the colony, which wasn't that far from where the cave exited.

As the two rushed into the lobby where the meeting was being held, the secretary, sitting behind her desk just outside the meeting room, tried to stop them. Dismissing her, Kaia opened the door to the meeting, letting Lucas slip through. She immediately closed it behind her, locking it.

A video from the salvaged server tower was playing in the dark room, and everyone was focused on it.

"The global conveyor belt stopped due to global warming," the translator said, showing images of a planet as Kaia moved a little closer. Her mother saw her and motioned for her to stay quiet.

"That set in motion a series of events that proved to be a catastrophe for us. Warming oceans flooded our cities, but that was just the beginning. As the ice caps melted, the ground under them rose, pushing the tectonic plates against each other. There must have been an enormous amount of tension between some of these plates because some of them flipped upside down. Entire, once-thriving cities are now under the crust, billions of people dead and buried. Who knows if anything recognizable even survived there to tell some alien race that we even existed? As far as we know, we are the last people left alive. And we will stay here to make sure..." The sound of rushing water interrupted the audio and the video shortly after.

"Oh my..." Shivers ran down Kaia's spine as she stared at the last image frozen on the projector. Her mother sank into her chair, making eye contact with Kaia, who had both her hands on her mouth as though to stop from crying.

In that fleeting moment, they both realized that Baishan's tales, passed along their entire line, were not ramblings of a drunk like those around them had believed to be. What he, and indeed their entire line, had experienced for hundreds of years was the demise of a race too careless with their planet. Kaia and her heritage had experienced the slow despair of a species realizing they were doomed, deliberately unraveling through some ancestral connection.

"They seemed civilized, and might I add very much human. And they saw their demise. Does this mean we will end up like them as well?" Una asked as soon as the lights came back up.

"I believe we passed that barrier when we realized we could harness energy from our sun. We will not end like them. We are a little wiser and have better technology. Unfortunately, we weren't quicker in our process."

"If we had arrived a couple of hundred years ago, we could have saved them," another added.

"Or warred with them. Humans are humans," Engel interrupted. "Now we know what happened to this place. We will make sure to mark it on our records that the previous inhabitants were humanoid, we will run the DNA tests to confirm that theory. For the time being, we need to expand and make sure we further our species here. We can change. We are capable of learning."

"What does this mean for us?"

The large room filled with chatter. As the councilmembers began to talk to each other, Una got up from her chair and approached Kaia and Lucas, standing by the door.

"What are you doing here?" she whispered to the two. "You shouldn't be here."

Kaia didn't react to her scolding whisper, keeping her hands by her sides and following her mother with her eyes, as if she wanted to tell her something.

"What is it?" Her mother felt that something was wrong as Engel finally got up again, addressing the council.

"Ladies and gentlemen, here are the facts." He looked at Kaia, Lucas, and Una. "Hansel is in the Goldilocks Zone, and it will be here for a very long time. The star it orbits is stable. The system it is in is stable. In fact, it is so suitable for human life that it did house humans at some point. We still don't know enough to decide if they were colonists from another civilization or spontaneous appearances from parallel evolution."

He walked to the piece of equipment the engineers had brought from the cave and continued, "In fact, we have firsthand accounts that whoever lived here previously *did* overheat the planet, perhaps through global warming, perhaps through some other process that we yet have to discover. However, I can say that whatever happened here, as documented by the translators, was a human-made disaster and not a disaster that happened as a matter of natural causes. It appears we have a better understanding of these systems than they did."

As his voice faded into the background, Kaia made eye contact with her mother, lost in her family's history. Goosebumps erupted over her body.

"Grandpa was right all along," Kaia whispered to Una, tears in her eyes.

Her mother hugged her as her lips trembled, and Engel continued with his speech.

"We might as well be this planet's, this system's, second chance. We have the technology and know-how. Let's do it right this time. Not with fear and destruction, but with expertise—" he again looked at Kaia and Una hugging "—and love."

The End

"I seriously hope that Helsey 8K won't be like Hansel." Irene closed the back cover, looking at the book before she got up and walked through the narrow corridor to her room. Sitting on her bed, she took her shoes off and looked at the closet where her clothes were, thinking she should pack up for tomorrow's journey. *I'll do that tomorrow.*

Irene turned the light off, placed her head on her pillow, and closed her eyes. Though she didn't want to sleep, she knew she had to.

#

"This is a message to all the remaining crew-members of the Morning Star," Irene heard Chief's voice say through the Morning Star's speakers. "We are preparing to move the rest of our operation down to the surface. Please prepare all the necessary equipment. Chief out."

Taking a deep sigh, she reached for her nightstand and turned the light on. Irene got up, yawning and stretching. She walked to the dresser, took a change of clothes, and headed for the shower. Outside, the remaining crew members were now wrapping up preparations and filled the corridors with their chatter. She stopped in front of the closed shower room and knocked on it. Someone opened the door exiting as Adam walked by.

"Good morning," he greeted Irene, zipping up his copilot's jacket.

"Good morning," Irene replied. "Did I miss the pre-launch briefing?"

"I think the chief will make another..."

"This is a message to all Morning Star Crew." Chief's voice over the speaker system interrupted him.

"Final pre-launch briefing will be held in the control room in a few minutes. Chief out."

"There you have it," he said as the transmission ended with a long beep.

"Let me get a quick shower. I'll see you there." Irene closed the door.

Adam walked to the control room that most of the remaining crew was already in. As usual, some were standing, some were sitting, and others were talking via their communicators.

"To all those who just walked in," the chief said. "Check the situation desk, right here," he pointed to the desk, "and pick the box with your name on it. Each one of these boxes represents a shuttle."

Adam walked to it, looking at the contents. Some boxes were missing, picked up by their respective members. *Here it is.* He saw his and Irene's name on a piece of paper and box number 7 on top of it. Inside the box, there was the symbolic Shuttle Seven key. The one Control used to manually mark the situation board whenever shuttles would be out on supply or support missions.

Passing his fingers along the raised number on the small box, Adam walked to the corner. Though almost all the remaining crew was inside this room, it was eerily quiet, broken only by fabric shuffling or the occasional electronic beep coming from the corridor where the EVA suits were stored.

"Where is everyone?" Irene said as she entered,

approaching Adam.

"Over the past several hours, the chief authorized launches, so a good portion of the crew is already down on the surface," Adam replied, kissing her as she leaned toward him. "Here is our chariot." He smiled, handing Irene the symbolic number 7 key.

"Ladies and gentlemen," the chief said as he got up looking around at the crew, "this is it. Today is the day we stop being astronauts and become colonists. We are faced with uncertainty, and there is so much to be done, but I am a firm believer that we," he paused, looking around the room, "will be the finest colonists humanity has ever seen."

"That's all," the chief added. "I'll see all of you down on the surface."

All the remaining crew members got up and walked out, passing Adam and Irene.

"I'm going to get some things from my room," Irene said, joining the crowd exiting the room.

"I'll see you there," Adam said to her. He walked toward the chief.

"What else is left to do here?" he asked.

"Since the communications satellites failed, we'll need the repeaters switched on—that way, we can still use our communicators on the surface of Helsey 8K."

"We can do that, just remember that there will be times when the Morning Star will be invisible to us.

Communicators won't work then."

"Yeah, we'll deal with that when the time comes," Helmsey replied.

Adam walked through the busy corridors filled with personal backpacks on both sides. He stopped by the auxiliary airlock and put on his EVA suit. Fastening his helmet, Adam picked up his oxygen tanks, wearing it like a backpack. After the room decompressed, he went outside the Morning Star as a first shuttle disconnected from it. Usually, the antenna movements would be carried and controlled by the cockpit, but that was no longer an option. He manually operated it, ultimately extending the antenna elements.

"Antenna extended," he transmitted.

"We've got a good signal here," the chief replied as another shuttle disconnected and floated away from the Morning Star toward Helsey 8K. "Come back, Adam."

"Copy that." Adam floated toward the side hatch as yet another shuttle disconnected from one of the launch bays, which now were wide open. He entered the airlock and proceeded to the control room where the chief and Irene were.

"This is it," Irene said. "I put the Morning Star on standby. Only the solar panels are operational. Life support systems will deactivate in twelve hours."

Lights flickered, and a timer displayed on all screens.

"Thank you for being so kind to us," she continued, looking around as she addressed the ship, "but it's time we part ways. Hopefully, we'll see each other again."

Helmsey noticed that Irene and Adam couldn't get themselves to walk to the escape shuttle bays. "I know the captain is the last to jump ship. I'll give you three some space. See you on the surface."

"We will be behind you, Chief," Irene said, shifting her gaze toward the corridor lit up by the emergency strobe lights.

As the chief continued walking to his escape shuttle, Irene walked to the control room, checking the monitors, which were now displaying a countdown timer in big, bold red numbers. She looked around at the empty chairs as Adam slowly walked behind her. "Do you remember the first time we met?"

"Yeah, it was right there." She pointed at an empty chair, "You walked in through that door," she pointed to one of the doors leading inside the control room, "holding your pilot's hat."

Adam smiled faintly. "Carrier Hope had just launched 'First Contact' with two other seed ships and began planning for our eventual launch."

"Yeah." Irene smiled, looking at the blank monitor above her head. "I remember the name 'Morning Star' printed up there and all our crew names."

"I sure hope that Carrier Hope is still releasing seed ships."

The two remained silent, recalling that day before Helmsey's voice interrupted their moment. "Crew Chief is leaving the ship."

"Captain copy," Irene replied with a sigh.

As three very long beeps announced Helmsey's departure to Adam and Irene, the Morning Star's fuselage shook. Chief's escape shuttle disconnected from the bay clamps, slowly heading for Helsey 8K.

"Shall we?" Adam extended his hand to Irene.

"Yeah, let's do this." Irene grabbed his hand.

The two slowly walked through the now deserted corridors toward the shuttle bays.

"Let me do a last inspection of the shuttle bay doors," he told Irene, who headed for Shuttle Seven.

Adam walked to the end of the hall, where one of the docks was shut entirely as all the shuttles scheduled to leave from there had already departed.

He went back to Shuttle Seven and bent down, looking inside. Irene was already in her seat, preparing for departure.

"It's time," he said as the Morning Star shook again as two more shuttles released the clamps holding them in place in the bays.

"How about the babies?" Irene looked at the direction of the cryogenic pod section, which was empty.

"Look." Adam pointed at a screen in front of them, showing the evacuation process. The section was floating together with two transport shuttles.

"I guess this is it, huh?"

Adam smiled. "The sight of you strapped up in that chair turns me on."

Irene looked at Adam with a smile on her face. Adam walked in, closing the door behind him.

As the Morning Star began to shut down its systems, the red evacuation lights lit up, and an alarm filled the ship, indicating that life support systems would be shutting down soon.

"One last thing." Irene reached for a panel in front of her, tapping a digital button labeled "Audio." She scrolled down a list and picked up her microphone.

"As per tradition," she tapped on the screen, "here's to good beginnings and good luck."

The sound of "Johnny B. Goode" sung by Chuck Berry echoed through the transport ship as it headed for their new home planet, Helsey 8K.

ACKNOWLEDGEMENT

Nothing happens in a vacuum.

I would like to thank all of those who supported me while writing this book during the Covid-19 pandemic times.

Book editor : Cath Lauria
Beta reader and co-author of "Fuses" : SJ. Turner
Cover art designer : Antonio Del Esporti

And all the amazing people that surround me every day.

*Special thanks to my wife, for the late night talks about plot points and general story direction. Without her this book wouldn't have been possible.

BOOKS BY THIS AUTHOR

Imprint Legacy, 2019

Detective Robert Miers is in trouble. His partner is missing, he's suspended from work, and he's got a gap in his memory that he can't explain. Uncovering the truth means plunging into a bizarre new reality far beyond his comfort zone, an inescapable reality where memories can transfer from body to body, secret factions fight for control, and human life extends far beyond Earth. Is taking sides worth the risk-to his job, to his family, and to himself?

And does he even get to choose anymore?